The Mumbai School for Murder

ALSO BY MEETI SHROFF-SHAH

THE MUMBAI SCHOOL FOR MURDER

MEETI SHROFF-SHAH

JOFFE BOOKS

Joffe Books, London
www.joffebooks.com

First published in Great Britain in 2025

© Meeti Shroff-Shah 2025

Cover art by Cherie Chapman

ISBN: 978-1-80573-286-0

For Maulik — how's this for a good word?

PROLOGUE

Nobody quite understands what it takes to be accepted into the North Star High School in Mumbai. Certainly not money. Money is a given. The school's astronomical fee-structure ensures that only those with disposable millions bother filling out application forms. It isn't luck, either. Unlike some other schools in the city that have an actual lottery system to decide who they accept, the North Star conducts four elimination rounds over three months to arrive at an admit list. Admission doesn't seem to rest on parental qualifications either. Or else children of surgeons and bankers wouldn't routinely be found languishing on waitlists. Neither does pedigree seem to play an important role. Regret letters have found their way into the homes of too many North Star alumni for a past association to really count. The parents who finally make it never really find out why they were chosen or how they got in. They just learn that they must always be grateful and never forget that the school is always right.

CHAPTER 1

Monday

Radhi watched the North Star silk banner with its green-gold lettering stir ever so slightly in the oppressive, mid-morning April heat, and marvelled at the unfaltering smiles plastered on the faces of the scores of parents mingling with each other in the school garden. Dabbing at the thin film of sweat that had formed above her upper lip within just a few minutes of arriving, she thought that only a school as inflated with its own sense of self-importance as the North Star could host a Garden Fest on a working day, and expect parents to be thrilled to have been invited.

She transferred the large watering can in her hand to the ground, before rolling up the sleeves of her rani-pink linen shirt and wondered if removing it altogether, so that only her white tank top and jeans remained, would be too basic for the Derby-ready mums flitting about with their oversized solitaires, sunglasses and smiles. You had to hand it to the women of Temple Hill, she thought as she overheard a plan for poker-and-panipuri-with-the-husbands come together rapidly among a group of mothers to her left. They could network just about anywhere.

Radhi gathered her dark shoulder-length hair into a high bun, so that the nape of her neck could breathe, and was struck, not for the first time, at the sway the school held over the parents. All the invitation email had to say was that it would be 'wonderful to see *both* parents', and the dads had left their respective diamond bazaars and trading desks during peak market hours to be there.

'Radhi? Radhika Zaveri? OH. MY. GOD. Is it really you?!' A high-pitched voice pierced the air, startling both the pigeon as well as the cat that had been waiting patiently to pounce on it for the past quarter of an hour.

Squinting in the bright sun despite her sunglasses, Radhi looked up to see a woman with strappy, neon stilettoes and platinum highlights in her hair, making her way purposefully towards her. Smiling uncertainly, Radhi got up from the vegetable patch she'd been squatting over and dusted her dirty hands. The woman seemed vaguely familiar, yet with her face partially covered under a wide-brimmed straw hat, Radhi couldn't place her until she was standing right in front of her.

'Oh . . . Vedika, hello!' Radhi smiled half-heartedly at her old classmate from school.

They'd never really been friends, and Radhi found it difficult to muster enthusiasm for someone she remembered as decidedly catty.

'What a surprise to see you here!' Vedika squealed, as she leaned in for a hug.

'It's lovely to see you too,' Radhi said and then, because she'd promised herself she'd be more social that year, she added, 'But look at you — you look just the same!'

'By same if you mean my waist-size, I'll take it.' Vedika giggled as she held up her arms and did a little shimmy. 'Though I definitely can't say the same about you.' She flicked a finger at one of the turquoise, silver peacocks dangling from Radhi's ears.

Radhi laughed despite herself, remembering what a tomboy she'd been in school. Skinny, with long, awkward limbs and hair which she kept perpetually short so that she could swim without hassle every day, she'd been the last girl in her class to fill out and get a bra.

'I'm serious. I wouldn't have recognized you with that sexy nose pin and that full red mouth, had it not been for this cute mini-Radhi beside you!'

Radhi smiled down to where her niece was mucking about in the soil and had to admit that Amayra, with her large coffee-coloured eyes and broad forehead, was a complete replica of her.

'Can you believe they're making us do this in bloody April?' Vedika hissed.

'It's nuts,' Radhi agreed. 'But why do people put up with it? I mean, I know they're the best in the country and all that, but surely parents can have some say?'

Vedika rolled her eyes. 'Don't be absurd. There are always repercussions if you're too vocal.'

Radhi made a disbelieving face.

'I swear!' Vedika dropped her voice a notch. 'A couple of years ago, they introduced compulsory lunch at school for everyone. And one of the mums created a WhatsApp group with some other parents where they complained about the amount of sugar in the fruit juices the school served as dessert and things like that. Eventually, the school found out about the group and put a stop to it with a stern email. But guess what happened when that mum's younger daughter was eligible for admission last year?'

Vedika paused to see if Radhi had an answer before continuing. 'She didn't get in! Now that poor mum has two daughters in different schools in different parts of the city, with completely different holiday calendars! She is going mad, I hear.

'Anyways, chuck that. Come, let's get a picture together.' Vedika fished out a phone from her oversized Louis Vuitton bag and posed with an arm around Radhi. 'Just wait till the rest of our class sees you. They're going to fall off their chairs!'

'Don't exaggerate!' Radhi smiled belatedly for the camera as Vedika clicked a series of pictures of them from different angles in rapid succession before putting her phone away.

4

'No, I mean they'll be surprised to see you appear so . . . so . . . normal.'

'What's that supposed to mean?' Radhi frowned.

'Just you know . . . all of this.' Vedika waved at the almost bucolic scene of parents helping their children to plant and water their seeds. 'You look so good, you have a daughter in school, you're back on Temple Hill . . . It all seems so well-adjusted and . . . normal.'

Radhi realized that her former classmate had mistaken her niece for her daughter, but she was too irritated to bother correcting her. 'And why wouldn't it be? Normal that is?'

'No reason. It's just that there were some really stupid stories floating about you.' Vedika shrugged dismissively. 'Of course, it's not like one believed everything one heard.'

'What kind of stories?' Radhi's nose flared. She knew perfectly well that the rumours about her wouldn't be pleasant, and yet she couldn't help herself.

'Forget it, no. Look, there's old Fernandes coming up to make her big speech.' Vedika pointed towards the podium. 'She loves her mic, that one!'

Radhi watched North Star's straight-backed principal making her way to the raised dais at the centre of the large garden. But before she could climb the stairs she was stopped by a group of gushing mothers.

'Well?' Radhi turned back to her classmate, unwilling to drop the subject. 'What did you hear?'

Vedika rolled her eyes. 'Something absurd about how you were shacked up in the US with a man old enough to be your father. And taking therapy for depression or something.'

'All of that's true. What else?'

'Haha very fun—' Vedika stopped abruptly when she realized that Radhi wasn't joking. Her eyes widened and travelled down to where Amayra was raking the soil with her plastic gardening tools. 'Is this *his* daughter, then?'

'This is my *niece*. I'm just helping out my sister!' Radhi snapped. 'Tell me, Vedika, is it "normal" to have a niece? And what about a divorce. Is *that* considered normal in the

5

twenty-first century? Because I've had one of those as well, you know.'

'Oh God . . . Radhi! I'm so, so sorry.' Vedika seemed embarrassed. 'I had no idea . . . I didn't mean to . . . I . . . I just thought . . .'

'A very good morning to all the North Starians gathered here today. Thank you for being part of our Garden Fest. You know how much this garden means to me . . .' The principal's voice floated out towards them, saving Vedika from saying anything further. As Fernandes launched into her speech, Vedika squeezed Radhi's arm and murmured something vague about catching up again before quickly walking away to where her own twin boys were beginning a mud fight.

Radhi's cheeks burned. She was so livid at herself she could hardly breathe. She was well aware that the life choices she'd made in the past were unconventional. She also knew, when she decided to move back home after a decade abroad, that there were plenty on Temple Hill who'd judge her for them. People could be narrow-minded and unkind. But that was true of people everywhere in the world. The plan had been to ignore people and focus instead on the reason she'd returned. Bruised from a failed relationship, her aching and tattered heart had craved the familiarity of home. The briny smell of the Arabian Sea at high tide, the summer scent of a hay-covered crate of ripe mangoes, and the fragrance of the sandalwood paste that rose up from the temples of Temple Hill in the mornings, had all but filled her dreams and senses until she felt that if she could just breathe in the air of the city she'd grown up in, she might feel whole again. That was why she'd returned home. And now she couldn't believe she'd let a minor irritant ruffle her so completely.

'*Maasi*, if Peter Parker were normal, he wouldn't be Spider-Man.'

Radhi looked down to see her niece studying her with big, serious eyes.

A wave of tenderness washed over her, and she squatted down, pressing a grateful kiss to the child's forehead.

Amayra had been listening to their conversation and had grasped what Radhi had completely failed to. She didn't need to be offended that people's definition of 'normal' was so narrow. She just had to accept that 'normal' wasn't for her. She kissed the child once again, before getting up, glad that she'd offered to pitch in today. Her older sister, Madhavi, had to accompany her mother-in-law to a doctor's appointment, and was going to be late, while her brother-in-law was travelling for work, which meant Amayra and Radhi had had the morning to themselves.

A smattering of claps and cheers from the parents and teachers gathered in the garden brought her attention back to the principal's speech.

'It was a small twelve feet by eight feet patch of earth when I first joined North Star, fourteen years ago, and now, thanks to the enthusiasm with which all of you've embraced it, and of course the invaluable support of our managing director Sri Ravi Kamble, our garden has spread across 3,000 square feet and meets over twenty-five per cent of our school kitchen's vegetable and fruit requirement.' Fernandes swept her hand in the direction of the neat rows of plants laden low with plump apricots, striped, green cucumbers, slender-waisted bottle gourds and teardrop-shaped lemons, that marked the perimeter of the square garden. 'Together, we've shown the next generation a way of life that's more sustainable, responsible and kinder to this earth. As you all know, I retire at the end of this year. In the last decade, North Star has been India's School of the Year every single year.' She paused and smiled as some parents cheered and clapped before continuing. 'And yet, this garden, more than anything else, is what I'll be proudest of. Happy gardening! Get dirty!' She ended her speech amid more applause and stood beaming at the podium for a few moments, before turning and beginning to make her way down.

A slight, sprightly woman, clad in a dark, georgette saree with a large, floral print, Fernandes had jet black dyed hair, smooth, walnut brown skin and the posture of a kathak

7

dancer. Her trademark, bushy, white eyebrows the only discernible sign that she was almost sixty-five years old.

'She hasn't changed at all, has she?' a voice remarked beside her.

Radhi turned to find Madhavi by her side and smiled. 'I know, right? Just look at her, as cool as a cucumber, even in this dreadful heat.'

Before she joined North Star, Rose Fernandes or Ms. Fernandes, as she was known to her students, had been the maths teacher at Radhi and Madhavi's school when they were growing up.

'Same attitude also. Still thinks she's God's gift to mankind,' Madhavi muttered then belatedly turned to check if Amayra had heard her dissing her school principal. Luckily, the child was busy with a friend, burying a slipper in the earth.

'I think the reason you never liked her, *Didi*,' Radhi grinned, 'is because you couldn't stand algebra.'

'No *normal* person likes algebra, Radhi,' Madhavi joked, with a pretend shudder, knowing well enough that maths was one of Radhi's favourite subjects in school.

Radhi smiled. There it was again, for the second time in the day, the word 'normal'. Almost, as if the universe was trying to drive home a point.

'Not that I'm complaining, mind you,' Madhavi continued. 'I'm glad you did. She's always liked you. Which makes my life easier right now.'

Radhi's other niece, Madhavi's younger daughter, Kavya, was eligible for admission that year, and since North Star didn't automatically take siblings in, Madhavi had been especially anxious to make a favourable impression on the school.

'Look, she's free.' Madhavi pointed to Fernandes who'd just walked out from the small cluster of parents around her. 'Come, let's go say hello and remind her that you and I are related.'

'She knows, *Didi*.' Radhi rolled her eyes. 'I think you made it ample clear when you so generously loaned me to the English Department!'

'Still,' Madhavi grinned and took Radhi's hand, 'It can't hurt for her to see us together.'

Radhi had recently begun conducting a three-month-long creative writing workshop for the ninth and tenth graders at North Star. Madhavi had found out that the English Department was looking for a published author to teach the kids the basics of fiction writing and had offered up her sister in a bid to win some big brownie points from the school.

'So, what do you think of our Garden Fest, Radhika?' Fernandes smiled at Radhi when the two sisters approached her. 'And how are you liking North Star, so far?'

'They're both lovely.' Radhi smiled back. 'And the students — they're so bright! It's a pleasure to teach them.'

Fernandes nodded. 'I take great pride in the quality of the minds at North Star.' She nodded at Madhavi. 'Your sister knows we admit only the best.'

'Like you said in your orientation speech, it's all about the quality of the seeds, isn't it?' Madhavi said.

'Glad to know you were listening.' Fernandes dipped her head. 'The seeds are critical yes, but you know what a good gardener never overlooks?' She paused and scanned the ground before bending down to pull out a short weed. She held it up for both sisters to see. 'Weeding. If left unchecked, the weeds compete with your plants for resources. Which means, they go after the sunlight and water that your plants need. And we can't have that, can we?'

Her eyes swept across the six-storeyed, Victorian, stone edifice of the school. Built originally in the nineteenth century in the Gothic style, the building had UNESCO heritage status and had been carefully preserved, with modern appendages like pool and playground, constructed in a way that complemented the original structure. Her gaze came to rest on a few mothers huddled in conversation in a tight group. 'There was a time when gardens were left to the sole discretion of the gardeners, but things are changing now,' she said with an eyeroll. 'People watch one YouTube video on growing basil, and think they are experts on horticulture.'

Radhi and Madhavi laughed on cue.

'Tell me, why do parents feel like they need to have an opinion on everything, now?' Fernandes turned to Madhavi, a serious expression on her face. 'Do you tell a pilot how to fly a plane? Or give your doctor your "views" on his diagnosis? Why teachers then? We are trained professionals too, why not trust us to do our jobs?'

Madhavi's eyes darted towards Radhi in a plea for help. This conversation had taken an alarming turn. Radhi knew she had an opinion on the school's dictatorial ways, but she could hardly tell the principal.

'It's uncalled for,' Radhi agreed quickly. 'But you know what hasn't changed, in all these years? The pressure to succeed. It still seems as ruthless . . .'

'More, I'd say! I find there's no place for mediocrity in this day and age.' Fernandes paused and glanced at Madhavi with a twinkle in her eye, 'Of course, there's one more thing that's still the same . . . People still don't like maths!' She laughed and patted Madhavi's arm.

'Luckily, both my girls are like their *maasi*,' Madhavi smiled back, refusing to take her eyes off her goal. 'They both enjoy numbers.'

'Good! I hope they do something with it, unlike this one here.' Fernandes tilted her chin at Radhi and smiled.

Radhi winced remembering the conversation she'd had with Fernandes after they got the results of her high school board exams. The then maths teacher had been disappointed to learn that Radhi had opted to pursue the liberal arts. She'd felt it was a waste of Radhi's natural aptitude for logic and numbers and had minced no words in telling her parents so. Luckily, Radhi's mum and dad had supported her decision — but it had been hard, and Fernandes had done her best to make it harder still.

Radhi was about to respond when she saw Venus Pereira, the head of the English Department, stalking purposefully towards them. The pallu of her saree fluttering angrily behind her, matching the thunderous expression on her face.

'Who does he think he is?' she hissed in her clipped accent, as she came to a stop near Fernandes. 'Foolish, shortsighted man!'

'Ms. Venus! What's wrong?' Fernandes asked, looking alarmed.

'Everything! The whole management!' the English teacher announced loud enough for the parents around them to hear.

'Let's talk in my office.' Fernandes quickly put her hand on Venus's arm and turned her around, trying to usher her towards the direction she'd come from.

But Venus flung her hand away. 'They have no moral compass! No sense of right and wrong!'

'Not here, Venus. Please,' Fernandes said sharply, her voice low but firm. 'This is not the place.'

Venus paused and looked around her at the curious parents who had stopped to stare. Her scowl deepened, but she turned on her heels. And together the two teachers walked briskly towards the school building.

CHAPTER 2

'You should've seen Kamble's face.' Mr. Bottlewalla shook his head so that his jowls wobbled, as he cut himself a large slice of the chocolate cake. 'He almost burst a blood vessel!'

The rotund vice principal, who was also the senior school history teacher, seemed unconcerned that more than half the other teachers were still in the line behind him. Radhi watched as he served himself a second slice of cake along with two samosas and a handful of potato wafers before he walked over to the staffroom table and lowered his considerable bottom into one of the narrow wooden chairs. 'It's a good thing Fernandes was there. Or else Venus would have given that man a stroke.'

The Garden Fest had ended an hour ago, and Radhi, who had come to the senior school staffroom to have her lunch, had found it buzzing with chatter. It was Ms. Lily's birthday, the petite, forty-year-old maths teacher had just cut her cake. But apart from the customary birthday samosas and wafers, and the green-gold gift bag of stationery that she'd received from the school, the occasion had been relegated to the background. Everyone was far more interested in the events of the morning when Ms. Venus Pereira had a showdown with Ravi Kamble, the managing director of North Star.

Radhi, who'd had a glimpse of Venus's fiery temperament at the Garden Fest, almost wished she had followed Ms. Fernandes to the scene of the altercation. Apparently, Venus's argument had been almost Shakespearean in its fury and theatrics.

'How is Ms. Venus not afraid of being fired?' asked Ms. Savant, voicing the question, also on Radhi's mind. 'I mean, what nerve!'

Almost as new as Radhi at North Star, Ms. Savant taught English literature to the eighth graders. From the conscientious touch of vermillion in her hair parting and the large and shiny managalsutra, which she kept on full display in front of the folds of her saree, Radhi knew that the young Ms. Savant was newly married and wanted the world to know it.

'Fire Venus Pereira?' Mr. Bottlewalla snorted, his samosa suspended mid-trajectory on its way to his mouth. 'Come, Ms. Savant, don't be naive.'

'Why? Just because she won that award, doesn—'

'*That* award is the Sahitya Akademi, madam,' Mr. Bottlewalla interrupted. 'The highest honour for any Indian writer, may I remind you.'

'Yes, yes. She's a good poet. Nobody's denying that. But does it automatically mean she's a great teacher?' Ms. Savant said, refusing to back down.

'No, but it certainly means she can't be fired!' Mr. Bottlewalla shot back. 'The school's very proud of having her on staff.'

Ms. Savant took a sip of her coffee, seeming unconvinced.

'What say, Bakshi?' Mr. Bottlewalla asked the lean and tall, soft-spoken chemistry teacher, just as Radhi took a seat beside him.

Mr. Bakshi, who had been cutting the three-layered bean lasagne in his lunch box into precise, bite-sized squares, nodded. 'It's true, the other schools would be all over themselves to hire her if she ever left North Star,' he admitted.

'Exactly.' Mr. Bottlewalla forked a large piece of cake into his mouth and relished it for a few moments before speaking again. 'And let's not forget the parents. They just love to brag about how their kids are taught by such a legend!' He looked to Bakshi again for confirmation and got a nod in return.

Ms. Savant rolled her eyes and got up to get herself a second cup of coffee.

'So, you do eat things other than daal-rice.' Radhi turned to joke with Mr. Bakshi, who she had found was a creature of habit. He sat in the same place in the staffroom every day, got the same lunch and solved the daily crossword with the same-coloured pen, in their 10.40 a.m. break. She had taken to helping him with it and they'd become quite friendly.

Mr. Bakshi had an exuberant shock of black hair and deep dimples which he now flashed at her. 'Everything's a bit up in the air today.'

'I know! Seems like it was quite the morning. So, what happened exactly?' Radhi scooped some vegetable pulao from her lunch box with a potato wafer and took a bite.

'You know the Interschool Drama Competition that our school is hosting, next week?'

Radhi nodded. She'd overheard a lot of conversations about costumes and dialogues among the students of her creative writing class over the last few weeks.

'Well, Mr. Kamble dropped by to see how the rehearsals were coming along and discovered that our play is about a corrupt politician whose plans to raze a forest area and make a mall in its stead are foiled by a group of environmentalists.'

Mr. Bakshi paused to see if Radhi had understood why there'd been such a hullabaloo about it. When she appeared blank, he continued, 'Do you know who's the chief guest for this competition?'

Radhi shook her head.

'Ramakant Wagle.'

'Oh.' Radhi leaned back into her chair as the full implication of that name hit her.

Ramakant Wagle was a local politician who'd been in the news for having allotted a large public park on Temple

Hill to a hotel chain which planned to convert it into an entertainment zone. He had residents signing petitions against him and environmentalists staging protests outside his house. The parallels between his story and the script of the play were impossible to ignore.

'And you're sure this was on purpose?'

'Most certainly! It is Venus's script. She knew exactly what she was doing and just how thinly veiled it was.'

A slow, admiring smile spread across Radhi's face. 'That's very gutsy . . .'

'Is it though?' Ms. Savant interjected, crushing her paper plate in her hand before getting up to throw it in the bin. 'To me, it just seems spiteful. I mean why invite someone as chief guest only to insult them?'

Mr. Bakshi shrugged. 'I agree with you in principle, of course. But sometimes, to get the attention of these thick-skinned politicians, you need to be a little . . . direct.'

'But why bring your personal politics into the school, in the first place? If you feel so strongly about an issue, protest outside his house like the rest of the public. Why draw so much attention to yourself?'

'Please,' Mr. Bottlewalla said, heaving himself with considerable effort out of the narrow chair. 'The very last thing someone like Ms. Venus needs is more attention.'

'But those are *exactly* the kind of people who do need it,' Ms. Lily said softly, from the far end of the table. 'The ones who're used to it, the ones who thrive in the limelight.' The maths teacher hadn't spoken so far, but when she did, her words were precise and measured, exactly, Radhi thought, like the subject she taught.

'Thank you.' Ms. Savant inclined her head towards Ms. Lily. She stood up from the table and collected her books and things. 'What plans for the birthday, by the way?'

Lily smiled. 'Oh . . . I brought it in last night at The Salato with my daughter.'

'The new Italian place in Colaba? Lovely.' Ms. Savant made for the door, where she paused. 'You know . . . just because she's gone and named herself after a celestial body, doesn't really mean she's above everyone else.' She let the door close behind her with a careless swing.

'Boy, she really doesn't like our poet, does she?' Mr. Bakshi said when the teacher was out of earshot.

'Can you blame her?' Ms. Lily asked.

Radhi had watched and experienced the almost icy silence with which the two English teachers worked in the English Department room, but she didn't know the reason behind it. Before she could ask Mr. Bakshi or Ms. Lily to elaborate, the school bell rang, and it was time for the teachers to head back to their classrooms.

* * *

'Keep in mind that the place you pick must make you feel safe.' Radhi clapped her hands to get the attention of the grade nine students as they got their books and pens ready for the *Story Setting* exercise that she had just assigned them.

'It could be an actual place. Like a favourite bookstore or a park you love. Or say, the laundry hamper or attic where you hid as a child. Or it could be an imaginary setting. A new planet. An enchanted fores—'

'Miss?' A girl with fluorescent green braces waved her hand in the air.

Radhi paused mid-sentence to answer her, 'Yes, Preeti?'

Radhi, who had one of those eidetic memories that automatically filed away faces and maps and numbers and all kinds of lists, and was able to retrieve them at will, had surprised the students by remembering their names in the very first week of joining them.

'Miss, could our school be the setting for our story?'

'Yes, absolutely. It could be anywhere. But describe it in detail. Not only what it looks like but how it makes you feel. For instance, what does the air smell like? Is it warm? Are there trees? What kind? The more detail you can put in it, the better. Remember, I want you to observe it as if you were visiting it for the first time or after a very long time. Got it?'

Radhi heard a few scattered yesses around the room along with the sound of chairs being scraped forward, papers being shuffled, clarifications being sought and then one by one the heads dropped down and the room fell silent.

As she watched the students work, Radhi marvelled at how different these classrooms were from the ones her sister and she had sat in, less than two decades ago. Gone was the traditional blackboard with the perpetual cloud of chalk dust hanging over it, replaced by a smart board screen which came down with a smart woosh and a tray of colourful markers. Now, no sharp-eyed teacher could aim a piece of chalk at a distracted student, Radhi thought wryly, remembering how frequently she'd been called out for staring out of the class window. Not only because there were no chalks, but also because, she suspected, hyper-protective parents would swoop in immediately, in protest. Also gone were the infamous, bulging school bags from her school years which had found their way into city newspapers for being dangerously heavy for young backs. Now, the students had been assigned cubbies at the back of the class where they could keep their books and stationery. What had remained constant, though, were the large softboards which displayed the students' current work. There were art pieces, pictures of science experiments and field trips, and a list of duty monitors for the current month.

Radhi shifted uncomfortably in her seat as the air conditioner swung towards her again. Outside, it was the hottest time of day with the afternoon sun at its peak, but inside, with two 1.5 tonne air conditioners blasting crisp, cool air into the room, most students were wearing North Star sweatshirts. Cursing herself for having once again forgotten to carry a jacket, Radhi got up to walk around the room, hoping it would warm her up.

With just twenty-odd students in each division, it wasn't a very big classroom. But an entire wall was dominated by large windows, which ensured that there was enough natural light and that the room appeared more spacious than it really was. As she paced at the front of the class, Radhi's ears caught a sniffle and then another. The sound had been hushed, very soft, yet there was no mistaking it. She glanced towards the direction it had come from, but every head was bent low as the students focused on their work. She walked down the aisle to the back of the class and stood still to see if she'd hear it again, but the room was quiet, except for the scratching of pen on paper.

Radhi checked her watch and was about to announce that only the last five minutes remained, when she was interrupted by the arrival of the school peon. He handed her a sheet of paper with two names on it.

'Soam Mehta?' she read aloud.

A stout boy with strong, broad shoulders and an acne ridden forehead got up from the back of the class.

'Brij Aggarwal?'

A sullen looking boy with round glasses and the beginning of facial hair, in the form of a tuft under his lower lip, got up from beside him.

'You guys need to go with him.' Radhi indicated the waiting peon.

Neither boy looked very surprised. Nor did one glance at the other while they made their way to the front of the class and handed Radhi their completed assignments before shuffling out of the room.

A murmur had gone around the class with the arrival of the peon and grown louder, once the boys left. Luckily, Radhi didn't have to settle the students again. The bell rang and announced the end of the period.

* * *

Radhi was leafing through the assignments she had just collected, giving each sheet a quick, precursory glance before sliding it into an A4-sized folder when one page made her pause. It had wet spots where the ink had blurred. Radhi glanced up to see the name in the right-hand corner. *Kia Soni.* A bushy-haired girl with thick glasses and an impressive vocabulary. Was Kia the one who had been crying in class? As she gathered her things, Radhi wondered what had upset Kia. Teenagers, she knew, had a lot of drama in their lives. Some real and some completely imagined.

Radhi had one more class before she could go home for the day. She decided to make her way to the third floor, where an empty desk had been assigned to her in the English Department for the duration of the three months she was going to be there. In the same line as the principal's office, and diagonally opposite the staffroom where the teachers assembled for their tea breaks, the English Department was a small, square room full of dusty books, stacks of papers, potted succulents and the hushed atmosphere one usually associated with a library. Today, however, raised voices greeted Radhi as she rounded the corner that led to the room.

'He is a powerful minister.'

'What he is, is a goon.'

'You really need to step down from this moral high ground.'

'And you really need to grow a pair.'

Venus's sharp voice reached Radhi, making her hesitate at the door.

The head of the English Department was in an intense conversation with a man sitting across from her.

'Should I come back?' Radhi offered, reluctant to interrupt.

The man sitting opposite Venus turned around. 'No, no please come in. I've already taken enough of Ms. Venus's time.' He stood up and pushed his chair back.

He was dressed in a fitted, linen kurta and blue denims and looked like he subsisted on protein shakes. His hair was completely grey, but the skin on his face was youthful, and Radhi pegged him at about forty or so.

'Please tell your father, this conversation is not over,' Venus said, her face stiff with displeasure.

The man shrugged. 'I don't know what else there is to say, Ms. Venus. The way I see it, we have only two options.'

'And what if neither of them works for me?'

The man sighed. 'I would urge you to reconsider.'

He glanced curiously at Radhi as she put her things on her desk and hung her purse on the back of the chair.

'I didn't know we had appointed a new teacher in the English Department,' he asked Venus, surprised.

'We haven't,' said Venus, still glowering at him. 'Even though we could use one with some actual qualifications.'

The man smirked. 'Come now, Ms. Venus, you know very well that Ms. Savant's qualifications are fine. You've just decided to not like her because my father hired her.' He walked towards Radhi and offered an outstretched hand. 'Satish Kamble. CFO and MD at North Star.'

'Radhika Zaveri.' Radhi took his hand and smiled. 'Guest faculty.'

And then because he was waiting expectantly, she elaborated, 'I'm taking a creative writing workshop for the ninth and tenth grades.'

His expression turned from mild curiosity to one of interest. 'Does that mean you are a writer, yourself?'

'Yes, she is a writer!' Venus said sharply from behind him. 'And a good one at that! But can this conversation happen anywhere other than my office?'

Unruffled at Venus's tone, the man shrugged. 'To be continued,' he said to Radhi with a smile, before turning to the English Head. 'You know you aren't being fair. In fac—'

'Don't you dare lecture me on fairness!' Venus interrupted him. 'Is your minister being fair to the poor kids who play in that park? Where should they play now? Your fancy sports club?'

Satish's face registered annoyance for the first time. He began to say something hotly then clamped his mouth shut. Running a frustrated hand through his hair, he said, 'Look, I support you in principle. But we have a school to run. We have other practical considerations. And I'm afraid that's that. Let's please talk again.' He gave her a curt nod before leaving the room.

Radhi looked over at Venus. The slightly built sixty-year-old had a head full of tight grey curls which were now dancing angrily around her shoulders as she shuffled papers roughly and muttered to herself. She wore round, oversized tortoiseshell spectacles which kept slipping down to the bridge of her nose, giving her an odd owlish appearance. In the short while that Radhi had been at North Star, Venus had come across as an idealistic, ill-tempered genius. Radhi had watched her yell at the school security guard for allowing parents to linger at the drop-off gate, and she'd heard her telling off Mr. Bottlewalla, in front of all the other teachers, for leaving the lights on in the common staffroom. But she had also watched Venus teach a class on *Jane Eyre*, had seen her evoke Rochester's desperation, his quiet dread of the mad woman in the attic with an effortless facility. Venus was cranky and caustic. But she could also be charismatic. She could do a feminist reading of the Brontë sisters and keep sixteen-year-old boys engaged. A rare feat in Radhi's opinion, if her own recent interactions with teenagers were anything to go by.

In fact, Radhi had been so impressed with one of Venus's classes that she'd promptly bought Venus's new book of poems and read it in one big gulp. She had been looking forward to discussing it with her, but given the English teacher's current mood, she knew it would have to wait.

'Will you have to change the script of the play, now?' Radhi ventured after a few minutes of watching the teacher scribble furiously.

Venus looked up, surprised, as if she had forgotten that Radhi was even there. She sighed and pushed her glasses above her head. 'If I don't, Satish says his father will cancel the whole competition. These kids have been practising for months now! Not only our students but also the children from the other participating schools. I couldn't do that to them.'

She was clicking her ball pen repeatedly, clearly agitated. 'This Satish is the sly one. I'm sure it was his idea. His father just puffs and rants. What I'd like to know is who told him? Kamble never comes for rehearsals of any kind. In fact, he is rarely on the school campus in the mornings. So, why did he suddenly decide to drop by the auditorium today?'

Radhi remained silent while Venus tried to solve the riddle she had posed to herself. 'This wasn't a coincidence. He didn't come out of curiosity to see how things were going. No.' Venus dismissed the idea with a slight shake of her head. 'This was deliberate. He came to shut us down.'

'This is probably the last thing you want to hear,' Radhi began carefully, 'but I can hardly blame him for asking you to change the play — they can't possibly let you embarrass their chief guest.'

'Of course, I know that,' Venus snapped. 'But you have to do drastic things sometimes, to get results.'

Some more clicking of the pen ensued, while Radhi waited for the older woman's annoyance to subside.

'Wouldn't you lose your job over something like this?' Radhi asked her finally.

'So?' Venus scoffed. 'I'd find another. But imagine saving that park for those kids! And more importantly, imagine the kind of example I'd be setting for the students. The power of speaking up, of taking action, of being change makers instead of bystanders. In just one evening, I would have taught them values that can take a whole lifetime to learn!'

Radhi smiled. For all her flaws, Venus was quite the firecracker. 'So now?'

The clicking of the pen began again. 'Now — I'll have to go with plan B.'

Radhi waited for the older woman to elaborate, but she seemed preoccupied again. 'I read your new book, by the way,' Radhi said after a few minutes. '*Butter and Sunshine*. It was gorgeous.' She rifled in her handbag and placed her copy in front of Venus. 'I'd love for you to sign it.'

'Very different from the kind of stuff you write, isn't it?' Venus asked with a slight smile. She patted the book. 'Leave this here with me, I'd like to write you a note.'

'I didn't know you had read something by me.'

'Of course I did. I wouldn't let them just bring anyone in — even if it's as guest faculty. *Chalk and Cheese*. That's the one I read. Some excellent writing in there.' Venus got up and walked to the coffeemaker behind her. 'So, what's next?'

Up until a few months ago, this question would have gone through Radhi like a shard of glass. But after years of struggling with a block, she'd finally written a new book, and it was due to release that month.

Radhi smiled. 'A murder mystery, this time.'

Venus, who had been tinkering with the knobs and buttons on the coffee machine, turned to Radhi with raised eyebrows. 'That's new for you, isn't it?'

'True,' said Radhi whose past work had all been award-winning literary fiction.

'Well, I do love a good mystery. There's something very satisfying about following all those clues and crumbs.' Venus turned to her again. 'Coffee?'

'Yes, please.' Radhi stood up to help her.

She opened the glass cabinet above the coffee maker and got out two ceramic mugs. One, the cobalt of traditional Jaipur pottery and the other, a warm mustard with white stripes. This was the first time the English teacher had offered her coffee, maybe because this was the first time they'd spoken at any length, but Radhi had long admired the colours and textures of the cups and mugs Venus had in that cabinet, all in perfect pairs. She suspected that Venus needed that many cups not because she was in the habit of offering coffee to that many visitors, but because she herself consumed a cup on an almost hourly basis, and she couldn't be bothered to go across the floor to rinse them in the staffroom sink.

'So, tell me,' Venus said, walking back to her desk with two cups of coffee and handing Radhi one, 'Are you a plotter or a pantser?'

'A bit of both, I suppose.' Radhi took an appreciative sip once they were seated at their respective desks again. 'Mmm, this is good.'

Venus snorted. 'It's impossible to have the swill they serve in the staffroom masquerading as cof—'

'Ms. Pereira? Excuse me, where can I find Ms. Venus Pereira?' a voice floated towards them from the corridor, preceding a tall, heavyset woman who appeared in the doorway, a few moments later.

'Are you happy now, Ms. Venus?' she asked without any preamble, when she caught sight of the head of the English Department.

'I beg your pardon?' Venus put her coffee mug down on the table, looking thoroughly surprised.

'They've taken away his sports captaincy,' the woman said as she entered the room. Dressed in a blue ikat kurta and jeans, she was tall, with a broad upper body and thick, muscular arms.

'I'm sorry what is this about—?' Venus asked.

'You caught my son vaping yesterday and took him to the principal.'

'Oh,' Venus's face cleared. 'You are Soam's—'

'Yes, I'm Soam Mehta's mother.'

'Please,' — Venus pointed towards the chair in front of her — 'have a seat.'

'I just met with Ms. Fernandes.' The woman continued as if Venus hadn't spoken. 'They've decided to revoke Soam's sports captaincy because of this vaping incident. Do you know how hard and for how many years he's trained for that captaincy? And now — just because of one stupid mistake, they've taken it away.'

'I'm sorry to hear that,' Venus said quietly.

'Are you, though?'

'Of course! This wasn't my decision—'

'But it was! You *decided* to take them to the principal. Couldn't you have let them go with a warning?'

'That was not the precedent I wanted to set!' Venus glanced at Radhi as if she couldn't believe she had to explain this. 'Vaping is dangerous and addictive! And as an educator, I couldn't possibly overlook it. Besides, he's an athlete. He should've been doubly conscious of how bad this is for the body.'

'He is sixteen, Ms. Venus.' The woman dug her nails into the back of the chair in front of her. 'They try new things. They make mistakes.'

'And shouldn't mistakes have consequences?'

'But shouldn't consequences be proportional?!' the woman countered.

'Again — Ms. Mehta,' — Venus pushed her chair behind and stood up — 'I don't decide the consequences.'

The woman shook her head bitterly. 'This sports captaincy was his ticket to a good university. His grades alone are not going to cut it. You know that. I don't know what we're going to do now.' She suddenly seemed deflated.

Both women were quiet for a few moments.

'I'll talk to Ms. Fernandes and see if there's something we can do,' Venus offered finally.

The woman nodded but looked as if she didn't believe anything would come of it. 'Soam's father is going to be so disappointed. He expects so much from Soam. Oh God, this is such a disaster!' She shook her head and turned, leaving as abruptly as she had come.

Venus sat back down frowning, muttering to herself. 'I don't know why parents do this.'

'What's that?' Radhi asked, cautiously.

'Pressurize the kids so much! Somehow, as a country, we've just not been able to shirk off this ridiculous importance given to marks. We've tied up the poor children's self-worth in grades and percentage points. As if they're the sum total of their report cards! And this Fernandes is no less!' Venus got up once more and left the room, muttering to herself.

* * *

Radhi took a long puff of her cigarette and almost shuddered in relief as the nicotine coursed through her bloodstream and infused her with an immediate sense of well-being. This — this going without a cigarette for hours together — she felt had to be the hardest part of her new job. Not the many assignments which she had to grade each week. Nor the snarky attitudes of some of the students. But the fact that smoking was prohibited in school, and she had to walk out of the school campus, cross the road and all but hide behind a tree to grab a quick puff. This was what she found most harrowing.

She looked around furtively, hoping that she wouldn't see anyone she knew. This was usually a safe time. The students were still in their classes and would be for the next hour at least. Which meant that there would be no parents thronging the gates, nor teachers leaving the premises. Still, it couldn't hurt to be careful. The last thing she wanted was for her smoking to rub the school authorities the wrong way. There was no world in which she could ever explain it to her sister — who didn't even know she smoked in the first place. No, it was much easier to hide behind cars and trees for the whole duration of her term.

Sighing, Radhi wiped the thin bead of sweat that had formed on her upper lip with the back of her sleeve. The banyan tree she was standing under was doing little to mitigate the oppressive April heat. Still, as she felt her body relax, she was grateful for the mid-afternoon break.

'Radhi?'

Radhi whirled around at the sound of a familiar voice and went from panic at the thought of being caught out to instant delight at the sight of the man in front of her.

'Hrishi! What in the world are you doing here?' she asked, breaking into a big smile.

'Same as you, I suppose,' he grinned, 'sneaking in a smoke?'

Radhi knew Hrishi from college. Tall, with kind, coffee-coloured eyes, and a salt and pepper beard, he was, what she supposed kids today would call, an old flame. Though things between them had never gone beyond one very explosive and memorable first kiss. Perhaps because Radhi's parents' accident had followed soon after and it had sent her on such a downward spiral, that there had been no space for anything else. Or perhaps because it wasn't meant to be. Radhi had never found out. Now, fifteen years later, he was married, and she was divorced, and they lurked in the friend zone, where they contented themselves with following each other's lives from the sidelines, except when their paths crossed, and Radhi experienced a charge between them which no number of years seemed to diminish. She felt it again as he leaned in for a hug and their cheeks brushed against each other. He was wearing a light blue cotton shirt and khakis with sleeves rolled up to reveal deeply veined muscular arms that she knew came from years of playing basketball. His hair and beard had more flecks of white than when she'd last seen him, but instead of making him look older, it made him more distinguished. She pulled away.

'What *are* you doing here?' she asked again.

'Anoushka forgot her project on the planetary system at home,' he said, referring to his six-year-old daughter and jerking one thumb towards the school building. 'I came to drop it off . . . and *you*?'

Quickly, Radhi told him about the writing workshop she was conducting for the school. 'But I had no idea that Anoushka went to North Star!' She added.

'You would, if we met more.' Hrishi smiled and checked his watch. 'Tell me, do you have time for a quick cup of tea?'

* * *

As Radhi glanced over the beverage menu, her eyes lingered over the wine list and her mouth felt dry. She had fallen into the habit of drinking a few glasses of wine each night, to help her fall asleep. She tried to avoid it when she could, tried very hard, in fact, but then she found she was always thinking about it. She glanced at the black and white checker-faced clock on the wall. It was too early to order a drink, regardless of how much she was craving one. Four p.m. was always going to be teatime.

'Masala chai?' Hrishi asked, looking up from the menu. 'And something to eat?'

'Yes, please,' Radhi said, pushing all thought of alcohol from her mind, along with why she needed it. She shut the menu. 'You order.'

They were at Your Daily Bread, a new café that had opened up in a lane behind North Star, that led to the main Temple Hill Road. With its black mirrors and black chandeliers set against exposed white brick walls and six-feet palms potted in white marble urns, Radhi liked how the place had been done up. But she knew its days were numbered. Hrishi seemed to have the same thought.

'I don't see why they must insist on shutting the place down,' he said, putting the menu aside once the orders were placed. 'If you don't want to eat non-vegetarian, don't come in here. Simple. To say that the place shouldn't exist is just autocratic.'

He was referring to the protest the Jain community of Temple Hill had recently launched against the café. They were demanding that either the café offer only vegetarian fare or shut down altogether.

'I agree with you in principle, of course.' Radhi put down the glass of water in her hand.

'But?'

She shrugged. 'But, I suppose, I get it.'

Radhi, who was Jain herself, knew that the non-violent way of life was an important tenet of her religion, and understood why the Jains had a problem with Your Daily Bread whose menu was generously peppered with mincemeat pies and bacon sandwiches.

When Hrishi continued to look at her expectantly, she continued, 'The restaurant is literally in the same complex as a Jain temple.'

'So?' Hrishi said, taking a sip of his tea and being purposely obtuse.

Radhi rolled her eyes. 'SO, I can understand how this might upset some people.'

28

'Have these people forgotten we live in a secular democracy?' Hrishi said.

Here we go, Radhi thought wryly, amused at how quickly they had fallen into their old pattern of being on opposite sides of an issue. In truth, she did not even believe that the restaurant should be shut down. In fact, had she been having this conversation with some of the stauncher members of her own extended family, *she* would most likely be the one condemning this strong-arming. But with Hrishi, the temptation to argue for the sake of it was just too irresistible.

'Look, you know that the Jains are probably the most tolerant of all communities in the country. We are peace-loving, we rarely involve ourselves in any kind of politics—'

'That's because you are so busy making money! Everything else must seem like a waste of time.'

Radhi was about to protest but, when she considered the wealthy stockbrokers and diamond merchants of her community, she thought better of it and laughed. 'You're probably right. But the point is, we live and let live. All we ask is you don't slaughter animals so close to where we worship.'

'Technically, this goat was slaughtered *before* it got here,' Hrishi said, taking a bite of the Russian salad sandwich the waiter had just placed in front of them.

'Well, *technically* then this argument is moot. This place is going to shut down sooner or later even without the protests.'

Hrishi's eyes widened as realization dawned. 'Oh, this is that jinxed place! I had completely forgotten.'

Radhi nodded, adding a generous dollop of tamarind chutney to her puffed rice bhel. 'Three months ago, it was Jasmine, an Asian restaurant that served excellent kimchi rice.'

'And I think a year ago, wasn't it a café called White?' Hrishi asked.

'Exactly. I doubt anything has ever lasted here for more than a few months.

'Clearly, this belongs to some newcomer,' Hrishi said, looking around. 'No one who's familiar with its history would open here.'

'That would explain the non-veg on the menu as well,' Radhi said dryly.

Hrishi seemed about to retort but was sidetracked by another thought. 'You know, I'm surprised nobody has written about this before. It's such a curiosity. I'm going to commission a piece on this.'

Hrishi was the editor-in-chief at the *National Gazette*, a leading national daily.

'Hrishi!' said Radhi clutching Hrishi's arm as her own mind went off on a tangent. 'Come teach writing to the kids in my workshop! Take one class on how to write a good hook for a story.'

'No, no, no . . .' Hrishi put down his cup, seeming alarmed. 'I'm not cut out for teaching.'

'Don't no-no me. It will be good for the students to hear from someone other than me. It'll give them a completely different perspective. And—' Radhi paused here before continuing, 'It might help *you* win some brownie points with the school!'

Hrishi leaned back in his chair, contemplatively. 'Well, her mother certainly will be glad. Neha's always cribbing about how I'm not involved enough with Anoushka's school and studies.'

The light in his eyes dimmed a little as he said this, and he fell quiet. And for the first time since they'd met, Radhi noticed the shadows under his eyes and the downward turn of his mouth.

'How are things at home, now?' she asked, gently. 'Did the therapy help?'

A year ago, Hrishi had confided in her that things were rocky in his marriage, and that his wife and he had been consulting a counsellor.

Hrishi sighed and ran a hand through his hair. 'Well, it did for a bit. But then I got tired of trying so hard . . .' He shook his head as if trying to clear the clouds. 'Sorry. It's not as bad as I make it sound. We do have our good days.'

He rubbed his hands together. 'You know what? I'll take the class.'

* * *

Radhi put down her book with a sigh. She was at home, stretched out on the sofa, trying very hard to avoid opening a bottle of wine. She was reading *Lincoln in the Bardo* — a beautiful book but heavy in its exploration of grief, mortality and racism. It was fast occurring to her, that if she had any hope of resisting alcohol with a book, it couldn't be this one. Ordinarily, a mystery would've stood a better chance. A good Christie, with an intelligent, tightly wrought puzzle, would've sucked her in. But these days, the minute she picked one up, her thoughts leaped to her own book, which was due to release in a week's time. And she found herself comparing it unfavourably to whatever book happened to be in her hand. Which ultimately defeated its purpose and just made her anxiety worse. Her thoughts went back to her evening with Hrishi, but she was afraid to linger there as well, always unsure of where that would lead her.

Frustrated, she straightened up and walked over to the tall, four-columned, mango wood bookcase, arranged in an elegant L facing the dining table. Her eyes traversed across Márquez, Mahfouz and Mantel, and came to rest on the three-foot matching mango wood bar cabinet that began where the bookcase stopped.

'Fuck it!' she cursed, before jerking open the bar cabinet, bringing out a bottle of shiraz and pouring herself a drink, in one swift, decisive motion.

Only once she'd had a glass and felt calmer, did she stop to consider the state of things. The drinking had started when she moved back to India and decided that resuming therapy was too painful. In the US, the therapy had given her access to medication which had helped her sleep – something she'd struggled with ever since her parents' car crash. Over the years, her anxiety and insomnia would improve or flare up depending on how she was doing in life. When she moved back, she was at an all-time low. Shattered heart. Stalled, stale career. And interminable, sleepless nights. What started as one drink each evening, slowly became a few. The wine made her so nice and mellow that she didn't miss her pills. She hadn't realized when the drinking went from a choice to a necessary crutch. Or maybe she did but didn't care. Even when her housekeeper, Lila, disturbed by the sight of an empty bottle in the kitchen each morning, called her out on her growing dependency, Radhi found that she was unable to give it up.

Now, she carried her bottle and glass and went to stand by the window. Below, the Arabian Sea lay like a dark, star-speckled blanket, still and heavy. The lack of even a wisp of breeze meant that the perennially swaying palms stood unmoving like sentinels watching over the city. Still, after a day of sitting in air-conditioned rooms, Radhi welcomed the embrace of the warm air. She took a deep, lungful of the salty sea smell, and immediately felt comforted. The sea, as always, reminded her of her mother.

Unlike Madhavi and their father, Radhi and their mother had a shared affinity for water. They were the beach people. The ones who would jump off boats and into the ocean to catch sight of pretty coral. The ones whose idea of a lazy Goa holiday was being at the beach by 6 a.m. to catch a pink sunrise. They would jump waves, make sandcastles, collect shells and go on long swims, all before the rest of the world emerged from their hotel rooms and into the breakfast café. In fact, being in Goa meant that Radhi got more of her mother. Madhavi, who much preferred treks and hikes and solid ground, would go off after breakfast to play tennis with their father, which left Radhi with her mother, both of them nicely bathed, but still smelling of the sea, sprawled with their books on the king-sized hotel bed. Perhaps it was the thought of those long, precious afternoons with her mother or the wine doing an exceptional job, but a sudden, unexpected sense of well-being settled upon Radhi. She turned from the window and approached her laptop lying on the dining table, in the hope of capturing some part of this emotion into words. However, no sooner had she awoken it from sleep mode, an email in her inbox made her gasp. Shocked, she sat down and read ahead, the glass in her hand forgotten.

CHAPTER 3

Dear all,

It is with a heavy heart that I must convey to all of you some deeply disturbing news. Earlier tonight, our beloved Venus Pereira was found dead at her desk in the English Department. It seems she had an acute cardiac arrest, but the police have been summoned, as is due procedure, to rule out any foul play. The management and I are shocked and saddened at this unfortunate turn of events, but the need of the hour for us as educators is to first think about our students. While the police conduct their investigation, we must rally together to decide upon a course of action as to how to convey the news to the parent and student body, so as to ensure that there is minimal scope for speculation and that our students are not overly disturbed.

We've announced a holiday for the students tomorrow, i.e. Tuesday, 4 April, 2023. Requesting all faculty to come into school tomorrow morning at nine, so that we can discuss the best way forward. The police will also be there during this time and can speak to each of you individually.

The death of Ms. Pereira is a terrible loss for our school community, and we stand with each other and with every one of you in this time of grief.
 Best regards,
 R. Fernandes

* * *

Tuesday

'Good morning, everyone. And thank you for coming in.' Satish Kamble paused to look around the room at the dozen or so teachers gathered in front of him.

The high school faculty had assembled in the school hall — a wide, high-ceilinged, rectangular room with a row of windows on one side, a grand piano forte on the other, and a stage with heavy, maroon, velvet curtains in the front. Kamble however had chosen not to address them from the stage. He stood instead in front of them in a loose grey kurta, his hands stuck deep inside the pockets of his jeans.

'As you know, Ms. Venus passed away yesterday. She was discovered at her desk at around eight p.m. by Ms. Savant who'd come back to school to pick up some assignments. She immediately called Ms. Fernandes who, in turn, informed us. We don't know exactly when she passed and what suddenly brought this on. The police will certainly be able to tell us more once they've had a chance to run some tests. But before that they would like to speak to you.'

He paused at the low buzz that had gone through the room at the mention of police, before continuing. 'Everyone. Please. This is a difficult circumstance as it is. Idle speculation is only going to make things harder. What the board and I and the school really need from you right now is to cooperate. And to help us contain this in a way that the school and our students come out of it as unscathed as possible. Now, Ms. Fernandes would like to address you.'

35

Fernandes, who was sitting in the first row beside the senior Mr. Kamble, got up and walked to the front of the room. And for the first time since Radhi had known her, her shoulders drooped.

'Good morn—' the principal cleared her throat and began again. 'Good morning, one and all. The last twelve hours have been exceptionally challenging for me as I suspect for many of you. I've not only lost a great teacher but also a very dear friend.' She removed her glasses and wiped them, looking at the front row of teachers sadly. 'I don't know how I'll fill the large, Venus-shaped hole in my English Department. But for now, I must urge you to stay strong. To put your personal feelings aside, and to focus on our students. An email has already gone to the parent body informing them of Ms. Venus's demise on the school premises. Tomorrow morning, Mr. Kamble and I will address the students in a special assembly. On your part, please encourage them to come to you with any questions. I would rather that they discuss it with you than with each other.'

A peon entered the room and approached Kamble who had stood up again just as Fernandes had finished speaking.

'The police are waiting for you in the grade six classrooms. Please go when he calls out your names,' Kamble said, nodding towards the peon.

As the teachers began to disperse, Radhi turned her chair to face Mr. Bottlewalla and Mr. Bakshi who were sitting in the row behind her. 'Do you know what exactly happened?' she asked.

Mr. Bakshi shook his head, 'No more than what Kamble just told us.'

'But how so suddenly? Were there any pre-existing health issues?'

Mr. Bakshi glanced at Mr. Bottlewalla who shrugged and said, 'She was rarely absent or on sick leave. I doubt there was anything serious.'

'At least nothing she saw fit to discuss with us,' Mr. Bakshi added.

Radhi scanned the right side of the room where Ms. Lily and Ms. Savant were sitting with a few other teachers she recognized. 'Was she close to anyone?'

'Not them for sure,' Mr. Bottlewalla said, following her gaze. 'You know, I'm not sure she was really close with anyone at school. She spent most of her spare time reading at her desk or with her students.'

'Yes, her Lit Kids, as she liked to call them,' Mr. Bakshi said. 'Four or five very enthusiastic kids she mentored after school.'

The peon came to call Mr. Bottlewalla, who struggled for a few moments to get out of the narrow, wooden chair, before heaving his considerable girth out of the room.

Radhi's stomach rumbled, reminding her that she'd overslept and left home without any breakfast that morning. At the back of the hall, she could see a few tables had been set up with tea, coffee and bottles of water. After checking with Mr. Bakshi if he wanted anything, she made her way towards the back, where a group of teachers had already gathered.

'What was she doing here so late, anyway?'

'Working, what else?'

'I suppose when you live alone there's no incentive to go home.'

'Didn't she live with her mother?'

'Her mum died last year.'

'Oh . . . I had no idea. Was there a prayer service?'

'Yes, but she didn't tell anyone.'

'How do you know?'

'Ms. Lily mentioned it. They went to the same church.'

'Aah, okay.'

Snatches of conversation reached Radhi as she poured herself a cup of steaming ginger tea from a large, steel thermos with a black cap. It saddened her to think that the old teacher had been all alone in her final moments. A life spent in the pursuit of beauty and poetry should have had a more fitting, a more graceful end. She stirred in a spoonful of sugar, before picking up a few Bourbon biscuits with their trademark chocolate cream filling, from a tray covered with a net. As she began to make her way back to Mr. Bakshi, she saw the peon approach him and accompany him out of the room. Pausing, she glanced around the room and decided to walk towards Ms. Savant who was sitting with Ms. Lily and a couple of other teachers.

As she neared them, she saw that Ms. Savant looked shaken. Her eyes were red, as if she'd been crying or hadn't slept or both, and yet, strangely, she also seemed to be in her element. She sat with her handkerchief pressed to her lips, one hand clutching her head almost theatrically, while the other teachers spoke in whispers around her. Radhi chided herself for her unkind thought. She, who had stumbled upon a murdered woman at a matrimonial bureau, just a few months ago, knew, perhaps more than anyone else in the room, how hard it was to unsee a dead body.

'Are you okay, Ms. Savant?' she asked, sitting in the empty chair between her and Ms. Lily.

The English teacher bit her lip and nodded.

'Here, would you like some tea?' Radhi extended her untouched cup to Ms. Savant, who accepted it gratefully.

'The police really grilled her,' said Ms. Farah, whose hair with its electric blue highlights always struck Radhi as very fitting for the art teacher. 'Why did she come back to school? Why so late? Why not leave it till the next day? Was it really so urgent? Was somebody with her—'

'Did I see anyone else when I went up?' Ms Savant took up the narration midway, reluctant to miss a minute of her moment in the spotlight, 'Did I see anyone while leaving? Did I know Ms. Venus was going to be there . . .' The English teacher shook her head and took another sip of the tea. 'I told them I didn't see a thing! I wasn't there to sightsee, was I? But they went on and on! And you know what the funny part is?' She took a bite of one of the Bourbons before correcting herself, 'Well, not *funny* funny, but more in the weird-coin-cidence-sort-of-way — I was there *because* of Ms. Venus! If I didn't grade those assignments that evening, she would have bitten my head off!'

'Well, at least you don't have to worry about her sharp tongue now,' Ms. Lily said dryly as she got up, 'I'm getting myself a cup of coffee. Can I get anything for anyone?'

Radhi guessed that Ms. Lily had probably heard Ms. Savant's story more than a few times that day and was fatigued by it. But still she thought her remark had been insensitive. She wondered though about Ms. Savant's relationship with Venus.

'Wait, I'll come with you.' The art teacher jumped up, along with a couple of others, leaving Radhi alone with Ms. Savant.

A part of Radhi wanted to go with them. She was hungry and thirsty and, by now, really craving that tea. In fact, what she would have loved at that moment was a cigarette. But the other part of her, the one that got immediately sucked into puzzles, was curious to find out why someone seemingly healthy had died so suddenly.

'She did seem stressed when I left last evening . . . but I didn't think it was this serious,' Radhi said. 'It must've been a terrible shock for you.'

'It was awful . . . Her face was flushed bright red like a tomato, and she was slumped on her desk with a pen in her hand.'

'Oh . . . had she written something?' Radhi's eyes widened at the prospect of a note. 'Or had she been working?'

'I don't know about all that. Somehow, I thought she was alive, so I went over to her side to shake her awake and stepped right into a puddle of vomit.' Ms. Savant shuddered. 'I called out to her loudly and when she didn't respond, I checked her pulse. Then of course I calle—'

'Ms. Savant?'

Radhi and the English teacher looked up to see Satish Kamble.

'Ms. Savant, the police have said you can go home now. I understand you were here till late, last night. Please get some rest. If there's anything else, we'll be in touch.'

'Oh? Okay then . . .' Ms. Savant seemed almost disappointed at being sent home earlier than the others. She began to look around to see where she could keep her empty teacup.

'I can take that,' Kamble offered an outstretched hand.

'No, I couldn't possibly . . .' Ms. Savant clutched the cup tightly to her chest.

'I insist,' he said, waiting until Savant had handed her cup over.

Radhi got up with the English teacher, thinking to finally get herself something to eat or drink, but Kamble touched her shoulder gently. 'Please, Ms. Zaveri, I was hoping to talk to you. Can we step outside?'

Curiously, Radhi followed Kamble out of the hall and through a door to its right, into what was clearly the music room. There were tables and shelves against each of the four walls, lined and laden with gleaming cymbals and harmoniums, bamboo flutes, the trapezoid-shaped santoor with its ninety strings, a row of sheeshum wood tablas, that were only ever happy in pairs, and graceful, long-necked sitars made of teak with delicate fretwork and strings of steel and bronze. Radhi stared, amazed at the variety of Indian instruments on display.

Indian classical music had been a passion Radhi had shared with her father. A passion that she had given up in the wake of her parents' car crash, because it had been tainted with guilt and fraught with grief.

'A lover of music, I take it then?' Kamble asked with a small smile, nudging Radhi out of her reverie.

'Sorry,' she smiled. 'You have a beautiful collection. I didn't know schools these days invested so much in musical training.'

'Not all schools, only North Star. It's my father. He is very passionate about the performing arts. In fact, that's what I wanted to talk to you about.' He pointed Radhi to a pair of winged chairs and a coffee table in the centre of the room.

'May I assume, you are aware of the whole hullaballoo over the script of our play?' he asked once they were seated across from each other.

Radhi nodded.

'Well, then you may also know that Ms. Venus was supposed to be working on a new script for us. The play is less than two weeks away and now with her gone, we are honestly at a loss on how to proceed. Ms. Savant will be taking over some of Ms. Venus's teaching load. And we should be able to find a substitute teacher for the rest, but the question of the play still remains.' He paused and smiled before continuing, 'I guess this is my rather longwinded way of asking you, if you would consider helping with the script?'

Radhi, who had begun to sense where the conversation was going even before he asked the question, frowned apologetically. 'I'm so sorry. I really wish I could help, but I have never written a script. A book is very different from a play in the way it is structured, in the importance given to dialogue, in the way scenes are visualized . . .' Radhi shook her head. 'It requires a completely different skillset and—'

Kamble held up his hands before Radhi could say more. 'I know, I know . . . but the basic principles of storytelling remain the same, don't they? We need a clear beginning, middle and an end. Correct?'

Radhi seemed about to protest, but he hurried on. 'Look, a lot of the work in terms of designing the sets and costumes is already done. The music has been selected and edited. The students have also learned their lines. So, we aren't looking to create something completely new or drastically different. We have neither the time nor the bandwidth for that. We just need to take our existing script and give it a different spin, a more palatable end. And let's face it, you are more qualified than the rest of us.'

Radhi bit her lip. What he said was true and yet, she didn't know where she would find the time for it. Already, the workshop was eating into a significant chunk of her writing time. George, her agent, had been telling her that she needed to start writing the second mystery in the series, while she waited for the first one to release. Series-readers expected a book a year. That was the only way of gaining a loyal audience.

Kamble checked his phone and frowned, 'I need to take care of something. Why don't you think about it? And we can talk again?'

* * *

'Hello, Inspector,' Radhi said as she entered the classroom where the police were conducting their interviews.

The inspector looked up from his notes and gaped at her for a moment before finding his tongue. 'You, again?'

Despite the grimness of the occasion, Radhi couldn't help but grin at his almost comical astonishment. This was her third run-in with Inspector Shinde and his impressive pot belly. The last had been at the matrimonial bureau when she had helped him solve a murder despite his mulish resistance. He gestured for her to take the chair across from him and folded his arms in front of him. 'How is it ma'am that every time there is an unnatural death in this neighbourhood, I end up meeting you?'

'So, this is an unnatural death?'

'No . . . no . . . no, see, you are doing that thing again.' Shinde waved one finger in front of her face. 'Reading too much into things. This is *my* investigation. *I* am the one who'll ask the questions, and you will answer them. Okay?'

'After all the help I gave you last time, Inspector, I thought you would be happy to see me.' Radhi knew it was the wrong thing to say but she took perverse pleasure in riling up the man.

'Oh, believe me, ma'am — I am,' he said, surprising Radhi. 'But not for the reason you think. After talking to all those teachers who think I'm vermin because my English isn't any good, I'm almost happy to see a familiar face. But you need to let me do my job.'

'Of course,' said Radhi, feeling slightly chastened.

The class differences in their country were so many and so pronounced that not only your house and car but the very accent you spoke a language in could be used as a class marker.

Shinde had been expecting Radhi to come up with a rejoinder but when she remained quiet, he hurried on. 'So, tell me, ma'am, what are you doing here?'

Quickly, Radhi told him about the workshop she was conducting for the school, and how she had shared her space with Venus in the English Department office.

'Can you tell me about your last interaction with her? Did she seem agitated about something?'

'Are you trying to determine if the cardiac failure was brought on because of something that happened?'

Shinde rolled his eyes heavenwards. 'Ma'am, ma'am, please. I am the one who will ask the questions, remember?'

Radhi thought back for a moment before answering. 'Well, there was an altercation with the parent of a student.'

Shinde motioned for the constable standing behind him to take notes while Radhi told him about how upset Soam Mehta's mother had been and how she had blamed Venus for the loss of her son's sports captaincy.

'Anything else or anyone else?' Shinde asked when Radhi had stopped speaking.

'There was also a disagreement with Mr. Kamble about the script of the play.'

'Yes, yes—' Shinde drummed the table, impatiently. 'Everyone mentioned that Venus and the old man really went for it that morning.'

'I am not talking about the senior Mr. Kamble — but his son, Satish Kamble. Even he had a spirited discussion with Ms. Venus later that afternoon.'

'Is it? Hmm . . . Mr. Kamble didn't mention it to me when we spoke about it, earlier today.' Shinde said, looking at his constable for confirmation.

Radhi hesitated. 'It wasn't a loud argument, more of an intense conversation. But I'm sure Ms. Venus felt pressured by it,' she said, remembering how that conversation had ended.

Shinde frowned. 'Ma'am, don't mind, but you're again complicating matters. We don't need to go into every conversation, just the ones that could've triggered her.'

Radhi swallowed back an angry retort. She would've thought that after the way she'd saved his skin the last time, he would treat her opinions with a bit more respect. But he was like the proverbial tail of the dog, unable to change his ways.

'Anyways, if there's anything else you remember, please don't hesitate to call me,' he said, scribbling into his notepad. 'Not that you ever do. Hesitate that is.' He chuckled to himself.

* * *

Irritated, hungry and desperately craving a cigarette, Radhi was making her way down the corridor that led to the school entrance, when Satish Kamble caught up with her.

'Did you get a chance to think about it?' he asked, easily keeping pace.

Radhi *had* thought about it. Aside from the obvious commitment on her time, she had also felt that changing Ms. Venus's script would be a betrayal of everything the old teacher had hoped to achieve by taking this stance against the management and the politicians. Practically and morally, this job did not appeal to her. But before she could answer, he threw in a curve ball.

'Ms. Fernandes tells me that your niece is up for admissions, next year? Of course, it goes without saying that if you were to help us with this, the admission committee would take that into consideration.'

They had paused inside the main lobby. Above the entrance, was a large, almost six-foot replica of the rhombus-shaped school badge depicting a golden star gleaming against a backdrop of bottle green. And on the wall opposite was a row of plaques, one with the names of all the head boys and girls and sports captains of the school since the 1980s, another with names of the school houses that had won the school trophy each year. A third plaque, which was larger and embellished with an embossed copper moon and stars, announced North Star's ranking in the country, which for the last decade had been first every year. And a final, fourth one bore the names of the toppers at the international Olympiads and maths championships every year. A high, vaulted ceiling and a liberal use of dark wood for stairs and banisters gave the whole place a hallowed appearance.

Radhi bit her lip. He hadn't said what would happen if she refused to do the script. Would the admissions committee take *that* into account as well? And what about the writing workshop she was currently conducting pro bono for the school? Wasn't that a consideration in the first place? She was fast losing patience with the evasive equivocal nature of these things. She was a writer, sure, but she was also her father's daughter. And her father hadn't built one of the largest diamond export houses in the country by letting people take advantage of him.

'Well, if a guaranteed admission is what you're offering . . .' She extended her hand with a smile and put their deal into words in no uncertain terms, '. . . then consider it done.'

He shook her hand. 'Of course, I will let Ms. Fernandes know.'

But just when he thought it was over, she added, 'It's just that Ms. Fernandes . . . she's retiring next year, and I'm guessing there's bound to be some shuffling and restructuring at the school. What will really set my sister's mind at ease is if we have an early acceptance letter from the school for my niece.'

Kamble frowned. 'That is really not our school policy.' He motioned her towards a navy-blue tuxedo sofa. When they were both seated, he said, 'If the other parents find out, they would accuse us of playing favourites and create a ruckus about it.' He paused for a moment as two teachers passed them by before resuming again in a softer voice. 'I could not risk it. Everyone knows how selective we are with our admissions process. People are always giving us flack for not being transparent enough. I can't give you anything in writing. You'll just have to take my word for it.' Suddenly, he hit his own knee, as if he'd just remembered something. 'Also, I forgot to mention that we've decided to offer you a generous compensation for all the time you're spending with us.'

Radhi smiled. He had misjudged the situation if he thought money would motivate her. With the millions in her trust fund from her father, the properties she had received as part of the divorce settlement from her hotelier ex-husband and her own income as a former bestselling author, Radhi would always have more than she knew what to do with. Any proposed fee he offered was never going to tip the scale. 'I wouldn't hear of it. I'm only doing this for my sister. A written acceptance letter would be such a load off her head.' Radhi lowered her voice. Softness, she had learned was usually more impactful than any forceful gestures or proclamations. 'You can, of course, be assured of our discretion.'

Kamble ran a hand through his hair. 'We really can't be seen to be making exceptions.'

'And yet, these are exceptional circumstances,' Radhi said.

Kamble seemed to be studying her. Contemplating, perhaps, if he could push back. But something in Radhi's face must have convinced him that it was futile. He got up and slipped his hands into his pockets. 'Okay, sure. I'll have the paperwork drawn up in the coming week.'

Radhi stood up and gave him a dazzling smile. 'Thank you. I appreciate it.'

She had learned from her father that victory was always sweeter if the other side didn't feel its sting as much.

CHAPTER 4

'Lila, I could kiss you right now!' Radhi said to her housekeeper, as she surveyed the elaborate lunch spread on the table. 'I've been starving.'

'Good,' said Lila, as she placed a hot, ghee-soaked roti on Radhi's plate. 'If you could please eat it instead of looking at it, that would make me feel much better.'

Chuckling, Radhi dipped the fluffy, white, steamed dhoklas into the bowl of mango *ras* and closed her eyes for a moment, savouring the delicate tartness of the soft rice cake as it mixed with the sweet alphonso pulp. Next, she tore a piece of roti and scooped up some of the spicy, ivy gourd subzi, which had the exact degree of crunch she liked. Besides this, Lila had also prepared a yogurt-based mango curry, a yellow, lentil dry-dal preparation and a crumbly and lemony, raw-banana subzi which Radhi loved.

'I'm just one person, you know! This is too much,' Radhi protested in between bites, when Lila brought out some crisp papads and a plate of sliced cucumbers, before finally taking her customary seat on the window ledge, with a cup of tea.

'You skipped breakfast today,' Lila said to justify going overboard.

But Radhi knew that this wasn't the only reason behind Lila's elaborate efforts in the kitchen, these days. The fact was that her housekeeper was feeling guilty for working part-time for a full day's pay. Her son had his final exams that month and Lila was leaving early every evening, so that she could be home and keep an eye on his studies. She had requested Radhi to cut her pay so that it was proportionate to her hours, but when Radhi wouldn't hear of it, she tried to compensate by overdoing the cooking and cleaning.

'I'm going to put on weight at this rate,' Radhi said, as she reached for a second helping of the dhoklas.

'I would really like to see the day,' Lila joked, rolling her eyes at Radhi's naturally slender frame. 'Your type of body makes me so jealous!'

Radhi mixed a spoonful of rice with the mango curry and crushed a papad with her hand before sprinkling it on the rice. 'But you know thin doesn't necessarily mean healthy.' She proceeded to tell Lila about how the slim and seemingly healthy Ms. Venus had passed away so suddenly from heart failure.

Lila's expression turned sombre. 'Sometimes no, Didi, when people are carrying too much here . . .' — she patted her own head — '. . . it affects here,' she said, touching her heart.

They were both quiet for a few moments, then Lila put her teacup down. 'Let's celebrate your birthday, this year.'

Radhi raised her eyebrows at the sudden change of topic. 'We celebrated it last year, as well. You got me gulab jamuns . . . Amayra made me that birthday card and Didi took me out for lunch . . .'

'Phssh.' Lila swiped her hand dismissively. 'THAT's not a celebration, Didi. What we need is a proper party. With gifts and music and other people. Where everyone makes a fuss over you.'

Radhi spoiled her face. 'Why in the world would I want that?' She took a final spoonful of her mango ras before adding, 'I like quiet birthdays. It gives me a chance to reflect on

the year that's passed by. To think of what's coming ahead
. . .'

'*Hey Bhagwan* . . .' Lila called on the gods theatrically, 'You please do all your thinking-*shinking* a day in advance and get it done with! There's no need to be SO boring on the day of.'

Radhi laughed. 'Since when did you become such a fan of big birthdays?'

'Since my ex made it a point to beat me up on every birthday,' Lila said quietly, all trace of mirth gone from her eyes. 'Obviously, he did it on other days as well. But in the five years I was with him, he never missed a birthday. Got pissed drunk and pissed mad and never failed to create a scene. I decided then that if I ever got rid of him, I would make every birthday count.' Lila took a final gulp of the tea and got up. 'And that includes the birthdays of people I care about.' She straightened the folds of her saree and fixed Radhi with a challenging stare.

Radhi met her gaze quietly. There was a lot she wanted to say, but she dared not express sympathy. This was the first time her proud housekeeper had spoken about her abusive husband. Radhi knew parts of her story and knew that Lila had had it very rough. But she'd never gone into the details of it, and Radhi had never felt it right to ask. She could see that bringing it up now hadn't been easy for Lila.

'Okay,' she agreed with a small smile. 'Party, then.'

Lila smiled back broadly. 'Yes! Proper party. I'll fix it all with Madhavi didi. We'll surprise you,' she said walking out of the room.

'You know, it's not really a surprise if you've already told me about it,' Radhi called after her.

'Oh, don't be so by the book!' Lila shot back.

Chuckling to herself, Radhi followed her into the kitchen to put her plate away. She had promised herself that she'd get on with the new book that day. She had already plotted her second mystery while editing the first one. And now, she was in the research phase. Things had been chugging along at a good pace, especially when she could stop herself from worrying about how the new book would be received. But with all the new, additional demands on her schedule, she was afraid she'd lose momentum if she didn't use her spare time well.

Radhi's study was a large, airy room with windows overlooking the Arabian Sea, a floor-to-ceiling bookcase, a walnut brown, Burmese wood writing desk facing away from the window and, on the wall above it, something that was a constant source of joy for Radhi. A framed depiction of Trishlamata, Lord Mahavir's mother, exquisitely and painstakingly hand embroidered by her own mother. Once she had settled herself at her desk, Radhi continued where she had left off, adding a list of poisons and antidotes to the document on murder methods open on her laptop. She then proceeded to work for a few hours straight, stopping only to open a new bottle of wine and pour herself a glass.

* * *

Wednesday

Assembly, the next morning, was a sombre affair. Students from grade five to ten had gathered in the school hall in front of the main stage, while the teachers were seated in the aisles on both sides. Since she was not part of the regular faculty, it wasn't mandatory for Radhi to attend the weekly assemblies. But she had wanted to be there for this one as a mark of respect for the dead poet. An email had gone out to the parent body with the news of Venus's demise, the previous day, so the students were well aware of what had transpired before they got to school, but still a hush had blanketed the whole hall all through Ms. Fernandes's speech. The choir had followed with the school song and then Ms. Venus's favourite hymn, but despite the accompanying music from the piano and the violins, the feeling of unease didn't leave the room.

Now, as everyone filed out of the hall, in more order than she had ever seen in the place, Radhi had a decision to make. She had planned a field trip to the theatre for the ninth graders that afternoon but, given the circumstances, she was loath to continue. However, the tickets had been bought, and permission forms had been signed, and Radhi didn't know how the parents would take it if she cancelled the plan without a refund. Detaching herself from the main hoard of students which was making its way to the class-rooms, Radhi walked up to the third floor, where she waited for Ms. Fernandes outside her office.

The principal who met her seemed a mere shadow of her former self. Up close, Radhi saw the sunken eyes which she'd missed when Fernandes was speaking on stage.

'You don't look like you've got any sleep these last two days,' Radhi said once the two of them had settled in the principal's office — a large, sunlit room with plants in pots and mugs and cups and frames of students on stage and podiums winning at things.

'How can I? The police, the parents, the press . . . already I've got a call from a reporter who wants to interview me for an obituary on Venus. I am so worried this is going to become a whole circus. And God forbid should any student do something stupid . . .' She shuddered then shook her head to clear it of whatever internal nightmare she had playing on loop. 'Anyways, what did you want to talk to me about?'

'Remember the field trip we spoke about?' Radhi hesitated. 'The tickets were for this afternoon. Given all of this . . . is it okay to cancel?'

'Absolutely not,' Fernandes said immediately. 'I want things to be as normal as possible for the students. This is an important term for our senior grades. We need to avoid any kind of disruption. Please go ahead as planned.'

Radhi got up with a nod, glad to hear the firmness in the principal's voice. Fernandes might be temporarily shaken, but it would take more than a dead teacher to steer her off course.

* * *

Fernandes closed her eyes and rested her head back in her seat, desperate for a moment of respite. It was exhausting to constantly pretend to be strong, to always know the answers, to keep the school and its reputation before her own needs and wants. The last week or two had been relentless. If she could just shut her eyes for a minute and get some sleep, she'd be able to think more coherently, function more effectively. She considered telling her secretary to not allow any calls or visitors unless they were urgent, but she doubted the silly girl would know the difference. Her presence in Fernandes's life was a testament to how the balance of power had shifted at North Star in the last one year. Ever since the arrival of Satish Kamble. But she wouldn't think about all of that right now or she'd get riled up again. Luckily, this was the year she retired, so she had to hold up the fort for just a few months more. If she could just keep that in mind, she might breathe easier.

* * *

Radhi was sure someone was crying. She had just entered the girls' bathroom on the second floor to freshen up before the field trip, when a distinct sniffling sound made her pause and shut off the tap.

'Hey, are you okay in there?' She knocked on the door of the bathroom stall.

The sniffling stopped immediately but there was no answer.

'Are you all right?' Radhi tried again.

This time, she got a strangled, 'Yes.'

'Can you please come out when you are ready? I'll wait for you.'

A long silence followed. Then a girl with a tear-streaked face and a long, bushy-haired plait, stepped out.

'Kia! What's the matter?' Radhi asked, recognizing the ninth grader from her workshops.

The girl took one look at Radhi's concerned face and began howling in earnest.

'There, there,' Radhi put an arm around the girl. 'Is it Ms. Venus? Were you close with her?'

Kia didn't answer but continued crying.

Radhi held her until the worst of the sobs had subsided. Then she pulled out a few tissues from the dispenser and pressed them into her hands. 'The death of a teacher you love can be hard. Were you part of the Lit Kids?' Radhi asked.

Kia nodded but didn't seem inclined to talk. She splashed water on her face, retied her hair, and together the two of them left the bathroom.

* * *

'Soam? Soam Mehta?' Radhi was standing at the front of the bus with a clipboard in her hand, taking attendance before the field trip.

'He hasn't come to school, Miss,' Brij answered.

Radhi put an 'A' against his name for 'Absent' and continued with the rest of the names before putting the clipboard away.

'Now as you all know, the play we are watching is about Gauhar Jaan, one of India's first female voice artists. Does anyone know anything about her?'

'Miss!' One of the ninth graders' hands went up.

'Yes?'

'She is said to have recorded more than 600 songs in twenty languages.'

'True.' Radhi nodded. 'It's a fantastic and inspiring story, and you're going to love how it's rendered. But what I'd like you to pay close attention to is how real-life events have been organized to form a gripping tale. How the narrative shifts between the past and present and still moves the story forward. Because for our next assignment, you are going to take an episode or a sequence of episodes from your life and tell it in the form of a story. You might want to leave out some people or amplify a few parts or change the order of how some events occurred. You can take complete creative liberty. As long as you give me a good story. Okay? Got it?'

A chorus of yesses rose from the back seats of the bus, and a satisfied Radhi took her seat beside Mr. Bakshi at the front of the bus. It was school policy for two teachers to supervise on a field trip, and Fernandes had asked Radhi to choose between Mr. Bakshi and Ms. Farah, both of whom had free classes that afternoon.

'I never did thank you for agreeing to give up your free time for this trip,' Radhi said to the chemistry teacher. 'Do you enjoy theatre?'

Mr. Bakshi smiled. 'Well, I don't watch enough to know whether I enjoy it. But I don't mind it. Besides, with the mood in the school today, I'm more than happy to be away.'

Radhi looked outside the window as the bus snaked its way through the traffic at Kemps Corner, a popular shopping area lined with shoe stores on both sides. You could find handbags and purses and even cosmetics if you were desperate, but the street was known for its vast variety of cheap, local footwear that no international brand had so far been able to compete with.

'Do you think Soam didn't come to school because of the whole sports captaincy thing? Poor fellow . . . Ms. Venus was going to talk to Ms. Fernandes about giving him a second chance.'

'He is a fool! This *was* his second chance.' Mr. Bakshi snapped the book in his hand shut. 'A few months ago, do you know what some of these boys did?' He continued without waiting for an answer. 'They brought grapes and orange segments injected with vodka to school! It was the day of the Christmas party, but still — can you believe the audacity?'

The idea was so ingenious that Radhi, who had only recently assumed the role of an educator, found it difficult to muster the appropriate amount of outrage. However, she could tell that the chemistry teacher didn't find it even remotely funny.

'You know what I think?' Mr. Bakshi continued after a few seconds. 'Soam is just acting up. His father's pretty draconian, I hear.' He shook his head. 'I never thought I'd say this, but sometimes even too much discipline can be a bad thing.'

'Do you think Ms. Fernandes will reconsider? His sports captaincy?'

Mr. Bakshi scoffed. 'Have you met our principal?'

The chemistry teacher was about to elaborate but they were interrupted. One of the students seated behind them, lifted a laundry tag with the logo of a sun sticking out of Mr. Bakshi's collar and asked, 'Sir, is this a new fashion statement?'

Mr. Bakshi turned to him with a smile and pulled out the tag. 'Yes — just like the pants you boys wear, which seem to have forgotten that their main job is to cover your arses!'

The student laughed and Mr. Bakshi turned back to Radhi with a good-natured eye roll.

* * *

Mr. Bakshi had meant it when he said he was glad to be away from the school. Ever since he saw that graffiti on the wall of the boys' bathroom in school, it was as if a tight fist had closed over his heart. He hadn't said anything to anybody. He hadn't even tried to clean it up. For that would've meant to acknowledge it. He had thought if he ignored it, it would go away and for some time, it had felt like it would, but then it had resurfaced in the most terrifying way. Bakshi opened the top button of his shirt, and tried to take a deep breath, but his chest felt constricted and, despite the air conditioning in the school bus, a sheen of sweat covered his forehead. He took a swill of water from a Bisleri bottle and with an effort he reminded himself that it was over now, that somehow he had come out of it unscathed. Which, given his past luck, seemed almost miraculous.

* * *

55

Built in the 1900s in the baroque style by King George V, the Royal Opera House had only recently been restored to its original magnificence. With crystal chandeliers, intricate murals, wall etchings and statues of cherubs in Carrara marble, it was India's only surviving opera house and had a rich history of hosting plays, operas and musical concerts for the city's elite. Radhi tried to give the students some background on the place, but they were too excited to really focus. Out of school, they seemed to have left the news of Venus's death behind them. They were talkative and loud as they got into line to enter the auditorium, and Mr. Bakshi had to remind them that this was not a private show. Even Kia, who was deep in conversation with a friend, seemed composed. Fortunately, once they were seated, the chatter died down, as the students took in the grandeur of the red and gold auditorium with its imposing balconies and the ceiling in the unique shape of a gramophone horn which amplified the acoustics.

Soon the final bell went off and the auditorium darkened. The curtains rose to reveal Gauhar Manzil, the former home of the recording star, and Radhi lost herself in the luminescent performances and the live music. Fernandes had told her to keep an eye on the students, but Radhi didn't see the point of it. If they wanted to hold hands or kiss or do whatever it was that teenagers got up to these days, they'd find a way to do it anyways. However, when the intermission was announced, she realized she had to be more alert. As the students went off in different directions to purchase their samosas, sandwiches and cold drinks, and to stand in the bathroom queues, she was glad that they had their green and gold uniforms on, making them easy to spot, and glad of Mr. Bakshi, who had positioned himself outside the men's washroom to ensure that the boys came back out quickly.

'I need to make a quick phone call,' Radhi lied to Mr. Bakshi, as the interval was drawing to a close and the students were making their way back inside.

She really needed a smoke and knew that she wouldn't get another opportunity until they were back in school an hour later.

Outside the theatre, near the carpark, she stopped short. 'Oh, you've got to be kidding me,' she muttered to herself at the sight of Brij Aggarwal coming out from behind a car.

'Didn't you just get into trouble for this?' she said when he came closer.

'I . . . I uh . . . I had to make a call, Miss.' The boy looked petrified to see her there.

'Is that right?' Radhi extended a hand, 'In that case could you hand over your phone please? I know you aren't allowed to bring it to school.'

Brij's face flushed, and his forehead glistened with sweat. He made no attempt to slip his hand into his pocket.

Radhi studied him for a few moments. She had no experience in disciplining teenagers but was loath to escalate it to Fernandes. She wondered if a little honesty would work better than any punishment the teachers would mete out.

She slipped her hand into her own pocket and brought out her pack of cigarettes. 'Look, I came out to make a call too.'

Brij stared at her and then his shoulders dropped, and his body seemed to relax. 'I'm sorry,' he said. 'But I can't help myself.'

She extended her hand again and this time he brought out the vape from his pocket and put it in her palm.

'You're too bloody young for this, you know.'

'I know. I'm trying to stop!' He hung his head. 'But sometimes, I can't think beyond . . . you know . . . beyond the next hit.'

Radhi, who knew the feeling well, didn't need a more substantial explanation. 'How did you start?' she asked after a moment.

They had re-entered the theatre, but instead of going towards the auditorium, where she knew they wouldn't be allowed mid-performance, Radhi led him towards the seating area near the canteen.

'It was at a party. Some of us boys thought it would be fun to try it.'

'You guys have so much information about this stuff and still . . .' Radhi shook her head. She knew she was in no position to occupy the moral high ground, but she couldn't stop herself. 'Don't you think the price of this fun is too high?'

Brij looked down. 'It wasn't all fun. I was amazed at how focused I could be after a smoke. How easy it was to stay up for the revisions, to memorize things.' He ran a frustrated hand through his hair. 'There's so much pressure, with the board exams coming up next year.'

Radhi had been prepared to launch into a lecture on how debilitating these addictions were. But she had experienced the nicotine-powered gush of words and ideas hundreds of times and knew precisely the kind of focus he was talking about.

She bit back her words and sighed. 'Again, there's always a cost. Sooner or later, you pay. Look at your friend, he lost his sports captaincy.'

'Yeah, Soam's royally fuc—' Brij stopped mid-sentence, perhaps realizing that, smoker or not, Radhi was still his teacher. 'He's in a lot of trouble, I mean. His father will kill him.'

'Is that why he didn't come to school today?'

Brij shrugged. 'I guess so . . . I'll try calling him once I get home but knowing his parents, they've probably taken his phone away.'

'And you? Seems like your parents let you off easy — or you wouldn't be at it again so soon.'

Brij gave a bitter smirk. 'I've got a red mention. It's like a remark that will stay on my report card for the next two years and will go on the final academic record that the school shares with the colleges I apply to.'

'That doesn't sound very nice. Weren't your parents mad?'

'My parents were furious, and they grounded me. But they should be at home, no, to see if I'm actually in my room?' He shrugged again. 'They travel a lot for work. Which works out well for me.'

* * *

Back in school, Radhi thought back to her own addiction to cigarettes and how, for a few years, she had been able to give them up entirely with the help of therapy. It seemed to her that the school would be better served by providing students access to counsellors, rather than trying to arm twist their vaping habits away with the threat of severe consequences. She resolved to talk to Fernandes about it — but later. For now, everyone had their hands full, Radhi, with the pending revisions to Venus's play. She was in the staffroom, going over the existing script, when it occurred to her that Venus might've already started on the changes or at least made some notes.

'Do you know when the police plan to give back Ms. Venus's things?' she asked Mr. Bottlewalla, who was sitting across from her shovelling biryani into his mouth at record speed, and who as the vice principal, was most likely to know.

He shrugged. His mouth was full so it was a moment before he could answer her. 'Either once they've finished combing through all the files or once the medical results are in and are conclusive of natural death.'

'Why?' Ms. Savant, who had been on her way out, paused, surprised. 'What else could it be?'

'Nothing, of course,' said Mr. Bottlewalla. 'They just want to rule out foul play.'

'You mean . . . you mean . . . murder?' she asked, her eyes wide.

'I mean *no* such thing, madam.' Bottlewalla seemed alarmed at the turn the conversation had taken and his own role in it. 'It's all a formality.'

When Ms. Savant had left, Mr. Bottlewalla mopped his forehead with a napkin and muttered, 'Jesus. What an imagination the woman has. As if anyone would want to murder Venus.'

Ms. Lily, who had been sitting quietly so far, snorted. 'Oh, I can think of many.'

Mr. Bakshi looked at her sharply. The movement was so pronounced that everyone noticed, and Ms. Lily seemed flustered.

'C'mon, you know she rubbed plenty of people the wrong way.' She looked at Mr. Bakshi for confirmation but, when he remained silent, she continued, 'I'll tell you what her problem was. She'd climb up on her high horse of idealism and then get stuck on it. Uncompromising. Unable to recede and unable to get off it. She'd just declare herself on a subject and then feel compelled to protect her stance.' The maths teacher collected her books and stood up, her cool composure back in place. 'It might sound harsh to you all but it's the truth.' She had spoken to everyone in the room, but her eyes were trained on Mr. Bakshi.

When she had left, Mr. Bottlewalla who had finally finished his biryani, shut his steel tiffin with a loud click. 'Gosh, women can be quite critical of other women, no?' he asked Mr. Bakshi.

'True. Though in that respect Ms. Venus was also no less,' Mr. Bakshi said, wiping his hands with a tissue before gathering his things. 'I'm sure Ms. Savant would agree,' he added before leaving the room.

There it was again, thought Radhi, this reference to the relationship between both the English teachers.

'What was it with Ms. Venus and Ms. Savant?' Radhi asked Mr. Bottlewalla curiously. 'Did the two not get along?'

Mr. Bottlewalla snorted. 'Yes, I think you can safely say that.'

When Radhi continued to look at him expectantly, he elaborated.

'See, Ms. Savant was hired by the senior Mr. Kamble directly. She had apparently come through an important reference. Ms. Venus, as the head of the English Department, was sent her resumé, but that's it. She was not included in the decision to hire her. Ms. Venus threw a fit about it, of course — but for a change Kamble refused to back down.'

Radhi leaned back. 'Aah, so it became an ego thing for Ms. Venus.'

Mr. Bottlewalla shook his head. 'More than ego, for Venus it was about meritocracy. She thought Savant had got the job unfairly and she didn't let the teacher forget it.'

'Is Ms. Savant not a good teacher?'

Bottlewalla shrugged. 'She's good enough from what I hear. Has all her degrees in place. But Venus could be very rigid about things. It's like the usual practical and transactional considerations of living in society didn't make sense to her.'

* * *

Back from school that evening, Lily D'Souza sat beside her daughter as she did her homework. She was supposed to be correcting some papers, but she found it impossible to focus. She had hoped that with time it would get better, that her burden would be easier to bear, but so far there had been no difference. If anything, the weight of it had got denser, more concrete, more real. She looked at her daughter and was once again overcome with guilt. She went to the kitchen to check on the rice. It was still boiling. Just like her.

* * *

Radhi took a bite of her methi puri and brushed the crumbs from her diary, before continuing making her notes. She was back home, sprawled on her stomach, on her bed, engrossed in the research for her book. Pasoori from Coke Studio Pakistan was playing on the music system and Lila had left steel canisters of homemade puris, vadas and chakris by her side. All deep-fried and even more hazardous for health, Radhi supposed, than the rather perilous topic of her current research.

She had made a list of poisons easily available in India, derived from plants, pharmacies or household cleaning products and now she was researching their symptoms. She was just chuckling to herself about how alarmed someone would be if they were to look at her browsing history or the open tabs on her laptop, when the list of symptoms under cyanide poisoning made her spine tingle. She went over them again, her blood running cold.

CHAPTER 5

Thursday

'You know, madam, I was sure I would be seeing you sooner or later.' Inspector Shinde cracked open a pistachio shell and popped the kernel in his mouth before attacking another one from the pile of nuts on his desk. 'Tell me, what is your theory, this time?'

It was 10 a.m., and Radhi was at the Temple Hill police station where she had called ahead to ensure the inspector was available. She let his sarcasm pass without comment and launched straight into what had kept her tossing all night.

'Are Ms. Venus's postmortem results in?'

Shinde sighed. 'I should be telling you that this is none of your concern, but I've learned from past experience that this is futile. We should be getting the preliminary blood-work by this evening. Why?'

'All her symptoms seem consistent with cyanide poisoning.'

Shinde, who had been leaning back in his chair, straightened up in surprise. 'Oho madam, you can't just come in here and make these dangerous accusations.'

'I may be wrong of course—'

'How kind of you to allow that you might be mistaken,' Shinde interrupted Radhi, but his voice lacked the bravado of a few moments earlier.

Radhi ignored him. 'She had it all — respiratory failure, the cardiovascular collapse, the cherry red face, the vomiting . . .' She consulted her notes and rattled off the symptoms.

He frowned and reached for the files on his desk.

'Look ma'am,' he said, as he turned the pages, 'cardiac arrests and respiratory failures are not only very common symptoms for all sorts of health problems, but they are also usually connected. And as for red skin — I don't remember the paramedics mentioning it at all.' He stopped at a page and scanned it until he found what he was looking for. 'See — nothing about a red face or skin, anywhere.' He turned the file upside down, so that Radhi could see for herself.

Radhi frowned. She remembered very distinctly Ms. Savant's description of the condition she had found Ms. Venus in.

'But the teacher who found the body said Venus's face had been "red like a tomato", in fact—' Radhi began but Shinde cut her off with a raised hand.

'No, no, madam, let's not get into this he-said-she-said. That's a very risky game. Let's stick to the facts.' He tapped his finger on the open file. 'This is the initial report the paramedics submitted. Cold, hard science.'

He picked up a handful of the forgotten pistachios from his desk, cracked one open and was about to pop one into his mouth, when he stopped midway and grinned. 'In fact, I can do you one better . . .' He opened a drawer in his desk and brought out an envelope. 'These are the pictures of the scene from that night.' He rifled through them until he found the photograph he was looking for and studied it briefly, before placing it on the table with a flourish. 'There you go.'

It was a photograph of Venus lying on a stretcher, most likely taken just before she was carried out. Her face looked old and tired and grey. Not red. Not even pink. Just an exhausted, defeated, grey.

Shinde's smile, when Radhi looked up, was a gash of red, paan-stained lips and Radhi realized she had never seen his face arranged in that expression before.

The inspector stood up and pulled up his pants over his impressive pot belly. 'Can I give you some feedback, madam?' He didn't wait for an answer. 'You really must learn to trust the system.'

Radhi remained quiet. She could have reminded him about how magnificently his system had screwed up the last time their paths crossed, but she was still reeling from how wrong her own instincts had been this time.

'May I look at those?' she asked, indicating the envelope with the rest of the pictures in his hands.

Perhaps feeling magnanimous in his victory, he plonked it on the table in front of her. 'Be my guest.'

'Oi, one, here,' he instructed a young chaiwallah delivering cutting chai, to place a glass in front of Radhi, before swaggering away.

Radhi blew on the scalding ginger tea and took a few tentative sips before bracing herself to pick up the envelope. Death had a way of staying with you she had learned, long after the body had been burnt or buried. Inside, there were pictures of Venus from every angle, slumped on her desk. Apart from the pool of vomit at her feet, her desk looked much the same with books and papers and coffee cups strewn around. Radhi wondered at how much older the English teacher looked in death than when she had been living. Even the loose skin, the hair above the upper lip, the cluster of tiny moles on her right cheekbone, all stood out more starkly than they ever had when her eyes were open and sharp and bright. Radhi looked up and around. Shinde was nowhere to be seen. A couple of other officers were occupied, dealing with complainants and paperwork. One lady constable sat on a corner bench, busy on her phone. No one seemed to be paying much attention to Radhi, except for the garlanded portrait of Gandhiji on the opposite wall, who she didn't think would mind her pursuit of the truth. She slipped one of the photographs into her own bag. She was still having trouble letting go of her suspicion. Though how the photo would help, she couldn't say.

'Excuse me, where can I find Shinde ji?' Radhi asked a passing constable.

Hoping to get hold of Venus's notes or at least a timeline for when she could expect to receive them, Radhi made her way down the stairs to the rooms below. This wasn't her first visit to the Temple Hill police station, but the sprawling blue basalt complex with its graceful arched gateway, white casement windows, high ceilings and bright airy rooms, always struck her as at odds with the purpose it had been built for.

She found Shinde leaning against a desk, his mood foul, as two constables went through a box of files and papers, while four more boxes stood in a corner untouched.

'If you bozos had paid any attention in school, you wouldn't be moving at such a snail's pace!' he chastised his juniors.

'Are those Ms. Venus's papers?' Radhi asked from the doorway.

Shinde looked up with a frown, which deepened at the sight of her. 'Yes, unfortunately. Since she didn't use a computer, we had to carry all of this back with us. And now these idiots can't make head or tail of it!'

Radhi walked into the room and picked up a sheet from the top of the box nearest to her — it was the first in a pile of essays on the many tragedies in *Macbeth*.

'But why get into these? They are submissions from more than a year ago,' Radhi asked when she noticed the date on the page.

Shinde ran a frustrated hand through his sparse hair. 'Usually, when there's a computer, the nerds in the IT cell take care of it. We don't involve ourselves much with this . . . dog work.'

'Sir. Call for you.' A young constable entered the room and addressed himself to Shinde.

'Who's it?'

'Someone from that school . . . North Star.'

'Bloody hell!' Shinde swore. 'Tell them I am not here.' Then turning to the two men working on the boxes, he yelled, 'And you two, hurry up, this is the third time they've called to ask when we'll give this shit back!'

'Would you like me to help?' Radhi asked.

She didn't have to be back at the school until later that afternoon and was suddenly curious to see what was in the boxes.

'No of course not. This is police work, madam, I ca—' Shinde began but sputtered to a stop at the sight of the hopeful expression on his constables' faces.

His eyes narrowed. 'What do you want in return for your help?'

Radhi hadn't offered help with the expectation of an exchange, but she wasn't going to let the opportunity pass. 'Just tell me what the pathology reports say?'

Shinde scratched his bulbous nose, then shrugged and nodded, and left the room.

* * *

As Radhi made her way towards the staffroom, she was surprised to see Soam Mehta's mother crying on the couch outside Ms. Fernandes's office. She was wearing a crumpled cotton kurta and looked like she hadn't slept that night. Beside her, a man in a sharp pinstriped suit and thick, black framed glasses sat straight-backed, his hand placed awkwardly on her knee. Ms. Fernandes's secretary, a young girl with a bob and bangs, hovered around them offering tissue paper and bottles of water.

Radhi had just returned from the police station where she had spent close to two hours going over Venus's papers. There were assignments on nineteenth-century American poets, essays on the Romantic movement in literature, John Berger's *Ways of Seeing* and the relevance of Austen today, not to mention, old textbooks with faded notes in the margins, test papers and answer sheets from students going back a few years, and all sorts of other literary paraphernalia that can accompany a long academic career. She had found nothing out of the ordinary nor anything on the new script of the play, and had left, after big thank yous from the two constables whose lives she had made easier. Now, she entered the staffroom to find it buzzing with the news that Soam Mehta had gone missing.

CHAPTER 6

Soam Mehta had left home on Wednesday morning for school but hadn't turned up in class. His teachers assumed he was absent and at home, while his parents assumed he was in school and, post that, at the Temple Hill Gymkhana where he trained for cricket. It was only around seven that evening, when Soam didn't come home in time for dinner, that his mother had begun to wonder where he was.

Radhi slipped into the seat beside Mr. Bakshi, just as Ms. Farah, the art teacher, asked, 'What happened when they tried his phone? Switched off?'

'That's the problem,' Mr. Bottlewalla said. 'He didn't have his phone. The Mehtas had taken it from him because of the vaping incident.'

'What about his friends?' Radhi asked. 'Has he tried to get in touch with anyone?'

'Nobody. They asked his video game buddies and his friends on the cricket team, as well, basically everyone they could think of,' Mr. Bottlewalla answered.

'So now?' Ms. Farah asked.

'They have spoken to Ms. Fernandes and now they're waiting to speak to all his classmates and the kids in other grades who he's friendly with, to see if anyone knows anything.' Mr. Bottlewalla shook his head. 'Let's hope he turns up soon, otherwise they'll have to involve the police.'

'Gosh! Poor Ms. Fernandes is having quite the week, no?' the art teacher said to no one in particular. 'I hope that boy doesn't go and do something stupid. We really can't have another tragedy like last year.'

'That had nothing to do with us or the school,' Ms. Lily said sharply. She had been quiet so far, but her movements now, as she pushed her chair back and collected her things, seemed agitated. 'Anyways, I don't think all this gossiping is serving any purpose.'

A silence descended on the room after Ms. Lily left. By calling it gossip, she'd discouraged any further conversation on the topic.

However, after a few minutes had passed, Radhi leaned in towards Mr. Bakshi and asked softly, 'What happened last year?'

Mr. Bakshi, who had busied himself correcting some papers, put his pen down and sighed, 'One of our students committed suicide.'

'Oh! In school?'

'No, no — on holiday in fact. In Goa.'

'Why?'

'No one knows for sure. Even the parents were shocked. Who knows what goes on in these teen minds.'

Ms. Farah who'd been listening to their conversation cleared her throat. 'Well, one heard stuff—'

'I did too,' Mr. Bakshi interrupted. 'But honestly? Like Ms. Lily said, it's just gossip when things have no real basis.'

'Of course.' The art teacher pursed her lips.

* * *

Radhi cut a sliver of the gooey, black pepper-coated brie and spread it on a rice cracker. Her sister had sent her a small platter of herbed cheeses from a new store she'd visited, and Radhi had taken that as a sign from the universe to crack open a new bottle of wine. She'd resisted the day before, but nobody could deny that a chilled merlot would completely elevate the cheese-cracker experience. She was working on the script of the play and had just poured herself a second glass when the phone rang.

'The preliminary lab results are in,' Shinde said without preamble when Radhi picked up the phone.

'And?'

'Inconclusive. They can't tell one way or the other. It could be natural causes, or it could be something else, but without further investigation, it is impossible to say.'

'Oh, okay,' Radhi said, disappointed. Somehow, she'd really been sure that she was on to something. 'How soon can they do more tests?'

'We only do further tests if there's a reason to. If there's suspicion of foul play. Or circumstantial evidence suggests something's amiss. In this case, there's nothing. Even the coffee machine and cups are clear. I don't think the higher-ups will authorize it.'

'But she had no other prior health issues, isn't tha—'

'Ma'am, ma'am, is it possible that you enjoy this? Most ordinary folk do not like to dwell on death. In fact, they actively avoid it. Your interest in these things is . . . a bit strange.'

He seemed to be choosing his words with care, and that, more than anything else, shut Radhi up. She hung up, feeling uneasy. Surely, there wasn't even a kernel of truth in what the man had said, was there? Yes, there was a part of her that seemed to be drawn to understand the urge of violence in others. But was that really so weird? She tried to focus on her work again but found her attention continually wandering. The missing student. The angry exchange between his mother and Venus. The altercation the English teacher had with the Kambles. Frustrated with herself, Radhi put her pen down and flipped the pages of her diary to look at the photograph of Venus which she'd slipped into her bag at the police station. She saw it almost immediately this time and cursed.

Then she cursed again.

She called Shinde but the inspector didn't answer so she tried him again.

'What is it, ma'am?' he asked when he picked up.

'One of the cups is missing,' she said, ignoring the annoyance in his voice.

'What's that now?'

'Ms. Venus had exactly a dozen mugs. All in pairs of two. I've been admiring them these past few weeks. There are only eleven in the pictures you showed me. Four unused, two on her desk and five used ones on the surface of the cabinet where she used to keep them for the cleaners to wash and return.'

'Maybe one broke or maybe someone borrowed it?'

'All the pairs were intact when she offered me coffee that afternoon. And you clearly didn't know Venus, if you think anyone would come to her to borrow a coffee mug.' As soon as she said it, Radhi knew it had been the wrong thing to say to Shinde. The inspector had been listening without his usual dismissive attitude, so far, but now he bristled at her words.

'We'll look into it, ma'am. Thank you for letting us know.'

'If she was poisoned, then someone would have had to come back to remove the mug from the room. There was no sink there, so they couldn't have washed it there. This is the kind of circumstantial evidence you nee—'

'Ma'am, ma'am, please.' Shinde raised his voice. 'Again, you're trying to tell me how to do my job. Like I told you, we'll look into it.'

When he'd hung up, Radhi finished the wine in her glass and poured herself some more — feeling too unsettled to sleep.

* * *

Friday

Radhi looked out of the car window at the fruit and vegetable vendors on the footpath, their displays mini feats of physics and audacity. Pyramids of muskmelons, pomegranates and oranges jostled for attention with fortresses of cauliflowers and bell peppers, and despite her raging hangover, Radhi marvelled at how they managed to stay upright under the onslaught of the careless and handsy early morning shoppers. She hadn't slept well and had woken up with a staggering headache made all the more unbearable because of how irritated she was with herself, her tendency to get fixated with problems where no one else seemed to see any and her inability to stay away from alcohol both contributing to it in equal parts. She had popped a couple of aspirins, but she didn't know if she'd feel better in time for her first class at North Star. At the moment, any loud sounds, especially the wanton honking that drivers in Mumbai seemed to enjoy so much, was setting her teeth on edge. She was considering sending an email and excusing herself from her first class, when Ramzan bhai, her driver, stopped the car at a signal, and her eyes fell upon the headlines of a newspaper stacked up at a newsstand.

However, it wasn't until she'd rolled down the window, bought herself a copy and begun to read in earnest that she gasped. Not because the article was particularly shocking, but because she had just noticed the byline. Quickly, she scanned the article and then, because the paper was the *National Gazette*, she called its editor-in-chief. Hrishi answered on the first ring.

'Hey, that story on the front page today — is it really by—'

'Yep. We got it two days ago. You're the second person to call about it in the last five minutes, by the way.'

'Why? Who else called?'

'Satish Kamble — for some reason he seemed upset — he is MD at North St—'

'Yeah, I know him. What did he want to know?'

'Same, as you. But listen, I can't talk right now, I'm entering a meeting. I'll see you tomorrow for that workshop thing. Unless it's been cancelled, what with poor Ms. Venus dying and all that?'

'Don't sound so hopeful.' Radhi chuckled despite her foul mood. 'It's happening.'

It was only once she'd hung up that she remembered she hadn't received a response from Ms. Fernandes to her email requesting permission to invite Hrishi over for the workshop. Radhi guessed it had been lost with everything that had happened since Venus's death and resolved to go talk to the principal about it in person. But first, she wanted to read the news story properly.

Beginning with a catchy headline, 'The Public has Questions. Does Ramakant Wagle have answers?' the story went on to talk about how, despite the widespread dissent among the residents of the area, the politician was going ahead with his plans for allotting a large public park on Temple Hill to a hotel chain that planned on converting it into an entertainment zone. It spoke about how in the past he had directed the MMRDA (Mumbai Metropolitan Development Agency) and the Municipal Corporation of Greater Mumbai (or the MGCM) into leasing open government land to mall developers and builders and what the ecological impact of such actions could be in the future. The story further went on to allege that Wagle was in the habit of routinely parcelling out government land to further his own business interests and urged the government to look into it. The byline for the story belonged to Venus Pereira.

CHAPTER 7

'Is Ms. Fernandes free?' Radhi asked the principal's secretary.

'No, sorry. She's with the police. I've no idea how long she'll take,' the young woman said.

She was clearly new at her job, Radhi thought, as she took a seat on the sofa in the waiting area. No secretary with any real experience would offer more information than was absolutely essential. Radhi didn't mind waiting. She hadn't had a moment to herself since she got to the school and rushed to take her first class. Now that she was free for a couple of hours, and her head had cleared up, she found that she had lots she wanted to think about. To begin with, she fished out the newspaper from her bag and read Venus's article again. She was in awe of the English teacher's audacity. Venus had told her that she would have to switch to plan B when the Kambles asked her to change the script. But when Venus sent this article out, she couldn't have known then that she wouldn't be alive to see it printed. Which meant she had been prepared to face the consequences. Prepared to face the Kambles and even lose her job, if necessary. She admired the older woman's faith in all her different convictions, but wondered if that had been what finally got her into trouble. Radhi didn't care if Shinde believed her or not. There was something fishy about Venus's death. She could feel it in her bones.

The door of Ms. Fernandes's office opened, and Shinde stepped out, followed by Soam Mehta's parents. Shinde appeared to have not seen Radhi. He shook the father's hand and promised to be in touch before leaving. The mother had swollen red eyes, and she stood with a handkerchief pressed to her mouth. When the inspector had left, the father attempted to console the mother by putting an arm around her, but the woman immediately flung it off.

'This is all your fault,' she hissed. 'You always pushed him too much. You and this bloody school!'

'Komal, please . . .' the man began.

'I swear if something has happened to him, I'm never going to forgive you!'

Then perhaps realizing that they had an audience, the two of them walked away towards the elevators and the secretary indicated that Radhi could go inside.

'Yes, Radhika, tell me. How can I help you?' Ms. Fernandes asked, pointing her to a chair.

The principal seemed to have lost weight in the past few days. She had always been thin, but now she looked gaunt. A copy of the *National Gazette* lay on her desk.

'Soam is still missing?' Radhi asked.

The principal sighed and nodded before taking a sip of water from a glass. 'His parents have checked with everyone — friends, cousins, neighbours — and have come up with nothing. And now they're blaming the school and our actions against him for the boy taking this rash step. Isn't that convenient? My point is — it wouldn't have reached this stage had they been paying attention and had nipped this vaping nonsense in the bud!'

It was a rare display of emotion for the principal, and she took a hold of herself almost immediately. 'Anyways, tell me, what did you want to see me about?'

'Did you see that email I sent you about the guest lecture? Though I understand if this is bad timing, and we can't do it. I'll just have to let the guest know.'

'Y-yes — would you? While I really want the school to function as normally as possible, I don't want any outsiders to come here, pick up on all that's going on and form the wrong impression of the school.'

'Makes sense. Though Hrishi is not technically an outsider. His daughter studies at North Star.'

Fernandes started to say something, paused and then spoke again. 'Hrishi Kamdar? This is his paper, isn't it?' She lifted the copy of the *Gazette* lying on her desk.

Radhi nodded.

'In that case, please by all means invite him to speak.' Then seeing the surprised look on Radhi's face, she added, 'At this point, the school needs some friends in the media. Don't you agree?'

Radhi smiled and stood up, then remembering something, she sat back down, hesitating before speaking. 'I know you already have your plate full. But have you considered having a counselling centre for the school? They can help with addiction and any other issues the students might have.'

Fernandes nodded. 'There was some talk about it last year. But personally, I am not a big fan of these newfangled coping mechanisms we have borrowed from the West.'

She held up her hand as Radhi began to protest. 'I know, I know. Some people find it helpful. But I am in the business of teaching my students self-reliance. I do not want them to be dependent on structures outside of themselves and their families. They need to learn to build support systems for themselves. I refuse to hand it to them on a platter at 2000 rupees an hour.'

She spread her hands. 'I suppose I'm old-fashioned in my views. So, it's probably a good thing I'm retiring soon. But that's how I feel.'

Radhi smiled, not wanting to press the point further. 'Please don't say that. North Star has been very lucky to have you.'

Fernandes shook her head. 'I've put my blood, sweat and tears into this school. But really? The school has done more for me.'

Radhi looked at her expectantly, and the older woman elaborated. 'It gave me a purpose to live when my son passed in an accident. A reason to wake up every day.' Fernandes crossed her arms and leaned back into her seat. 'Those were some rough times at home, and this was where I took shelter.' Then she smiled as if to say that all that was in the past. 'The school has given me a lot. Not to mention, an identity I could be proud of. So honestly? I've been the lucky one.'

* * *

Radhi stretched her arms and straightened her back. She was in the North Star library and had been working on the script of the play for the past hour and a half. Now that Venus had had a chance to say her piece in the paper, Radhi felt far less guilty about changing her script and had made significant progress in revising the premise and dialogues of the story. Radhi didn't come to the library very often, but every time she did, she realized how much better it was than going home. To begin with, there was no mango wood bar cabinet, which meant she didn't keep thinking about pouring herself a glass. And there were other people, which meant her thoughts didn't turn dark quite so quickly. Besides, it was a beautiful space with high ceilings and arched windows of stained glass in shades of green and gold, which let soft, dappled sunlight into the room. Bulging, floor-to-ceiling bookcases stood in one half of the room, while one section was lined with long, twenty-seater tables, and yet another section had been fashioned into a computer lab where a couple of senior students sat right now, doing some research.

Radhi did a few stretches holding the back of her chair, before walking up to the fiction section to take a break to browse and to stretch her legs. She had just moved from Rendell, Roy and Rushdie to Shakespeare and Shelley, when she heard two girls whispering. She couldn't see them because they were on the other side of the bookcase, but she could hear them clearly.

'I didn't know what to do, so I just kept quiet.'

'But you can't *not* tell his parents.'

'But what if he gets into even more trouble?'

'Yeah . . . his parents *are* like bloody Hitlers. But I can't believe he'd go away without saying a word even to *you*.'

'I know right — some girlfriend I am.'

'He must've been really upset.'

'He was hopping mad at everyone — especially Venus. He pleaded with her that he would really get in trouble if she reported him, but she didn't listen.'

'So, what was he planning on doing?'

'Not sure. He just said, "I'm going teach that bitch a lesson."'

Their voices had dropped even lower, and Radhi didn't catch the girl's next question. But she'd heard enough to figure they were talking about Soam. She walked around the bookcase to where two ninth-grade girls were sitting on the floor with books open on their laps. Radhi knew them well.

'Sorry, girls,' she said, 'I couldn't help but overhear your conversation. You were talking about Soam, weren't you?'

The girls gaped at her, too surprised to deny it.

'If you know anything about where or why he has gone away, you must come forward.'

'But we don't want to get him into more trouble,' said one of the girls with braces and a cute button nose, and Radhi recognized her voice as the one who'd called herself his girlfriend.

'Yes. What if the school expels him?' added the other girl.

'Don't tell the teachers then. Just his parents,' Radhi said, 'Can you imagine how worried they might be?'

'The only thing his father worried about were his grades and the only thing his mother worried about was keeping his father happy,' the first girl said.

'Don't be mean, Piu. You know about his brother,' the other girl chided her friend.

The two fell silent.

'Come girls, you know what the right thing to do here is.'

* * *

'But what did he mean by it?' Mrs. Mehta asked. 'What did he plan on doing?'

Piu hesitated. 'He didn't tell me.'

It was after school, and Radhi and the two girls were sitting on the four-seater chesterfield in the Mehtas' drawing room, with the Mehtas in matching black and white Jacquard armchairs across from them. The Mehtas lived in a sea-facing art deco building on Marine Drive, ten minutes away from North Star. Piu had just told them about her last interaction with Soam.

'Is that it?' Mr. Mehta, whose left leg had been shaking incessantly, said with a hint of more than a little impatience in his voice. 'Listen, child, I hope you're being honest with us. If there's more . . .'

'Shailesh please,' Mrs. Mehta chided her husband. Then, looking at the girls, she added more gently, 'Girls, if there's anything else you remember, you must tell us . . .'

Both the girls nodded.

'Teach the bitch a lesson . . . phish!' Mr. Mehta muttered to himself. 'That boy needs to be taught some manners, first. Is this any way to talk about a teacher?'

'He was just upset, Shailesh!' Mrs. Mehta said. 'As were you and I. May I remind you what you said?'

'That's enough, Komal,' Mr. Mehta snapped.

'Mamma, who are these people?'

The question made them all turn to where a stout, young man with a flattened face and upward slanting eyes stood at the door.

'They are friends of Soam, beta,' Mrs. Mehta said.

'Can they stay for dinner?'

'No Omee — they can't.' Mr. Mehta got up with a frown and walked towards him.

'Can they ask Soam to come back, then?' the young man said.

'Yes, of course they will,' Mr. Mehta said, as he led him away with an arm around his shoulders.

'Sorry about that,' Mrs. Mehta said, when her husband and son were out of earshot. 'That is Omee, I mean Omkaar, Soam's elder brother. He uh . . . he has the Down syndrome. He has been asking for Soam every hour.' Her lips quivered as she said it.

Radhi marvelled at how different she seemed from the angry, broad-shouldered woman who had come barging into the English Department a few days ago to give Ms. Venus a piece of her mind. The Mrs. Mehta in front of her, sat hunched, hair dishevelled, eyes watery, all the fight gone out of her.

She picked up a frame from the corner table beside her and ran her hand over the picture of her two boys. 'I suppose it's our fault, also. We put too much pressure on him. With Omee being . . . the way he is . . . all of their father's expectations were pinned on Soam. It's as if Shailesh needs Soam to excel, to succeed, so that *he* can feel like a successful father.' Mrs. Mehta put the picture frame down, frowning, perhaps feeling like she'd said more than she intended to. She fixed her attention on Radhi. 'I know it's not always fair to Soam. But it's for his own good. Isn't it?' She bit her lip. 'Do you have children, Ms. Zaveri?'

Radhi, who had been sitting quietly so far, shook her head.

Mrs. Mehta nodded. 'Just as well. It's the hardest job I've ever done. This parenting thing.' She closed her eyes for a moment before opening them. 'God, I miss my mother.'

'So . . . this plan of his.' Mr. Mehta walked briskly back into the room, picking up the conversation where he'd left it. 'Sounds more like an empty threat. Did he tell you when he was going to do something?'

The girl hesitated. 'All I know is that he was going to go to her office after football practice on Monday.'

'Do you think she was still in office at that time? That she caught him?' Mrs. Mehta asked eagerly. 'Could that be why he ran away?'

'Monday . . . that was the third,' Mr. Mehta said as if Mrs. Mehta hadn't spoken. 'That's the day the teacher died, isn't it? At least that's what the school email said.'

Mrs. Mehta nodded. Her fingers made deep grooves in the right arm of her chair. Nobody said it aloud, but they all seemed to be wondering the same thing: What kind of lesson had Soam planned on teaching his teacher?

* * *

Komal Mehta continued to sit in the same chair, long after Radhi and the two girls had left, questioning some of the choices she'd made in life. She was asking herself where she'd gone wrong and what she could have done differently. Whether she could have protected Soam better from her husband's ambition? When he woke Soam up at four and five in the morning to go swimming before his tennis training began, could she have stood up to her husband and told him to stop, that he was overdoing it? When he monitored what Soam ate and took away the Diwali laddus his grandmother had sent him, could she have protested and told him to let the boy be? When he refused to let Soam go for birthday parties that clashed with his cricket coaching, should she have put her foot down and told him to let their son enjoy his childhood? Her husband had always seemed so certain, so adamant about his vision for their son's future that she'd let him have his way. She'd looked away and focused all her own energies on Omee, saving all her softness for him, because he seemed to need her more and because her husband seemed to have no expectations from him at all.

Komal wished now that she had cared less about maintaining the peace in the house and fought harder for her younger son. If she could go back and do things differently, she would never tell her husband that their son had been caught vaping. No, *that* she felt had been her biggest mistake of all. That was why her husband had gone ballistic, had raised his hand at their grown son. And that was why the boy had run away.

If only she could put her arms around her son again and breathe in that scent of sweat and freshly cut grass, she promised herself she'd shield him with her life.

CHAPTER 8

Radhi couldn't get one thing out of her head. Not the fact that Soam had gone to Venus's office on the day she died, no, *that* she had filed away with all the other irregularities about Venus's death, to work through later. What was bothering her ever since she came back from the Mehtas', and through the four glasses of wine she'd finished since, was what Mrs. Mehta had said about how hard parenting was. It wasn't anything new, and yet, Radhi had never thought about it in the context of her sister. How hard had it been for Madhavi — how much harder without her own mother to lean on? Without a mother *and* father, both of whom Madhavi had lost in the course of a single day, all because of Radhi.

Radhi had spent many years in therapy working through the guilt she felt on account of her sister. The fact that Madhavi had to navigate her teenage years and come into adulthood without her parents. But she had never considered that Madhavi might be feeling their absence as acutely even now, while she raised two young kids, while an oblivious Radhi continued to be completely preoccupied with the drama of her own life.

'Fuck!' Radhi cursed as she shut the book in her hands, frustrated with herself.

'Fuck, fuck, fuck!' she said a moment later, as her careless movements caused her elbow to topple her glass and spill the wine.

She supposed it was for the best. A fifth glass would have meant an excruciating struggle to wake up on time the next day. Though, she thought a moment later, eyeing her empty glass and licking her lips, she didn't really need to wake up on time considering it was the weekend.

* * *

Monday

As Radhi darkened her lipstick and gave her mustard-coloured kalamkari harem pants and top a last once-over in the mirror, it occurred to her that she'd taken extra care with her appearance that day. She wondered if it had anything to do with Hrishi coming over for his guest lecture. Then, alarmed and irritated with herself for even having thought it, she turned away from the mirror.

'You really need to get a life,' she muttered, as she brushed her hair and tied it into a severe, no-nonsense bun as if to discourage herself from any further ridiculous ideas.

'I know you're turning a year older, Didi, but surely you can't be senile already,' Lila said from the doorway to Radhi's room watching her talk to herself.

'Very funny.' Radhi grinned, glancing her way, before turning back to line her eyes with her customary dark kohl.

The area below her eyes seemed puffy, and Radhi knew it was because of the alcohol, but it was nothing she couldn't fix with a little concealer.

Lila waved a sheet of paper. 'I've spoken to Madhavi didi about your surprise party, and this is the guest list we've come up with. Will you take a look at it and add whoever else you want?'

'Thank you, Lila,' Radhi said as she slipped a delicate parrot earring into each ear. Crafted in pure silver, each bird had green enamel wings and a red ruby for an eye. Both of which matched the colours in the thick, engraved bangle she wore at her wrist.

'Just look at you!' Lila said, when Radhi finally stepped away from the mirror. 'It's a wonder the poor boys in your class get any studying done at all.'

'Why?' Radhi turned back to her appearance, alarmed. She'd been taking great pains to choose appropriate outfits for school, these last few weeks. In fact, so conscientious had she been about high necklines and long hemlines, that she'd gone shopping to meet her self-imposed criteria.

'These are perfectly respectable clothes for a teacher, Lila,' she protested.

'But who is looking at the clothes, Didi?' Lila chuckled. 'When you tie your hair like that, how is anyone to take their eyes off that long, long neck?'

Radhi rolled her eyes. 'So, tell me, have you planned the surprise menu for my surprise party?'

'Planned and finalized — all with Madhavi didi. You just have to show up. You and that gorgeous neck of yours,' Lila cackled as she left the room.

There she was again, Radhi thought, her sister, stepping in to ensure Radhi had a full life. In fact, when had she not been there? Through Radhi's divorce, through her depression, through her breakup with Mackinsey, she'd shown up for Radhi, regardless of what was going on in her own life. Playing sister, friend, confidante, and very often, mother — but who had essayed that role for her?

* * *

'How are you, Didi?' Radhi asked Madhavi when she picked up the phone.

She was in the car, on her way to North Star and had realized, as she made the call, how seldom she checked up on her sister.

'I'm fine. What happened? Is everything all right?' her sister asked immediately, the concern in her voice further proof of how rare such a call from Radhi was.

'All good, Didi. And the kids? What are they up to? Tell me, do you need any help with them?'

'What's going on, Radhi? Where are you?' Madhavi asked, now clearly alarmed. 'Are you okay?'

'Jeez, Didi! Can't a girl just call her sister?' Radhi chuckled. 'I've been around kids so much these days that I'm realizing how much work they are.'

When Madhavi was finally convinced that there was really nothing amiss with Radhi, she relaxed.

'You know who's more work than both the kids put together?'

'Your darling mother-in-law?' Radhi guessed correctly, knowing fully well that the woman was not only a bit of a hypochondriac but also full of her own sense of self-importance.

'Yes! She's had me running to cardiologists this time, convinced she's having heart trouble. Honestly? I think it's just gas. But we finally convinced her to check into a hospital and get all her tests done once and for all.'

'Good, at least she's out of your head for a few days now.'

'Pshh!' Madhavi scoffed. 'She expects us to visit twice a day. Not to mention, send hot meals from home because she refuses to eat hospital food. By the way, you need to go see her one of these days.'

'Ugh, Didi, no! Anything but that,' groaned Radhi, who considered the woman an absolute bully and couldn't stand to be nice to her.

'Please, Radhi, or it will just give her one more thing to taunt me about,' Madhavi said. 'Besides, remember how you left things the last time?'

'Fine, fine, I'll go,' said Radhi, hurriedly, reluctant to touch upon the subject of her last interaction with Madhavi's mother-in-law.

'So, how are things at the school?' Madhavi asked, changing the subject. 'What with Ms. Venus dying and all that?'

'About that . . .' Radhi began and filled her in on all that had happened in the last few days, including the missing student and her own suspicions.

'Oh God, not again . . .' Madhavi said, when Radhi had finished. 'How do you land up in these situations every time?'

'*You* put me in this particular situation, may I remind you?'

Madhavi sighed. 'I want to tell you not to get involved and to just focus on why you're there, but I doubt you'd listen.'

They discussed the school and its teachers some more, and it was only once Madhavi had promised Radhi that she'd ask her the next time she needed help with the kids that Radhi agreed to hang up the phone.

* * *

Tick-tick one . . . Tick-tick two . . .
The day's here,
it's almost time
Did you like my pretty rhyme?

Radhi! Isn't my little limerick sweet? I wanted to write the whole thing in rhyme but got stuck at 'publisher'. Finisher? Extinguisher? Nothing seems to rhyme with it!

Anyhoooo, how are you, you gorgeous thing?

So, listen, the publisher (Fisher? Disher? See nothing!) has started sending out copies of your book to the media for reviews. It's also up on NetGalley for early readers. Which means, by next month the reviews will start coming in. At some point, you need to fly down to New York for a book launch. But more on that later. Until then, take a deep breath and relax. As the Americans say, you've gaat this!

For my part, I'm spectacular, as always. Off to Ecuador for an ayahuasca retreat. Wish me luck. The hope is to come back calmer, wiser, more zen. And if nothing else, a better poet! Hahaha! Toodle doo, darling.

XOXO, George

Radhi grinned. She was at the North Star lobby, waiting for Hrishi and had just finished checking her mail. George was her literary agent. A Londoner at heart, he was based in New York and was one of her dearest friends. They'd been together ever since her first book, almost a decade ago, and he'd stuck with her even when she'd stopped writing, missed deadlines, allowed commissioned projects to languish uncompleted and refused to answer his emails.

* * *

'Ms. Zaveri. Mr. Kamdaar.' Satish Kamble smiled and nodded at Radhi before introducing himself to Hrishi.

Radhi had just met Hrishi in the lobby, and they were about to head to the school canteen for a cup of tea, when Kamble had all but accosted them. In a fitted Lacoste T-shirt, the MD of the school looked even more beefed up than he did in the cotton kurtas he usually wore.

'I just wanted to thank you for taking the time to do this,' Kamble said. 'The school, as well as I personally, we subscribe to the *Gazette*, so it is very special to have you talk to our students.'

'The pleasure is all mine,' said Hrishi. 'Though you have Ms. Zaveri to thank for it. She can be very convincing.'

'Oh, *that* she can,' Kamble said, his eyes resting on Radhi for a beat longer than necessary.

'I don't know if you remember, but we spoke on the phone on the day the *Gazette* carried Ms. Venus's article.' Kamble turned to Hrishi, all businesslike again. 'I just wanted to reiterate that that is — was — her own opinion, entirely. As a school, we do not take political stands nor offer our views. In fact, we hate to be connected in any way, so I'm really glad that you left our name and Ms. Venus's connection with the school out of it.'

Hrishi nodded. 'Ms. Venus's article was published as is. The editor who she was in touch with said that she didn't want to be introduced as a teacher here. I guess she was trying to protect the school.'

'Yes, exactly as it should be,' Kamble said. 'Reputations are built over so many years and they take mere moments to be undone. Don't you agree?'

Then before Hrishi could answer, he changed the topic.

'So, Ms. Fernandes tells me Anoushka is a clever girl. Very diligent with her work. In fact — and these are her words, not mine — she's proper prefect material.' Kamble flashed his empty palms at them, to suggest that he had nothing to do with the high praise. 'Anyways, I'm so glad we got a chance to catch up.' He shook Hrishi's hand again, before turning to Radhi. 'By the way, Ms. Zaveri, should we meet on the script sometime this week?'

When Radhi nodded, he added, 'Excellent. Let's do it outside school. Over a nice lunch.' Then he turned to leave as abruptly as he had come.

'Did he just ask you on a date?' Hrishi asked, frowning at Kamble's retreating back.

'What? No. Don't be absurd!' Radhi said. She checked her watch before adding, 'Though I think he did try to insinuate that if you keep the school's name out of the papers, they might make Anoushka a prefect.'

'Yeah, I caught that! But I wasn't sure. What the hell was that about?'

Radhi shrugged. 'Let's just say, this is his way of trying to be friends with you. What with the dead teacher and the missing student, the school may be expecting some rough weather.'

'What missing student?' Hrishi asked.

'I'll tell you, later.' Radhi tapped her watch. 'It's time for your talk.'

* * *

Back in his office, Satish Kamble hung up the phone, furious with his father and his meddling ways. He didn't know what it would take for his father to trust him. He knew he hadn't been his father's first choice for this job. His father would've much preferred handing the reins of his precious school to his eldest son. But his brother had refused, preferring to live in the US to India. While Satish had accepted. For a whole year, ever since he returned from the US, he had dedicated himself to learning its ways. Putting in effort and time to get to know the teachers and the parents of the PTA, trying to understand their issues and challenges. But none of this seemed to hold any water with his father, who when it came to important decisions preferred to listen to Fernandes. Between him and the principal, they were second-guessing every step he made. Kamble ran a frustrated hand through his hair and went to stand by the window.

It had been his decision to host the Interschool Drama Competition at North Star and to invite Wagle as the judge. He'd been quite pleased with how smoothly the thing had worked out. He hadn't an inkling of Venus's vendetta against the politician, nor that she would carry it all the way to a national newspaper! That woman was causing him so much trouble even after she was dead. The missing boy was also her doing. Hers and Fernandes's. In his opinion, old women really couldn't understand what went on in a teenage boy's mind. Much less, be in charge of disciplining them. But they were. And now he was expected to clean up their mess. His father was on the phone with him every second hour for updates. Insinuating, with his numerous calls and suggestions, that perhaps he'd made a mistake in asking Satish to come back. That perhaps running a school was not for him, after all.

* * *

'I'll have a three-bean quesadilla with extra jalapenos, sour cream and the mango salsa on the side,' Radhi told the waiter before handing back the menu.

'Nothing to drink?' Hrishi asked.

'On a working day?' Radhi raised her eyebrows. 'Wow, aren't you living on the edge,' she teased.

He grinned and Radhi's heart gave a little lurch at the sight of his dimples, her own reaction surprising her so much that she almost missed what he said next.

'It's just that I could do with a drink, today,' he said as he studied the menu.

He didn't say why, and she didn't ask. She watched as he ran a hand through his short salt and pepper hair. He had beautiful hands with long fingers and rough callouses from years of basketball. Suddenly, without any warning, she remembered his hand, the gentle coarseness of it, warm on her bare knee when they kissed all those years ago, and she felt her face burn. With an effort she pulled herself to the present.

'You were great with the kids today, by the way,' she said.

Hrishi's talk had been a success. It had taken him a few anxious moments to warm up, but once he began talking about story hooks and leads and headlines, his eyes had shone, and his enthusiasm for his subject had rubbed off on the students. Now, the two of them had stepped out for lunch and were at a cosy Mexican restaurant watching the server grind their fresh guacamole with a traditional, black stone mortar pestle, while they waited for their mains.

'Let's do red-wine sangrias?' Hrishi asked. 'A pitcher? Or will that be too much?'

'Not too much,' Radhi said, wondering what Hrishi would say if he knew just what her drinking habits were like, lately.

'You look gorgeous by the way,' Hrishi said, once their orders were given.

He'd said it casually, but Radhi blushed and wished she hadn't. 'Thanks.'

'This new relationship clearly agrees with you,' Hrishi said.

'What relationship?' Radhi frowned.

'Weren't you dating someone? A Nishank or Nishant?'

'That's old news Hrishi. Been months since we broke up.'

'Is it? Then *not* having a relationship agrees with you.' Hrishi grinned.

'Very funny. Who told you, anyway?'

'Heard it on the college grapevine.'

'You always were quick to pick up on gossip,' Radhi teased.

'Hey, perils of the job.'

'Speaking of college, I'm having a bunch of friends over for dinner this Saturday. You must come. And bring Neha along, of course.'

'This Saturday . . .' Hrishi pulled out his phone to check his calendar. 'Aah, your birthday.' He smiled. 'Done. We'll be there.' He put his phone away. 'Tell me about this missing student now.'

As they polished off their cheesy quesadillas and ordered burrito rolls stuffed with spicy bell peppers, beans and soft, crumbling cottage cheese, Radhi filled him in on the goings-on at North Star, ending with her suspicions about Venus's death and the missing coffee mug.

'At one point I thought it was cyanide poisoning because the teacher who found her said her face had gone completely red, but the pictures the police took—'

'Didn't show the red skin, right?' Hrishi put down his wine glass hastily so that some of it spilled onto the white tablecloth.

Radhi nodded, surprised.

'That's a classic symptom of cyanide poisoning! The red flushed skin lasts only for about thirty minutes or so. We reported on a case like this a few years ago. In fact, the longer it takes to discover the body, the lower your chances of proving any kind of poisoning because cyanide metabolizes very quickly and rapidly clears away from the body.' Hrishi frowned. 'But what I'd like to know is why? Who in the world would want an old English teacher dead?'

Radhi bit her lip as a number of people occurred to her.

CHAPTER 9

Shinde was sitting with one hand on his head, the ladyfinger subzi, rotis and green pickled chillies lying forgotten in his open tiffin box, as he processed the new information Radhi had just shared with him. Judging from the expressions on his face, Radhi guessed he was sorry to have ever laid eyes on her and harrowed at how complicated she'd just made things. Expecting him to criticize her for being a busybody, she'd come prepared to argue, but his next words surprised her.

'Okay, ma'am,' he said, finally straightening up. 'Leave it with me. I'll make a few calls and see what we can learn from the path lab. This bloody school has given me so much grief, I'd love to give it back! Especially that Fernandes. Every time I go there, she reminds me that we are at an educational institution and that she expects my men and me to conduct ourselves accordingly. As if none of us has gone to school before!' He snorted and resumed eating his lunch with a furious bite of the pickled chilli. 'Finally, I had to tell her that, ma'am, we are aware of the concept of schools. We haven't come here for a picnic either!' He scooped some ladyfinger with a piece of roti and said with a stuffed mouth, 'I can't wait to see her face when I tell her this is now a murder investigation!'

Across from him, Radhi had still not recovered from how smoothly this had gone. This was the most Shinde had ever spoken to her, and all of his own accord. The look of glee on his face right now would have been comical had it not been for the gravity of the subject at hand.

'So, you'll let me know once you hear back from the labs?' she asked.

'Yes, yes.' He waved aside her request and continued with his fantasizing. 'You know, I'm going to get some more books and boxes from the school, just to mess with her. The last time, that Kamble had my station manager dancing on my head to return everything quickly! As if they are government secrets not Shakespeare—'

'What about that missing boy?' Radhi asked, interrupting his rant. 'Any leads on where he could be?'

Shinde blinked and frowned as if he had suddenly remembered why he found Radhi annoying. 'Ma'am, ma'am, one second—' He put down the glass of buttermilk he'd been sipping on. 'While I appreciate your help in this matter with the school, this is where it needs to stop. We'll take over from here. You please don't go and involve yourself in that missing kid problem. They're separate cases altogether.'

* * *

As she waited outside the police station for Ramzan bhai to bring the car around, Radhi had to shield her eyes from the blazing mid-afternoon heat. The April sun was fierce, the champaca and banyan trees were all deathly still in the absence of even the whisper of a breeze, and though she'd been standing for only a few minutes, she could feel droplets of sweat trickle down her back. She watched as a small group of Jain monks walked past her — heads bent low, feet bare — nothing in their expressions to betray the agony of walking on scorching concrete. She marvelled at the degree of their detachment, especially when she compared it with how impossibly entangled she tended to get with the world and people around her.

Hrishi called just as she got into the car. He'd had to leave after lunch for a meeting at work, but he'd promised to check up on how it had gone with the police.

'Why was Kamble so keen on getting Venus's things back?' he asked when she'd finished telling him about her conversation with Shinde.

'I don't know.' Radhi frowned. The thought had never occurred to her. 'There was nothing in there except old notes and assignments and such.'

'So then?' Hrishi asked.

* * *

Back at North Star, Radhi made her way to the English Department. She didn't have any classes that afternoon and school was about to be done for the day, but now that Hrishi had said it, she wanted to take another look at Venus's boxes to see if she'd missed anything. At the entrance of the room however she paused, surprised. Ms. Lily sat at Ms. Venus's desk going over her files. The maths teacher seemed startled to see her but recovered herself quickly.

'Ms. Fernandes asked me to help Ms. Savant sort out these papers,' Lily said, to explain her presence there.

'Oh, I can lend a hand too, if you like,' Radhi offered, wondering where Ms. Savant was. 'I'm free for the next few hours.'

'Thanks. But this is almost done,' Lily said, then because Radhi continued to stand there, she asked, 'Did you need something?'

'Uhm . . . Yeah . . . I couldn't find my glasses,' Radhi lied, glancing at her desk which was completely bare. 'But they are clearly not here.'

She turned to leave and then paused as something else occurred to her. 'I'd given Ms. Venus a book of poems to sign. Did you come across it by any chance?'

Radhi had thought that perhaps Lily would let her look for it, but the maths teacher reached for a pile of books on the floor to her right and with a precision of movement that seemed to characterize all aspects of how she conducted herself in life, she pulled out a copy of *Butter and Sunshine*.

'This?' she asked, holding it up for Radhi to see.

'Yes! Thank you.' Radhi took the book and turned to leave — completely out of excuses now.

Back in the car, she wondered what she had missed. And what Ms. Lily had really been doing there. Had Ms. Fernandes really asked the maths teacher to sort through essays on John Berger and literary criticism — it definitely didn't seem like a good use of her time.

Sighing, Radhi turned her attention to the book of poems in her hands, wondering if Venus had got the chance to sign one last book. She opened it and stared at Venus's scrawl on the first page, in surprise.

* * *

Instead of a sentence, signature or quote, the poet had written the number '5' on Radhi's book. The handwriting was shaky and uneven, but there was no mistaking it for anything else. Radhi flipped through the book to see if she'd written on any other pages, but the rest of the book seemed untouched, except for the lines which Radhi had herself highlighted.

Intrigued by the scrawl, Radhi turned the pages again, this time to page number five to see if it had any annotations or significance. It was a poem titled 'Flower', a melancholy yet beautiful musing on how the beauty of a flower springs from its transience.

Radhi read it carefully once again to see if the poem itself held any special meaning, but unable to find anything hidden between the lines, she went back to the first page to look at the scrawl again. This time, focusing on the unevenness of the handwriting.

While rifling through Venus's boxes and files at the police station, Radhi had gone through a lot of her writing. There'd been side notes in books, remarks on student assignments and even scribbled lines of poetry on scraps of paper — the English teacher had had a steady hand — clear, bold and elegant. Nothing like the scrawl on the first page. Which, Radhi thought, could only mean one of two things: a) It wasn't written by Venus or b) that the English teacher had written it with great difficulty. The more Radhi looked at the number, the more she felt that the teacher had written them while in pain, or in a hurry, perhaps in the moments just before her death. Why? Radhi wondered. What had the teacher been trying to say?

Back home, she changed into a pair of parrot green cotton shorts and a white ribbed singlet, before fixing herself a strong cup of cardamom and ginger tea. Then she switched on the air conditioner, put it on power chill and settled herself into her favourite winged armchair with a quilt and a blank diary. She would analyse later why the prospect of solving a new murder excited her so much. For now, she had work to do.

On an empty page, she wrote the number five and then began to make a list of all the possible things the number could mean.

5 (five)

Page number? Of? This book? Some other book? Of a newspaper?

Date? Of what? The drama competition? Of when her article would be released? Of when she was due to meet someone? But then why put it in Radhi's book?

Roll number of a student? Who? Soam? Brij? Anyone else?

Time? Was she going to meet someone at five?

An amount? But of what? Number of students? Money?

At one point, Radhi picked up the book again and gave it a nice shake to see if any chits or folded sheets of paper were hidden between the pages. When the book of poems remained mute, she turned the page of her diary and wrote down Ms. Venus's name. Under it, she began to name the people who were pissed off at her. Soam and his mother. Kamble and his father. The snubbed Ms. Savant. Not to mention Brij. In the hullabaloo surrounding Soam, Radhi had forgotten Brij and the red remark he had seemed so bitter about. Piu had told them that Soam planned to teach Venus a lesson. Wasn't it likely that he had enlisted his friend's help? Regardless, when Radhi surveyed the names she had so far, none of their grouses seemed serious enough to inspire violence. Let alone, murder.

Sighing, Radhi put her diary aside and wandered into her kitchen in search of something to munch on. On the platform beside the stove top, Lila had laid out Radhi's dinner in neat, glass containers with blue lids. There was a capsicum subzi sprinkled liberally with roasted peanuts, a potato-pea subzi in a red tomato and cashew gravy and a chunky yellow daal which Radhi liked with a dash of lemon. Lila was perpetually guilty about the fact that she wasn't around to make hot rotis for Radhi and apologized at least once a week for leaving the rotis in a casserole, like she'd done today. Radhi shook her head, amused. She had tried to explain to her several times that after a decade of living abroad, she didn't mind simpler meals, but Lila wouldn't hear of it.

As fond as she had grown of her housekeeper and the luxury of having elaborate, homecooked meals every day, the truth was that, every now and then, Radhi liked to have her kitchen to herself. She liked cooking and baking and the aroma of well-being that filled a home when something delicious had been whipped up in the kitchen. Acting on an impulse, she opened one of the lower drawers and pulled out an old apron with flamingo prints. She'd make banana bread and give it to Lila to take home as a surprise for Shiv. Pleased with herself for having thought of it, she brought out a bottle of merlot from her mango wood bar cabinet and put on an album by Jasleen Royal on her phone. For the next hour and half, she worked contently, sifting the cinnamon with the flour, folding in the banana puree and brown sugar with a touch of vanilla essence and stirring the batter to the beat of the music, all while her mind wandered.

At the end of it, she had two thick loaves the colour of gold, cooling at the counter, and a vague idea of what she could try next. She carried her half-finished bottle of wine out to the living room and brought out her laptop. It had occurred to Radhi that Venus's article in the *National Gazette* was sure to have pissed off Wagle, but the politician's name was not on the list she had made that day. Who else had the English teacher written about in the past? Were there others she had antagonized?

A quick Google search turned up over two dozen articles that Venus had written over the years. Radhi scanned them briefly, most of them were opinion pieces — some on the craft of writing poetry and the practice of reading, others on the current systems of education and the dilemmas of being young, and still others on environmental issues. Only three were written in the last six months, and each had appeared in the *Gazette*. Radhi focused on these. One was the recent story about Wagle which Radhi had already read. She scrolled down and clicked on an article written about two months ago.

Here, Venus spoke about the importance of green spaces in urban landscapes, the impact of parks and promenades on the emotional and physical health of a city and its people, what happened when these public spaces were appropriated for other uses and how it deepened the dissonance and disparity between the haves and the have-nots. Venus hadn't named names in this one, but she *had* cited the common ground on Temple Hill as an example of the way spaces were being withdrawn from the public domain by the government.

Radhi poured herself another glass of wine and clicked on an article which had appeared less than a month ago, where Venus had spoken about the importance of public dissent. About how, when people mobilized themselves against a common cause, they were loud enough to make themselves heard. Again, she had cited the ongoing protest against Wagle and how the people had come together to save the green spaces on Temple Hill. Unlike the most recent one, published posthumously, these articles were pointed but not accusatory. It was almost as if Venus had lost patience with the powers that be to take the right steps and had decided to call out the minister publicly.

Radhi stretched and got up from her chair. She had forgotten that she'd been hungry and hadn't eaten anything since her early lunch with Hrishi. The wine and the baking had put all thought of food from her mind. But now she felt a hunger pang in earnest. She went back to the kitchen and served herself some food on a plate which she heated in the microwave. Then, taking her plate out to the living room, she texted Hrishi asking him if she could drop by the next day to meet the editor who had been in touch with Venus.

* * *

Tuesday

'Miss, this is sick!' said one of the ninth graders, his mouth full of banana bread.

'Yeah! Bussin, Miss. Totally delish!' said another.

'Thanks, guys!' Radhi laughed. 'But could we please speak actual English?'

'It's all going into the *Oxford Dictionary* in a few years' time, anyway,' said the first. 'You might as well learn it now, Miss.' He moved ahead to make way for the student behind him.

Radhi's class had just finished an exercise on writing evocatively about food. A couple of students had read out their work for the class, and Radhi had helped the rest of the students to gently critique their pieces. Now, they were all digging into the banana bread loaf which Radhi had brought from home.

'You know who else used to bake?' asked a bushy-haired girl called Naisa, as she helped herself to a slice.

100

'Ms. Venus!' said Anika, whose name Radhi remembered with the help of the unfortunate acne on her forehead. 'Boy was she good! All those apple pies and chocolate chip cookies . . .'

'Yeah, but that was only for you precious Lit Kids,' said Preeti, eating delicately so that crumbs wouldn't get stuck in her fluorescent green braces. 'Never for the whole class.'

Naisa shrugged. 'True. But any one of you could've joined the Lit Kids. It wasn't like she stopped anyone.'

'Puhhlease . . . no number of pies would tempt me to read those dull books,' Naisa said.

'So, the Lit Kids were a . . . book club?' Radhi asked.

By now the class had cleared out and just a couple of girls remained behind helping Radhi clear her desk and rearrange the chairs and tables into proper front facing rows.

Anika shook her head. 'Reading books was only one part of it. We discussed films and shows we'd watched, or articles we had read. Some of us also brought her our own writing to read. She gave such great advice.'

'And for those of us who didn't write, she encouraged journaling,' Naisa added. 'Said it was the best therapy.'

'Yeah, remember how she helped Nattu work through that whole thing after her sister's death?' Preeti asked. Then, turning to Radhi, she elaborated. 'Our friend's sister committed suicide last year. Nattu was traumatized. And Ms. Venus helped her write about her feelings and the whole experience. In fact, she wrote such a wonderful essay on it, that Ms. Venus said it was good enough to be published. Was it though?' Preeti turned to Naisa with a frown, trying to remember.

'I don't think so. Something about her parents not agreeing,' Naisa said as she put away her books and things into her cubicle.

'Where is she now? This girl — Nattu, did you say?' Radhi slung her purse on her shoulder and tucked the empty Tupperware container under her arm.

'Short for Natasha,' said Preeti. 'She left school at the end of last year. I think being here, where everyone knew her sister, made her too sad.'

'By the way,' — Radhi paused on her way to the door — 'speaking of sad . . . where's Kia? I know she was upset about Ms. Venus's passing. She was also a Lit Kid, wasn't she? I haven't seen her these last few days.'

Preeti nodded but at the mention of Kia, her face turned serious, and her expression became guarded. 'She's got the flu, Miss.'

CHAPTER 10

'Miss! Miss . . . Miss Zaveri!' a voice called as Radhi got out of the elevator and made her way to the English Department.

Turning around, Radhi saw Piu climbing up the last few stairs to the landing. She waited as the girl caught up with her, coming to a stop with her hands on her waist to catch her breath.

'Miss . . . I just wanted to know if there was any . . . any word on Soam?' the girl inquired nervously about her missing boyfriend.

'No, sorry nothing,' said Radhi apologetically. 'At least nothing that I know of.'

The girl bit her lip. 'I don't know who else to ask. I'm terrified of Soam's parents. Ms. Fernandes is equally scary! And the rest of the teachers don't know anything!'

'If I hear something . . . I'll definitely tell you, okay?' Radhi said, 'And if you hear anything from his friends or classmates yo—'

'You know that signed Maya Angelou poster on Ms. Venus's wall,' Piu asked in a rush, 'the one she was mad about?'

Radhi nodded, surprised at the sudden change of topic. She was well aware of the poster Piu was referring to. Venus had three signed posters on the wall opposite her desk, one of Angelou and the other two of Morrison and Simone De Beauvoir.

'Soam was going to deface that. Draw horns on it and big breasts and say something nasty — I don't know what . . . but he was going to ruin it!'

Radhi frowned. 'But the poster is intact.'

'I know. When he went to do it, Ms. Venus was still in there. Having this intense discussion with Mr. Bakshi. So, Soam said he would check again in a while.'

A hoard of younger students, on their way to the canteen for lunch, passed them by in a great gaggle of stone-paper-scissors and Pikachu claps and snaps, and Radhi and Piu moved against the wall to make way.

'Do you know if he went back?' Radhi asked Piu, when the students had gone.

'He did. At least that's where he was heading when we parted ways after his football practice and my debate meet.'

'Okay . . .' Radhi crossed her arms and leaned against the wall trying to think about this from Soam's perspective. 'What about Brij? Do you think Soam had involved him in this plan?'

'I'm not sure,' Piu said with a troubled expression on her face. 'I'm so sorry I didn't say anything sooner!'

When Radhi didn't reply, she added, 'I just didn't want to get him into any more trouble! He went to deface the poster. But the poster's intact and now Ms. Venus is dead, and he is missing, and I don't know how to think about all this!' She'd begun to cry now, but she wiped her tears impatiently with her sleeve.

'I'm sorry, Piu,' Radhi said after a moment. 'But we need to give this information to the police and the Mehtas. I don't know how it will help find him, but we can't keep this to ourselves.'

'The police?' Piu's eyes were wide and watery.

'Yes, and your parents as well.'

'Why my parents?' Piu shrank back looking horrified. 'What did *I* do?'

'We need their permission before you can talk to the police.'

'But they don't know about Soam and me! They'll kill me if they find out I've been dating behind their back!'

'Come Piu, surely—'

'No, I'm serious, Miss! Soam is not Jain, like me. In fact, he eats egg and chicken for extra protein . . . He needs it for all those sports. But that's a big no-no with my family.'

Radhi didn't reply immediately. She knew just how staunch some of the Jain families on Temple Hill could be. She put an arm on the girl's shoulder, partly to comfort her and partly to draw her attention to two approaching teachers who'd soon be within hearing distance.

'I'll get into too much trouble!' said Piu, her voice lower but no less hysterical.

Radhi smiled at the teachers as they walked past and waited until they were out of earshot before continuing. 'You don't have to worry about that. We don't need to give anyone a relationship update. You just need to tell the police what Soam told you. Even friends can talk to each other, no?'

Piu nodded, looking more resigned than convinced.

* * *

When Radhi finally entered the English room, she found a harried-looking Ms. Savant going through one of Ms. Venus's boxes.

'This Ms. Venus had zero organization!' She grumbled to Radhi when she looked up and saw who it was. 'How am I supposed to find her notes on the Brontë sisters in this mess?'

Radhi, who had come to put final touches on the script of the play, put her things on her desk and surveyed the scene. She had wanted to give the script one last read and cross all her Ts before she showed it to Kamble, later that week. But now, watching Savant have a mini meltdown and considering she had wanted to look at those boxes again anyway, she decided to offer help.

'It *is* a lot for one person to go through. Why is no one helping you?'

'Ms. Fernandes asked Ms. Lily to help me. Why a *maths* teacher? Great question. Maybe if you can do maths, you can do everything else?' Ms. Savant said, rolling her eyes. 'In any case, she needs to turn up first, right, to be of actual help?'

Radhi, who had seen Lily there just the day before, hid her surprise.

'Here, let me give you a hand.'

They worked silently for a few minutes. Radhi, who found it hard to forget a thing once she'd seen it, knew not only exactly which box the folder was in but also that it was below a file of essays on 'the mad woman in the attic and the subconscious mind'. But she took some time to rifle through all the other boxes once again, to see if she'd missed anything important at the police station, before finally pulling out the folder Ms. Savant was after.

'Aah, thank you! Hopefully, this will make things easier,' Ms. Savant said, clutching the notes to her chest, relieved. 'I'm teaching one of Ms. Venus's classes. The ninth graders. And they can be such bitches! Especially, those Lit Kids! Excuse my language, but they're constantly trying to correct me. It's always, "Miss, but Ms. Venus said this, and Ms. Venus said that," and I want to ask them does Ms. Venus also shit gold? I mean, *she* did not actually write *Wuthering Heights*. It is literature. It's open to interpretation for heaven's sake!'

Ms. Savant paused and took a deep breath. She smiled at Radhi. 'Sorry, I don't know what got into me.'

Radhi smiled back sympathetically. 'You have very big shoes to fill. It's bound to be hard at the beginning.'

Ms. Savant nodded, tucking the folder into her bag and slinging the bag over her shoulder. 'I don't mind hard, but I've always felt she has poisoned the students' minds against me.' She walked to the door and turned back. 'Anyways, easy enough to fix things now, right?' She smiled. 'Thank you once again for your help.'

* * *

106

Savant's smile slipped off her face the moment she left the room. She had the ninth graders to teach now, and she was terrified of them and their cruel ways. She had spent all night practising her notes on the Brontë sisters so that she didn't falter and fumble when they asked her their purposely obtuse questions. Now, she brought out a bar of chocolate from her bag and unwrapped it hastily, stuffing a block of four pieces in at once. She had gone back to her stress eating ways, but a few kilos more was a small price to pay for the strength she derived from the sugar.

* * *

On her way to the offices of the *National Gazette*, Radhi watched from her car window at the passing tableaus playing out against the city's famed Queen's Necklace. The sun was just setting and there was still time for the sweeping, sea-facing promenade to transform itself into its glittering, bejewelled self. At the moment, it was still a stage to catch different vignettes of the Bombay life. Lovers, sitting on rocks facing the sea, necked with abandon in the twilight. Perhaps believing themselves to have been rendered invisible in the midst of so many other similarly occupied couples. Or perhaps thinking that because they had turned their backs to the world, the world had also turned its eyes away from them. College students out for corn on the cob and office workers newly escaped from their nine-to-five-cells had stopped to catch the sunset and, failing which, the fleeting wisteria-purple of the evening sky. Hawkers of puffed rice, peanuts and flattened chickpeas ambled about carrying mini-kitchenettes around their necks, fully prepped with chopped tomatoes, onions, coriander, lime wedges, bottles of spices and cones made of paper where guilt-free bites and snacks could be assembled according to personal preferences. Men and women in sneakers, some in groups, some alone with their music, some on their phones, walked up and down the seafront, trying to clock-in a few last steps or breaths or thoughts, before the demands of dinner and home and children swooped in.

Radhi, who had stuck her head out to feel the warm, salty sea breeze, now rolled the window back up and got out her compact to fix her hair in its mirror. She'd had so many conversations that day, but there had been no time to dwell on any one thing, or to pull at any of the various threads of this story to see where they led. In her diary, however, she jotted down everything she'd learned. How it was connected, though, or what it all meant, if anything at all, she would get to later. She redid her lipstick now, and then shut the compact with an irritated snap, when a tiny flutter in her stomach reminded her that she was about to see Hrishi again.

Housed in a handsome Victorian building made of rough, brown basalt, with steep, marble stairs and elegantly curved, wooden banisters running the length of its eight floors, the offices of the *National Gazette* were a far cry from the workspaces of the twenty-first century. There were no gleaming glass doors, linoleum floors or identical cubicles with white laminate desks laid out at right angles. Nor was it flooded with bright panel lights. The place, in fact, was poorly lit. The windows were many but small, and though the ceiling was high, the incoming light was obstructed by pillars which seemed to have been constructed almost willy-nilly across the room. Yet, as Radhi waited in the visitor's area for Hrishi to finish a meeting, she felt that she liked the place. It had character. A great, big, bustling energy. Phones were ringing. Printers were whirring. And ancient window air conditioners were wheezing, as if in protest. And even though it was almost the end of the official workday, the place was swarming with people walking in and out of cabins and meetings with files and folders and smiles and scowls. The designated smoking area was in a narrow balcony outside in the lobby, but the air inside the office smelled strongly of cigarettes, as if nicotine was coursing through the place, through the cracks in the walls. The furniture seemed worn, the chairs threadbare at the arms or missing a wheel. But the people in them seemed comfortable, nibbling at their pens, hacking at their keyboards, taking bites of their sandwiches, happy enough to be there.

'Ms. Zaveri? Thomas.' A short, bespectacled man with a goatee came up to Radhi, and offered her a sweaty palm. 'Hrishi is still tied up in a meeting. He may be a while, but he mentioned you wanted to talk to me?'

'Yes. About Ms. Venus.' Radhi got up and shook his hand, suppressing the little bubble of disappointment that had surged up at the news that Hrishi may not be able to join them.

The man led her across the office and into a corridor, where the first door opened into an empty, plain looking conference room. When they'd settled into their seats and tea had been offered and accepted, Thomas turned to Radhi expectantly.

'So, tell me, how can I help you?'

'I understand you were the one who edited Ms. Venus's articles?'

'Yes . . . not that they needed much editing, but yes, I did some fact checking and looked them over.'

'Can you tell me how that came about? Meaning, were they commissioned by the paper, or did she approach you with the idea?'

'*She* approached *us* with the finished articles. Just to be clear, this is not how we usually operate . . . new writers need to pitch their story ideas first, there's a whole process to it . . . but in the case of Ms. Venus, considering her reputation . . .'

'You made an exception,' Radhi offered.

'Exactly.'

'I'm assuming they were handwritten? Since she didn't use a computer.'

'Yes.'

'So how did she send them across? By post or courier or did she come to the office herself to drop them?'

The editor studied Radhi with a frank curiosity. 'Sorry, but these questions . . . are they . . . are they in any way connected to her death?'

Radhi hesitated. 'I don't know, yet,' she admitted after a moment.

The editor nodded. He seemed to have more questions, but he held back, answering hers instead. 'My mother and Ms. Venus go . . . sorry, *went* to the same church. They weren't exactly friends, I doubt Ms. Venus had many of those, but they knew each other well enough. My mum's always telling her congregation about my articles and urging them to subscribe to our newspaper. You know how mums can be, right?' Thomas paused to grin at Radhi, who forced herself to smile back. She remembered only too well how mums could be. In fact, she remembered, every single day.

Thomas continued, 'Anyway, I think that's how Ms. Venus knew that I worked for the *Gazette*. A few months ago, she gave a handwritten article to my mum and asked her to pass it along to me. Told her, "They can publish it if they see fit." I showed it to Hrishi, and we agreed it was well-written and relevant, so we carried it.' Thomas paused just as the door opened and the peon came in carrying a tray with cups of tea and a plate of Marie biscuits. When they had both stirred the sugar in the tea, he continued, 'The next time round was again through my mother. But the last article, the one where she accuses Wagle, she mailed it to us by courier.'

Radhi put her teacup down. 'When was this?'

'We received the story one day after she passed. It came to us in a North Star envelope.'

Radhi leaned forward. 'Would you happen to have kept the envelope?

'Sure,' said Thomas, putting the biscuit he had just picked up, back on the plate. 'We always save any communication we receive from our contributors. Regardless of whether it's physical or digital.' He stood up, 'It'll be in one of the drawers of my desk.'

He returned a few minutes later and handed Radhi a white envelope with a green and gold star. Turning it around, Radhi saw that the name and address on it were in Venus's hand. And the date on it was the same as on the day she died.

'Why do you think she couriered this one? Why not hand it over to your mum, like always?' Radhi asked, putting the envelope away. The speed at which Ms. Venus had executed plan B had surprised her. The old English teacher could not possibly have known that she'd be dead later that day. Why then the urgency?

Thomas shrugged. 'I told her to. When she called to tell me about this piece, I told her to send it across if it was ready. I knew that this Sunday's Mass had been cancelled, which meant she wouldn't have met my mother until the week after. And I didn't know if her story would have stayed relevant until then. So, I told her it was better to just send it to us directly.'

That, Radhi supposed, made sense for Venus. Considering the date of the play was fast approaching, and the Kambles were pressurizing her to change her script, Radhi could understand Venus's need for speedy action.

Leaning on the desk, Radhi made a steeple of her hands and rested her chin. 'When she called you that day, what time was it, do you remember? And how did she sound?'

Thomas frowned. 'Must be . . . sixish? Wait, I have it here in my incoming calls records.' He brought his phone out and scrolled down. 'Yes, says here 6.37 p.m. And yeah, she sounded exactly like herself. Maybe a bit agitated. But other than that, all right — if that's what you are getting at.' He shook his head. 'I was pretty zapped when I learned that she died later that day. I mean, there were literally no signs.'

'True,' said Radhi.

They fell quiet for a moment, then Radhi asked, 'Did she say anything else?'

Thomas smiled wryly. 'She was never one for small talk as you may already know. She just told me to give her regards to my mother.'

Radhi nodded and straightened up. The editor hadn't been able to tell her anything new that might give her a clue about what had happened to Ms. Venus, but she wondered if anyone at her church might know more. 'By the way,' she said, as another thought occurred to her, 'Does the number five mean anything to you?'

'Five?' Thomas frowned, then shook his head. 'No, nothing I can think of . . .'

'Anything connected to the article, perhaps?' Radhi tried to jog his memory.

'Sorry, no . . .' he began to say, then, suddenly his eyes widened. 'Oh, but speaking of articles, she did tell me that she would be sending us one more after this one.'

'Meaning apart from the one on Wagle?' Radhi clarified.

'Yes. She said it was written and ready, but she needed to tie up some loose ends, so it would take a little longer to send.'

Radhi was quiet as she thought this through.

'Was it connected to this one?' she asked finally.

'I'm not sure. We didn't really discuss it.' Thomas scratched his cheek. 'I wonder if anyone found it in her things . . . I'd love to get my hands on it. Will you please keep an eye out in case it turns up? She'd usually date it and give it a headline and subhead and everything.' He grinned wryly again. 'Basically, she'd do my job also.'

Radhi nodded quietly. But her mind was already whirring in all directions. What could the new article have been about? Radhi hadn't found anything like what Thomas had described among Venus's papers. Could Venus have kept it at her home? Or had someone else got their hands on it already?

And also, was any of this actually connected to Venus's death? Or was she just barking up the completely wrong tree?

CHAPTER 11

'You can't just eat the sides and waste the stuffing!' Hrishi laughed as he watched Radhi nibble at the outer crust of the kachori, without touching the stuffing inside.

'Who said I'm wasting it?' Radhi said, her mouth half full. 'I just want to enjoy both the textures separately.' She held up an uneaten kachori in front of him. 'First, the crisp and biscuit-y layer on the outside and then the soft and crumbly pea and coconut filling inside. Why confuse both the tastes?'

'And what about the chutney?' Hrishi asked, taking a sip of his black coffee. 'Are you still as particular about chutneys?'

'Of course. You know what I always say — a well-made chutney elevates the whole meal experience. But a mediocre chutney is a disgrace. Any cook worth her salt should give the chutney as much attention as the main course.'

'For someone who didn't know how to make a cup of tea, you've always had many opinions on food.' Hrishi grinned and leaned back into his seat.

'Well, I now have opinions *and* skills, I'll have you know.' Radhi raised a shoulder with fake haughtiness.

'Hey, only one way to prove it.'

'Done,' said Radhi. 'You let me know when.'

Hrishi had come to find Radhi, just as she was leaving the conference room, and now the two of them were sitting in Hrishi's cabin, where Radhi had just finished telling him about her conversation with the editor and everything that happened at the school that day. They'd tossed about some ideas about everything that was suspicious about Venus's death. The suddenness of it. The missing student. The missing article. The strange scrawl on the front page of the book of poems. Nothing seemed to add up to anything. But Radhi had enjoyed exchanging theories with Hrishi. His mind had a way of seeing things which was very different from hers.

Hrishi's phone rang and he excused himself to take the call. As he stood by the white, colonial-style window, Radhi gazed about his office. The wall behind his chair had a whiteboard with a long list of who was covering what. Random news items had been cancelled or circled or ticked and underlined. Some had dates against them, others had exclamation marks, perhaps to indicate a level of urgency. On the wall beside the door, there were shelves with books on current affairs and autobiographies, mainly of athletes and artists. There were also a couple of trophies for excellence in journalism almost hidden by the books which, knowing Hrishi, was probably intentional. On a third wall, there were black and white photographs of monuments, the Qutub Minar against a clear Delhi sky, the Gateway of India amid a flock of pigeons in mid-flight, and the Taj Mahal, standing aloof and exquisite, despite the throngs of tourists. His desk had the usual clutter of laptop, files and stationery. The only personal item was a picture frame of his wife and daughter in sun hats on a beach. Radhi had just picked up the frame to see the photo better when there was soft a knock, and the door swung open a moment later.

'Hrishi?' a woman stuck her head in.

She had short, tight curls, dangling earrings and creamy white skin, the same as the woman in the photograph in Radhi's hand. Radhi put the picture frame back on the desk and the woman entered the office just as Hrishi finished his call.

'Neha! What are you doing here?' He crossed the room to greet his wife with a peck on the cheek.

'I was just on my way home after running some errands and I thought I'd check if you were ready to leave. I tried calling but you didn't pick up,' she said in a pointed manner.

'Yeah, sorry, I was on a work call. Anyways, here, meet Radhika, she's an old friend.'

Neha turned to Radhi, an appraising look behind her smile. 'How nice to meet you.'

'Likewise,' said Radhi, getting up to shake Neha's hand.

'So, is this also where you socialize, now?' she said to Hrishi, then turning to Radhi, 'I'm always telling my husband that he practically lives in this office, eats his meals here, spends holidays here, and now seems like he is even catching up with friends here.' She was smiling, as if she had meant to say it as a joke, but Radhi felt it hadn't come out lightly enough.

'This isn't a social call,' Hrishi answered. 'Radhi had come to meet one of our editors for something she's working on.'

'So, how do you know each other?' Neha continued. 'Let me guess, journalism school? Almost all of Hrishi's friends are writers!'

'Not journalism school,' Radhi smiled, 'but still a writer, I'm afraid.'

'Radhi writes books. Literary fiction and now murder mysteries,' Hrishi said. 'Some of them have even won awards. I bumped into her at North Star, the other day. She's teaching creative writing to some of the senior grades there.'

Neha's eyes widened. 'Oh, so you must be the one who convinced him to speak at the school that day! I was so surprised when he said he had volunteered.' She turned towards Hrishi and swatted him on the arm playfully. Her tone, however, when she spoke had an edge to it. 'All these years, I've been telling him to be more involved with Anoushka's school and nothing. From now on, I should just ask other people to persuade him.'

'To be fair, he didn't need much persuading,' Radhi said, glancing at Hrishi who looked ill at ease. 'He said you'd be thrilled about it.'

'Did he now?' Neha glanced at her husband thoughtfully, before turning back to Radhi again, 'Well, that's nice to know. Anyways, what are you guys doing about dinner? Or was this it?' she said, looking at the half full plates of kachoris and khaman dhoklas on Hrishi's desk.'

'No, of course not,' Hrishi said hurriedly. 'I'll be eating dinner at home.'

'Good,' Neha said. 'Anoushka will be happy to see you home early for a change.' She turned to Radhi. 'We would love it if you could join us for dinner, Radhika.'

'Oh no, I couldn't possibly,' Radhi said immediately. 'I need to get going actually. Besides, dinner is already made at home.'

'No, no,' said Neha. 'I feel bad about interrupting your evening. If not today, then how about tomorrow?'

'Don't worry about it, Neha, please,' Radhi said. 'We were almost done here. In fact, I'm going to be seeing you soon, anyways.' Radhi glanced at Hrishi, 'I don't know if Hrishi's had a chance to tell you yet, but please consider it a personal invitation for dinner at my place on Saturday night.'

Hrishi passed a hand through his hair and smiled sheepishly. 'Sorry, I completely forgot.' He turned to his wife. 'It's Radhika's birthday on Sunday and she's invited us for dinner, along with a bunch of other college friends.'

A look of displeasure crossed Neha's face before she forced herself to smile at Radhi. 'My husband never tells me anything. Now, I'm really glad we met.'

* * *

Radhi took a spoonful of yellow lentil daal with one hand and clicked on the TV remote with the other. As *Monk*, the show about the eccentric private detective, began with its usual opening scene of bloody murder, Radhi wondered whether it was preferable to have dinner alone in front of the television every day like she did, or with a family, albeit with its undercurrent of tensions, like Hrishi might be facing that night. She imagined him with his wife on one side and daughter on the other. The atmosphere at the table stiff because of everything that was tightly held in. They'd probably focus on the child and her day at school, something safe and neutral, to ensure that they didn't bicker in front of her. But what happened once the child had been put to bed? Did they watch TV, sullen, resentful, offering each other perfunctory good nights before turning their backs to sleep? Or did they let loose? Did it begin with the aiming and throwing of tiny pebbles, which dislodged larger rocks, which in turn caused a landslide? And then? What happened then? Bruised and angry, did they lie awake, festering in different rooms? Or did they soften? Did she tear up, and did he feel the need to kiss the tears away? And then did the warmth and scent of his breath on her face stir something, kindle something else?

Radhi blushed at this strange direction of her thoughts and tried to bring her mind back to the show. It had been a long day, and there was much she'd learned, but no part of her felt inclined to make sense of it. Even her calls to Shinde that day had gone unanswered, but she didn't feel like following up. For now, all she wanted was to not think. And perhaps, a glass of wine. Or two.

* * *

Wednesday

Shinde looked alarmed when he saw Radhi at the entrance of the Temple Hill police station the next morning. He got up from his seat and came to her as fast as his giant belly would let him.

'Ma'am, it is such a pleasant day, shall we talk outside?' He wiggled his eyebrows at her, insinuating that she should follow his lead without any argument.

Outside, the blistering April morning was far from pleasant. The sun hadn't climbed overhead yet, but already the branches and leaves of the trees around were limp in the heat. Shinde put on his sunglasses and looked around him, his manner almost comical in its surreptitiousness.

'We can talk in my car if you like,' Radhi offered, suppressing the urge to grin.

'Yes, please,' he said.

Radhi led him to where Ramzan bhai was waiting with the car in one of the adjoining lanes.

Once they were inside, Shinde whipped aside his sunglasses almost immediately and turned to her. 'Ma'am, you can't keep coming to the station or I will lose my job!'

'Whatever for?' Radhi asked, surprised. 'I just wanted to know when the test results were expected. And you didn't answer my calls.'

'There's not going to be any further testing, ma'am. I don't have permission from my seniors.'

'What do you mean? Didn't you tell them about the red skin?'

'They're saying it's not enough to go on.' Shinde mopped his forehead despite the cool air conditioning inside the car. 'I have been told to be more mindful of public resources and to use my team's time and energy on more critical matters.'

'A woman's dead! How's that not critical enough?' Radhi asked.

'An old English teacher dying of old age is not exactly the mystery of the century.' Shinde put up both hands before Radhi could protest. 'My senior's words, not mine.'

There was a knock on the window of the car and a young homeless woman with a toddler at her hip flashed a fan of magazines at them. Radhi shook her head, but the peddler continued to stand there, pressing an issue of *GQ* about balding men to the glass pane for so long that Shinde adjusted the cap on his head self-consciously.

'The old teacher wasn't old enough to die of age. If yes, her health records should reflect that. Where are they?'

Shinde shrugged. 'Probably at her house. We have the keys, but as of now I can't spare the men to go take a look.'

'That's ridiculous. I'm going to come and talk to your seniors,' Radhi said, waving at the woman with the magazines to move on, but to no avail.

'No, no, no!' Shinde's eyes widened with alarm. 'Ma'am, why are you hell-bent on making things difficult for me? The new station manager will have my head if he knows I've been discussing the case with you.'

The woman outside the window was now flashing an *MW* magazine with the headline 'Men, Middle Age & Metabolism', and the toddler at her hip was pressing sticky, snotty fingers to the glass. Radhi could sense that in the front seat Ramzan bhai was having a hard time not reacting to this gross violation of the beautiful car he had just washed and cleaned. She quickly rolled down the window, handed a hundred rupee note to the woman and took the magazine before rolling the window back up. The young woman grinned at her little victory and finally left them, and Radhi almost smiled at her tenacity.

Turning back to Shinde, she fixed him with a stern eye. 'Look, Inspector, you and I both know that I'm not going to let this be. So, either I talk to your senior, or you cooperate with me.'

Shinde shook his head and cursed in Marathi, the choice of words so colourful, that Ramzan bhai, usually the model of discretion, almost turned in his seat.

Radhi continued to look at him impassively.

The inspector cleared his throat. 'Okay. I'm going to be honest with you, ma'am, and I hope you won't make me regret it.'

Radhi shrugged, refusing to commit.

'Our new station manager is an arsehole of the first order. He checks our uniforms, our schedules, and has been going through all our current cases, deciding the order of priority we are to give everything, as if we are bloody rookies. Now, I can't openly contradict him. I'm up for promotion next year, and he can ruin things for me. But should I tell you something in the strictest of confidentiality?' He dropped his voice a notch as he said this.

Radhi nodded but he jerked his head towards the front seat.

Radhi caught Ramzan bhai's eye in the rearview mirror. The old driver nodded once imperceptibly before getting out of the car.

Shinde watched as the driver walked towards the paan shop up ahead, before speaking. 'Between you and me, ma'am, I think my senior is under some kind of pressure to close this case.'

Radhi stared at him. 'Pressure from within the system?'

Shinde shrugged. 'Could be the commissioner, could be some MLA or politician, I don't know, but one thing is for certain, he wants to wrap this up quickly.'

CHAPTER 12

Radhi was quiet for a few minutes as she processed this new information.

'Okay,' she said, 'I won't approach him — for now.' She held up a finger, seeing Shinde's relief. 'But we need to go to Venus's home.' She held up her finger again, this time to stop him from protesting. 'We can do it when you are off duty. But I need to see her health records as well as check if there's anything there that could have led to her death.'

'I will lose my job, madam,' Shinde hissed.

'Only if the station manager finds out. But if you don't help me, I'll have to go to the media and tell them what I know so far and how the police are refusing to investigate. Who do you think your seniors are going to throw under the bus when that article comes out?'

Shinde looked outraged, but before he could say something, Radhi hurried on.

'But imagine if we do find something and we can prove foul play. Can you imagine what kind of story we could give the media, then? Can you imagine your name on the front page of the *National Gazette*?'

At seeing Shinde's disbelieving expression, Radhi shrugged. 'The editor is a friend. A very good friend.'

Shinde stared at her. And Radhi could see him weigh his options, trying to think about the problem in every way that his limited imagination would allow.

'They'll have to give me my promotion, then,' he said, finally.

'Exactly,' Radhi agreed.

'And who knows, we might even be able to get rid of my station manager!' Shinde said, beginning to get excited.

'Exactly.' Radhi smiled.

The cop got out of the car after they had fixed a time to visit Venus's home. But just as he was leaving, Radhi rolled down the window. 'Oh, and Inspector, remember how you said the missing North Star student was unconnected to all of this?'

A look of dread came over Shinde as he bent to hear her better. When Radhi told him about her conversation with Piu, he cursed.

As she watched him walk up the lane to the main Temple Hill Road, Radhi considered sending Ramzan bhai after him with the magazine on middle-aged men, but she didn't think Shinde's fragile equanimity could handle any more that day.

* * *

Radhi hurried into the Shamiana, the all-day restaurant at the iconic Taj Mahal Palace hotel in Colaba, late for her lunch with Kamble. She'd reached the chandelier-lit lobby of the hotel much ahead of time, but then Hrishi had called to apologize for the abrupt end to their evening the day before, and she'd spent some time waving off his apologies and telling him about her conversation with Shinde.

'Pressure from the top, huh? That's a new angle. Who do you think it could be?' Hrishi had said, immediately zeroing in on the most critical piece of information to come out of Radhi's whole interaction with Shinde.

When Radhi didn't immediately answer, he had added, 'If you're thinking Wagle — you know the chronology is all wrong, right?'

Radhi's first thought *had* been Wagle, but she knew that Venus's article on Wagle had appeared *after* her death. The only way Wagle could be involved was if he knew what her article would say beforehand, and even then, her death hadn't solved anything for him. The story had still been published and read by millions in the country. Radhi's mind was so busy sorting through the various threads that Venus's death seemed to have unspooled that she almost didn't see Kamble and would've crossed his table altogether had he not got up and said her name.

'It's true what they say about writers then, how they always have their heads in the clouds,' he said, grinning once they'd taken their seats.

'I think you'll find that true for most artists,' Radhi smiled. 'A need to escape, to create.'

'What a luxury to be able to do it,' he said.

'And a torment when you can't,' she shot back.

'I read one of your books, by the way.' He handed her a menu card. '*Happy Now?* Such an authentic portrayal of a troubled marriage.'

'Thank you.' Radhi blushed and ducked behind the menu, always a little uncomfortable around compliments.

'I found myself wondering if you'd drawn any of it from real life. It certainly made me think about my own divorce. I had a rather bitter one and identified with so many of the issues that the couple in the book grapples with. But I have one complaint, why did you have to give them a happy ending?'

The waiter came to take their orders then, and it was a minute before Radhi could answer Kamble.

'I think I needed to. I needed them to be happy for my own selfish reasons,' she said lightly and left it there.

Radhi had gone through her own divorce at the time of writing the book, and the book had been her way of processing her grief over the death of her marriage or, more accurately, the death of that idea of herself that she had inhabited during the marriage, but she didn't intend to delve into any of it with the MD of North Star, whose scrutiny she found she didn't care for much.

'So, did you read the play?' she asked once the waiter had placed their fresh lime sodas in front of them along with crusty slices of avocado on toast.

Kamble had requested a copy of the play a day prior, so that he could review it before they met.

'Yes, it's perfect. I like how the public is now protesting against industrial emissions instead of the mall. The issue is still about the environment, so we're able to retain a lot of the original lines.'

'Along with the original spirit of it,' Radhi added, meaningfully.

Kamble nodded quickly. 'Yes, absolutely. Look, I was also loath to change this script. Especially now, with Ms. Venus gone, this is probably the last piece of writing she did, and it would've been nice to preserve it as is, and have our students perform it as a way of remembering her.' Kamble took a sip of his drink before adding, 'But I have to think of the school.'

Radhi studied him for a moment, then on an impulse she said, 'This is not the last thing she wrote.'

Kamble's mouth was full, so Radhi continued. 'The team at the *National Gazette* mentioned that she was going to send them another article, something she'd already written.'

The expression on Kamble's face remained neutral but his jaw stiffened. And Radhi could see that it was a carefully studied blank. He waited for the waiter to place Radhi's mixed vegetable dim sums and his soy burger in front of them before inquiring casually, 'What was it about?'

'No idea. But knowing her, probably something badass.' Radhi shrugged and smiled.

Kamble smiled back and said smoothly, 'She has left such a big hole in our English Department, which brings me to why I asked you to lunch.'

'I thought it was to personally hand over my niece's admissions letter.' Radhi joked.

He hadn't mentioned the letter even once, so she felt obliged to bring it up now that she'd handed over the script of the play and he had approved it.

He laughed at that. 'You know, with your negotiation skills, you should be in the foreign service.' He chuckled again. 'The letter's ready — it's gone to Ms. Fernandes for her signature. You can collect it from her office in a day or two.'

He watched Radhi soak her dim sums in chilli sauce before manoeuvring them expertly to her mouth with her chopsticks. 'Would you like a permanent teaching position at North Star?'

The question was so out of the blue that Radhi's dim sum almost slipped from between her chopsticks before she tightened her grip. 'That's the second career you've suggested for me in the span of two minutes,' Radhi said once she had recovered from her surprise. 'I thought you liked my book.'

He smiled. 'I did. And I'm not suggesting you quit writing books for even a moment. But how about a part-time position? Ms. Venus was quite happy with you. So, I thought, we'd offer you a couple of classes, nothing too heavy. You do enjoy teaching the kids, don't you?'

'I do, of course. But—'

Kamble held up his hand, before Radhi could talk. 'Please, you don't need to answer right away — just think about it?'

Radhi nodded. She took a sip of her fresh lime soda. 'So, what about you, Mr. Kamble? Did you always want to run schools?'

Kamble shook his head. 'I'm a lawyer, in fact. I used to practice in DC. North Star is my father's dream. He has the heart of an educator. Do you know he was the first person to go to school in our family? My grandparents were simple farmers in Vidarbha. My father came to Bombay to pursue further education and then never left. This school and its sister, which he opened in our village, is his life's work. But now he's getting old.'

'And he'd like you to take over?' Radhi guessed.

'Yes, I'll be taking over as CEO, next year.' Kamble smiled. 'And then, of course, I have some plans of my own.'

Radhi looked at him expectantly, but he didn't elaborate.

* * *

Kamble continued to sit there for a long moment after Radhi had left, thinking over their conversation. What he had told Radhi was true. It hadn't always been his dream to run a school, but it *was* his dream to make his father proud. When it came to temperament, his brother and father were more alike. Both hot-tempered, fearless and unable to comprehend how Satish could be so measured in his responses. He wanted to prove to them that his calculatedness wasn't a weakness, that when things got hard, he was able to face them with equanimity. Like now, if what Radhi had told him was true, if Venus had indeed written a new article, he suspected things were going to get even harder than they already were.

* * *

The first thing that Radhi heard when she entered the buzzing staffroom that afternoon was that Soam Mehta's mother had been hospitalized.

'It was because of high BP, I heard.'

'Obviously, it's the stress of these last few days.'

'So, still no idea where the boy has gone, huh?'

'I heard they are announcing a monetary reward for anyone to come forward with any kind of information.'

'Is that why the father was in school, then?'

'Yes, they want to email all the school parents.'

'And put up posters about the reward.'

'There's no way Fernandes is going to allow that!'

'Why do you think the father was flipping out?'

Snippets of conversation made their way to Radhi as she made her way into the staffroom, got herself a cup of coffee from the machine and pulled up a chair next to Ms. Lily. She had just finished one class and wanted to finish grading some assignments before her final class that afternoon.

Ms. Lily looked up and nodded at her but turned back to correcting the sheet of algebra equations in front of her. Around them, the conversation was thick with conjectures and guesswork, but the maths teacher remained uninterested and wholly focused on the hypotheses that could actually be proved. Her entire demeanour as she worked was stiff and closed, discouraging any uninvited conversation. But Radhi had a pressing question for her.

'Sorry, to disturb you, Ms. Lily, but I was just wondering if you saw a recently written article by Ms. Venus, when you went through her papers and things, the other day.'

Whatever answer Radhi had been expecting, she hadn't expected the maths teacher to actually flinch.

'No, nothing,' she said, recovering herself so rapidly that Radhi would've thought she'd imagined her initial reaction, had it not been for one curious detail.

Ms. Lily had not asked what article. Had not paused to consider her question, or to think back to all the files and notes and sheets she'd gone through. It was almost as if the maths teacher knew exactly what article Radhi was asking about.

* * *

Radhi was still thinking about Ms. Lily as she made her way down the crowded corridor to her next class, when someone hurled into her left shoulder with such force that the folder of assignments in her hand fell and the sheets scattered on the floor.

'I am so sorry . . . so sorry.' Ms. Savant grasped Radhi's arm in apology before kneeling to help her collect her papers.

The English teacher had tears in her eyes and a reddened nose which she had to wipe with the pallu of her saree to stop it from dripping.

'Are you okay, Ms. Savant?' Radhi asked.

'Yes, yes,' the other woman replied without meeting Radhi's eyes. 'Just allergies.'

When all the papers had been collected, Ms. Savant stood up and apologized to Radhi once more, before hurrying away. Curious, Radhi walked into the classroom the English teacher had just come out of. The ninth graders were standing in hushed knots of threes and fours, talking softly with each other.

'What happened here?' Radhi asked the class at large. 'Why was Ms. Savant so upset?'

The students turned around at the sound of her voice, but no one answered.

'Piu? Stuti?' Radhi asked the girls closest to her.

The two friends glanced at their classmates.

'Some of us thought it would be funny to . . .' Piu walked towards the smart board and switched it on.

On the screen was the definition of savant.

Savant (noun): A very learned or talented person, especially one distinguished in a particular field of science or the arts.
   Synonym: scholar, intellectual
   Antonym: Mrs. Savant

Radhi's eyes widened at the words on the board. 'This is nasty, you guys.'

'It was just meant to be funny, Miss,' protested Brij from the back of the class.

'Yeah, just some clever wordplay,' said one of the other boys.

'Ms. Venus always liked wordplay,' added a third.

'Well, she isn't Ms. Venus, and it is unfair to punish her for that,' said Radhi, turning to leave.

She considered going after Ms. Savant, but she had her own class to teach. Besides, she didn't know if the English teacher would welcome her concern.

'Brij, can I please see you outside for a minute?' Radhi asked.

'It wasn't my idea, Miss!' the boy said as soon as he had joined Radhi outside the class.

Radhi shook her head. 'That's not what I wanted to talk to you about.' She paused before continuing. 'It's about Soam. Did he tell you that he planned to teach Ms. Venus a lesson? Did he ask for your help?'

'No. Why? Who told you that?' Brij answered quickly, his eyes wide.

'That's not important,' Radhi said. 'But I really need to know if you went up to the English Department with him.'

The boy began to deny it again, but Radhi raised a hand to stop him.

'Look, I already know *he* went up there. The question is, were you with him?' She switched her folder of assignments to her other hand and dropped her voice. 'See, I get that you don't want to get into any more trouble than you already are and, as you already know, I'm not going to rat you out. But if you know something about what Soam did that day, you should speak now.'

Radhi could see conflicting emotions on the boy's face.

'You have to understand about Soam . . .' he began finally. 'He's not a troublemaker. He was just devastated after they took his sports captaincy.'

Radhi nodded.

'He wanted to trash her office. Rip out a few books. Scatter some files. Ruin her precious posters. He asked me if I'd do it with him, but I said no.'

Radhi raised her eyebrows.

'I swear, I went straight home.' Brij looked around, before continuing, 'I admit I was tempted. Ms. Venus could have gone easier on us. Even Ms. Fernandes. It was like they wanted to make an example of us or something. And if it was any other day, I probably would have. But I have band practice with some guys from school on Mondays and Wednesdays. We meet at my place, and I'd never miss it for something like this!'

The boy seemed to be telling the truth, Radhi thought, as she studied his face. In any case, it would be easy enough to check his story out.

CHAPTER 13

214, 215, 216 . . . Radhi walked down the corridor of the Temple Hill Hospital with a huge bouquet of oriental lilies, looking for Roma Bansal's room. She had promised Madhavi that she'd visit her supposedly ailing mother-in-law, but the closer she drew to the woman's room, the stronger she felt the urge to turn and run. Radhi detested her and found it very taxing to not let her feelings show. She reached the end of the corridor and was about to turn left when someone bumped into her again.

'Ouch!' she said, rubbing her left shoulder for the second time that day, growing increasingly annoyed with the world at large.

'Sorry,' said the man who had crashed into her, barely glancing her way, before walking ahead.

But Radhi had got a good look at him. It was Soam Mehta's father who had just stridden out of one of the rooms. A moment later, two nurses came out from it. One of them was crying.

'Don't let that man get to you, Bina. He's been awful with everybody. Just yesterday he got into a nasty argument with another patient's visitors for clogging the waiting room.'

Radhi glanced up at the room number. Komal Mehta was most likely admitted here. She considered checking on her but decided first to rid herself of the flowers and the onerous task she had set for herself.

'Aah, I was wondering when you'd show up,' Roma Bansal said with a self-satisfied smirk, when Radhi walked into the room. 'For me?' she added in mock surprise, as she took in the flowers. 'I suppose this is your way of saying sorry, hmm?'

'Hello, Aunty.' Radhi smiled, not trusting herself to say more.

'Apology accepted, of course,' said Roma, pressing on the lever of the bed to lift her from semi-reclining to a sitting position. 'I am magnanimous, if nothing else.'

The two women had had a heated exchange a few months ago, when Roma had called both sisters selfish — Radhi for not accepting an offer of marriage from her friend's son, and Madhavi for not attempting to give Roma the grandson she so badly wanted. Radhi had told the old crone where she could stick it, in different words of course, but still it had created some trouble for her sister. It irritated Radhi now that she had to turn up with flowers for the woman. She could think of no one more undeserving and felt genuinely sorry for the poor lilies.

'How have you been, Aunty?' Radhi asked, placing the bouquet on the TV cabinet opposite the bed and taking a seat on the visitors' chair.

Roma Bansal sighed. 'Surviving. Though with all the problems I have, even the doctors are surprised at how.'

The woman was in a hospital gown but other than that looked like she was about to go to one of her kitty parties. Her hair was done up in an elaborate bun, and she had on her trademark two-karat solitaires. Her brown lipstick, winged kajal and bindi had all been applied so precisely that she was sure the woman had bribed one of the nurses into helping her.

'How much longer will you have to stay?' Radhi asked, 'Have the doctors said anything?'

Roma shrugged. 'They're still running tests. Trying to figure what's wrong with me.'

Everything. Everything's wrong with you, Radhi wanted to say, but she kept mum, and the older woman continued.

'Honestly, I don't mind. So many relatives and friends have been coming to check on me that the nurses are joking they should have separate visiting hours just for my guests.'

The woman's sense of her own worth was so grossly inflated that one could die of boredom under the weight of it. But Radhi had long learned that the trick to surviving a conversation with Roma Bansal was to treat her as a possible character in one of her books. That way, every dull thing she said was fodder for writing and not something to be suffered through.

'The doctors have been telling me,' Roma continued, obliviously, 'that sometimes, the problem is not here but here.' She tapped her heart and then her head with two fingers. 'And I feel like telling them, did you really need a medical degree to figure that out? *I* could've told you that. I always have so much on my mind, that it's bound to have an impact on my body.'

She paused and looked at Radhi so expectantly, that Radhi felt compelled to ask, 'What are you so worried about, Aunty?'

'My son! His house, his children, his health! Your sister is out the whole day, so tell me who is taking care of them?'

Radhi could've told her that Madhavi was out *working* not gallivanting, that she managed their father's multimillion-dollar jewellery business singlehandedly, while always being back home when Amayra returned from school. But they'd had a version of this argument before, and it had gained her nothing but trouble. She stayed quiet now, refusing to take the bait.

Roma, who had paused in anticipation of protest from Madhavi's normally argumentative sister, seemed surprised but undeterred by Radhi's silence.

'Do you know the doctors say half my gastric issues are caused by these anxieties?!'

Radhi wondered if this was a good time to remind her of the ghee-soaked kachoris and deep-fried samosas she was so fond of, but she bit her lip. She had promised herself she'd behave. Instead, she said, 'I've heard naturopathy is great for a gut cleanse.'

Whatever response Roma had expected from Radhi, it was not this. She seemed almost irritated at her inability to goad the younger woman.

'I don't expect you to understand what it is to worry for your children . . . maybe someday, if at all, when you have one of your own . . .'

'So true,' said Radhi, her mind far away, thinking of ways in which she could dispose of a character like Roma in a murder mystery.

Adding something to her tube of saline would be most convenient, she thought. But wouldn't suffocating her with a pillow just be so much more satisfying? Radhi almost smiled at the thought, which annoyed Madhavi's mother-in-law even more.

How in the world was she to take offence to a smile?

* * *

Komal Mehta was alone in the room, listlessly flipping through a magazine, when Radhi snuck her head in.

'May I come in?' she asked.

At first, Soam's mother didn't recognize Radhi. Perhaps it was the unexpectedness of the setting. But then her face cleared, and she asked almost immediately, 'What is it? Have they found him?'

Radhi frowned apologetically. She hadn't thought that the woman would construe her presence here in this manner. 'Sorry,' she said, entering the room, 'I was visiting a relative in the hospital and happened to realize you were admitted here as well. How are you?'

The woman shook her head. 'It wasn't anything serious, just BP. They should discharge me today. But the thought of going home without my Soam there . . .' Her voice trailed off and her eyes welled up with tears. 'I'm sorry,' she said, turning to the bedside table for a tissue. 'I keep thinking about what we could have done differently. How else could we have handled things?'

Radhi wondered if this was a good time to tell her what Piu had shared with her, but she decided against it. She would let Shinde get to it in his own time. The woman seemed fragile, and Radhi didn't see how this information would help her in any way.

'My husband can be so hot-headed. It's one thing to lose your temper at your own kids, but to scream at the school principal. No wonder Ms. Fernandes is not helping us now. She's refusing to put up posters in the school about the reward we've announced.'

'I'm sure that's not true,' Radhi began. 'Ms. Fernandes is probably acting in the best interest of the school and its reputation, not because she wants to be vindictive.'

Mrs. Mehta switched off the air conditioner in the room and rubbed her arms. 'Who knows? All I know is I shouldn't have let my husband go to school the day Soam lost his captaincy. He was so angry — I'm sure he behaved awfully.'

Radhi stayed with the woman for about a quarter of an hour, until a nurse came to take her pressure. As she left, she wished her well and promised to be in touch if there was anything she heard at the school, but all the time her mind was on what she'd just discovered — Soam Mehta's father had gone to the school on the day Venus died. This was news to her. And she filed it away, to mull over it later.

* * *

Radhi entered Venus's apartment guiltily. Having convinced Shinde that she needed to search Venus's home, she now felt like she was violating the old teacher's privacy. She had to remind herself that Shinde and his lackeys had already been here, and any poking around that she did now was with Venus's best interests at heart. How the English teacher would have hated the clichéd phrase, Radhi thought with a smile.

While Shinde switched on the lights and fans, Radhi drew the curtains and was surprised to see that Venus's apartment was exactly like she'd imagined it. She wasn't sure when but somewhere between the turning of the key in the lock and the opening of the door, she'd formed an idea of a room filled with books and art and dark, wooden furniture almost as if she had seen it before.

The apartment was a large three-bedroom-hall-kitchen in an old and leafy Bandra neighbourhood. There was such a clutter of Burmese teak armchairs and loveseats and settees that, had they not all been piled up with books and papers, a stranger would have assumed that Venus was very fond of having people over and entertaining. According to Shinde, Venus had lived alone with a pet cat for company and had seldom had any people over. At one point she'd been married, but a decade into it the couple had separated and the husband, a photographer by profession, had moved to London. There were no children, no siblings and no parents. But there was a lot of art. On the walls, in great splatters of frames made of wood, lacquer and gilded metal, there were oil paintings of classical Indian mythology, impressionist renderings of bustling streets and blooming gardens, and kitschy abstract art, maddeningly unfathomable in its abstractness. There were also postcards and photographs, pictures of parks and people and pillows in empty beds. Radhi walked closer to examine the beds captured in soft morning light. Most gave the impression of having been slept in, rollicked in. Perhaps there had been lovemaking, or a pillow fight, or a worry-ridden tossing and turning. It was left for the viewer to imagine.

'You know where most people keep their medical reports?' Shinde asked, drawing Radhi out of her thoughts.

She turned around to find the inspector sitting on one of the sofas, in the process of removing his socks and shoes.

'Either under the mattress of their beds or on top of cupboards. That way all the X-rays or MRI reports and so on stay intact.' He smiled at his own cleverness and pulled a footstool towards a wooden cabinet with glass shutters before proceeding to climb it. 'I'm going to check out here. Maybe you can look in the bedroom?'

Agreeing with his suggestion, Radhi walked out of the living room and down a narrow corridor, pausing at a door on the left. Venus's bedroom got a lot of light that slanted into the room through the thin, wooden slats of the old-fashioned windows and the sheer, lemon-yellow, cotton drapes which covered them. The room itself was neat. A tall sheesham wood bookcase with a built-in desk dominated one corner of the room. Another was taken over by a trio of dying potted plants. There was no television. The bed had a Sanganeri print bedspread in a deep indigo blue. And on the bedside table there was a tube of hempseed hand cream, a spectacle case and a couple of medicine bottles which turned out to be vitamin and calcium pills.

So, this, thought Radhi was what it was to grow old alone — with only books and ideas and your own thoughts for company. It could be a neat, little existence without the hot mess of relationships and responsibilities and expectations that plagued most ordinary lives. As smooth as you desired, as pretty and predictable as you cared for, as without attachment as you wished. And yet, Radhi found herself wondering, as she lifted the mattress off the bed with one hand, and slid the other under it to check for files or folders, could this chosen solitude also sometimes become that bristling, biting, bitter kind of lonely?

Radhi knew she'd always have her sister and nieces to share holidays and festivals with, but she was also aware that it wasn't the same as sharing a life with someone. Waking up next to them, waiting up for them, nursing them through a cranky flu, arguing over the temperature of the air conditioner, a Netflix show, a wet towel on the bed, or any of the thousands of little emotional transactions that were part of the business of living a fully entangled life with someone. Radhi felt a strange melancholy take hold of her and it was with an effort that she brought her mind back to the job at hand.

She had not only wanted to get a hold of Venus's medical history, but she'd also wanted to check if there was any sign of the article that Venus had promised the *Gazette* among her papers. For the next hour or so, she went through Venus's files and folders, methodically, pausing only when Shinde came into the room, triumphantly waving a plastic bag in front of her. He had found some medical reports and files and had rifled through the X-rays and cardiographs to find a recent prescription for some migraine medicine on a physician's letterhead.

'I'm going to call this number and see if she was Venus's regular doctor,' Shinde said. 'If there's nothing else in there,' he added, indicating the papers in Radhi's hands, 'we can leave now.'

Promising to join him in the living room in a few minutes, Radhi quickly finished scanning the remaining folders. She had discovered nothing surprising, revelatory or even new, most of the documents she had gone through had been dated. Sighing, she got up from the chair and began to put everything the way she had found it. Then, with one final glance around the room, she stepped out and closed the door behind her. Back in the corridor again, she noticed that even the corridor walls had a few frames on it. This time, there were personal pictures. Venus at the Duomo in Florence. A young Venus with an older woman, presumably her mother, wrapped in shawls at a hill station. A twenty-something Venus with a friend, both girls on horses. Venus receiving the Padma Shri from the President of India. And finally, Venus with a bunch of teachers, in what looked like a staff photo. Thinking that it was a North Star picture, Radhi leaned forward to take a closer look. But the banner above the teachers announced 'Victoria High' a different school altogether, and all the other people around Venus seemed unfamiliar, except one. Radhi registered with some surprise, standing second from the right, in the very last row, looking almost fifteen years younger, the tall and lanky frame of Mr. Bakshi.

Radhi scrutinized the picture again and then went out into the living room where she found Shinde looking at a newspaper on the centre table quizzically.

'Did Mr. Bakshi tell you why he had gone to see Ms. Venus on the day she died?'

Shinde looked up with a preoccupied frown and shook his head. 'I'm not sure — I'll check. But you know something strange? I could swear I had left the sports page of this newspaper open the last time I was here and now it has been turned over.'

'What do you mean?' Radhi asked.

'See, the last time, I was sitting here, going through the cricket news, while we waited for some animal shelter people to come and pick up her cat. Then, when we were about to leave, I kept the paper, like this, on top of these books.' He tossed the paper over the books on the centre table to show her what he meant. 'But today, when I saw the paper, it had been turned over to the front page.'

Radhi's eyes narrowed, and she spoke slowly, 'Are you saying what I think you're saying? That someone was here, after you?'

The inspector stood with his hands on his waist looking around the apartment. 'Can you think of any other explanation?'

CHAPTER 14

Radhi came home from Venus's place in a strange mood. Usually, after a day out, she welcomed the peace and quiet of her own apartment, but today, as she changed into a pair of flamingo-pink shorts and a white tee, she felt restless. The parallels between the English teacher's life and her own were hard to ignore. An early divorce and then a life filled with books and art and travel. If someone had asked Radhi just a few months ago, she would have said that this was sufficient for her, but now, suddenly, she wasn't so sure.

She was sitting on the couch in her living room, her feet on the centre table, checking and answering her email. Lila had left her dinner in the kitchen, but the thought of another meal alone, watching *Monk*, however endearing the eccentric detective was, didn't seem appealing today. She was glad that she had Venus's death to think about, because increasingly she found that when left to herself, she began to question her life choices.

Shaking her head as if to change the direction her thoughts seemed to be headed in, Radhi put her laptop away and picked up her diary. There were so many unanswered questions and loose ends surrounding Venus that it had become difficult to keep a track of them all. She began to jot them down, starting with the big one.

Had Venus been poisoned? Who could've wanted her dead?

What was her new article about? Was it really connected to her death?

What did the number five in her book of poems, mean?

How was Ms. Lily involved?

Who was pressurizing the police to drop the case?

Did the politician have anything to do with it?

Who had gone into Venus's apartment?

Where was Soam Mehta? What kind of prank had he pulled?

When his father met Fernandes, did he also stop to see Venus?

And what about Bakshi? Why had he gone to see her the day she died?

Radhi paused. This last question she could try and answer now. She picked up her phone and dialled Shinde whose 'hello' when he answered, was the least annoyed it had ever sounded. Was the inspector finally coming around? Radhi almost chuckled at the thought.

'Mr. Bakshi, why did he go to meet Venus that day? Could you check?'

As the inspector flipped the pages of his diary, Radhi thought back to that picture of Bakshi she had seen in Venus's home. She wondered how well the teachers had known each other.

'He didn't meet with her,' Shinde said.

'Sorry?'

'In the statement he gave us, he doesn't mention going to meet Venus that day.'

Radhi hung up the phone puzzled. Piu had specifically told her that when Soam went to the English Department after school, post his football practice, he saw Bakshi in an intense conversation with Venus. Those were her exact words. Why had the chemistry teacher lied to the police?

Radhi's phone rang and she answered it, pleasantly surprised.

'Busy?' Hrishi asked on the other line.

'Not at all, what's up?'

'I was just thinking about the article on Wagle that Venus wrote. What if there's more to it? It may or may not be why Venus was killed, but I would like to dig deeper into that story, in fact—'

'Hey,' said Radhi impulsively. 'If you have some time, would you like to come over? There are a few other things that came up today an—'

'Yes.' Hrishi didn't wait for her to finish. 'I'll be there in half an hour, but you need to feed me dinner, I'm starving.'

Radhi's mood, after she hung up the phone, had undergone an almost alchemical transformation. She felt light, almost buoyant, as she made her way to the kitchen. Lifting the lids of the pots on the platform, she saw that Lila had made some Mexican rice along with a red bean soup. It was enough food for Hrishi and her, but Radhi found she couldn't go back and simply wait. She felt restless and knew that cooking would help her process all of the emotions that she was feeling at that time. She checked the refrigerator and was glad to find a large piece of pumpkin along with a hunk of fresh, homemade cottage cheese. She decided to make a pumpkin sauce pasta and began by boiling the spaghetti. As her hands got busy with grating ginger and cutting the pumpkin into cubes to stew in vegetable broth, her mind puzzled over why the prospect of having Hrishi over, had made her so happy. Yes, it would be an escape from the strange and stifling loneliness of the last few hours. And she was glad she had someone to work through her questions about Venus's death with. But was that it? Was it just company she was grateful for? Or was it *his* company? She was reluctant to follow her own thoughts, afraid of where they'd lead.

Luckily, she was spared. Hrishi was at the door, just as she finished taking the pasta off the stove.

'You've changed the place completely,' he said, looking around the living room, taking in the bottle green wingchair, the Aztec print curtains and the mango wood bookcase that now dominated the space.

The last time he had come over was when her parents were still alive. When this was still *their* home and her mother's hand-embroidered frames hung on every wall in their living room. Radhi remembered that afternoon well. A bunch of them had been working on posters for a college event, and Radhi and Hrishi had been arguing about the rules of the competition, their voices and gestures growing more animated, fuelled by the steady supply of snacks and fruits that Radhi's mum sent from the kitchen. This was months before their first kiss, but even then the charge between them had been palpable, their friends sure about where they were headed. The only question was when.

'How about you pour us drinks, while I lay the table?' Radhi pointed him to her bar cabinet before heading to the kitchen to bring out the plates.

Hrishi whistled as he bent down to study the labels on the bottles. '*You're* well-stocked.' He selected a bottle of Jaisalmer and made them both large gin and tonics. 'Lemons?' he asked, following her into the kitchen.

'In the fridge,' Radhi said, tilting her head in the direction of the refrigerator, as she lifted the rice dish with a pair of potholders and carried it through.

While Hrishi cut lemon wedges and squeezed them over their drinks, Radhi finished laying the table and then, together, by some unspoken consensus, they went to stand by the window and lit cigarettes. They smoked quietly for a few moments, then Hrishi clinked his glass with hers and raised it. 'To old friendships and how uncomplicated they can be.'

Radhi took a sip of her drink and smiled at the irony of the toast. For her, there had been nothing but a complicated whirl of emotions since his arrival. His scent as he raised his arm to draw the curtains open, his proximity as he leaned in to light her cigarette, the slight brush of his shoulder as they stood side by side, smoking and watching the sea . . . she'd been hyper aware of it all, and confused about why. She was relieved when they moved from the window and sat down to dinner on opposite sides of the table. As they ate, she told him about her day and what she had learned. He listened quietly for the most part, asking questions, most of which were about the teachers at North Star whom he had little or no background of.

'Just ask Mr. Bakshi why he went to meet Ms. Venus,' he said when she told him about her last conversation with Shinde. 'You said you guys are friendly, right?'

Radhi nodded.

'So, just catch him off guard then. See how he reacts. Sometimes, when I'm interviewing someone, I'll throw in a question they least expect, and then if they fumble and flounder, you know there's something there.'

'Good idea,' Radhi replied, thoughtfully.

'Hey, for such good food there's plenty more where that came from.' Hrishi grinned. 'This pasta, especially, is outstanding. Are you still not going to tell me what's in the sauce?'

Before Radhi could respond, Hrishi's phone rang, and she saw Neha's name flash on the screen. Hrishi reached out to put it on silent, but a few seconds later it rang again and this time he pushed his chair back and stood up, before answering it.

'Yeah, sorry, still here,' he said, then paused to hear the question on the other side before replying, 'I think another fifteen, twenty minutes more.'

Even though he'd moved to the window to talk, Radhi could hear his softly murmured answers clearly, as she finished the last of her dinner.

'Yeah, sorry, the meeting lasted forever. Tell Anu I love her.'

When he came back, he seemed preoccupied. He finished the last two bites of his rice, in silence. Then he put his fork away and sighed.

143

'Sorry', he said, 'I just lied to my wife, and I hate it.' He looked away for a moment before shaking his head at some internal dialogue. 'It goes against everything I believe in, but I don't know how else to keep the peace at home.'

Radhi remained quiet, waiting for him to continue. Instead, he picked up their empty plates and stood up. 'Shall we?'

They cleared up the table in silence. Hrishi made a neat pile of the dirty dishes in the sink while Radhi put the leftovers away in smaller containers in the refrigerator. Once they were done, they made their way to the window again and lit up new cigarettes. They stood together wordlessly, watching a lone boat bobbing tirelessly on the dark sea. After a while, Hrishi spoke.

'Neha finds it hard to accept that sometimes I might want to meet a friend for a drink or just play cricket at the club instead of coming straight home from work. The newsroom . . . it can be intense and sometimes I just need to decompress before I head home, you know?'

Radhi nodded and he continued. 'We've spoken about it at therapy as well. That when I choose to watch some TV, instead of going to the mall with her, it's not a rejection of *her*. She takes it too personally and we have these massive fights at home.'

Hrishi laughed bitterly. 'Fuck, I can't believe I've become the kind of guy who finds it easy to bitch about his wife. Not to mention the lying. Textbook arsehole behaviour, right?'

'Hey, hey . . .' Radhi gave his arm a squeeze. 'Go easy on yourself, okay? Marriage is bloody hard, and it's okay to blow off some steam. The important thing is that you want to save it and you're putting in the work towards it.'

Radhi left him at the window and went to the bar, returning a few minutes later with fresh drinks. 'It's much easier to throw it all away.' She handed him a glass with a wry grin. 'Ask me, I should know.'

Hrishi turned to look at her, his gaze intense. 'Don't bullshit me, Radhi. Nothing about being a divorced woman on Temple Hill is easy.'

Radhi averted her eyes from his face and turned back to the sea.

'I think you are very brave,' Hrishi continued. 'You realized you made a mistake, and you weren't afraid to admit it. You didn't compromise and stay in a bad marriage for the sake of appearances.'

'It's simpler when you don't have kids,' Radhi interrupted. 'In fact—'

'Phish!' Hrishi made an annoyed sound. 'I know how unhappy your family was when you married outside your community. I can't even begin to imagine how the tongues wagged when you went through your divorce.'

Radhi took a sip of her drink and shrugged. 'It's easier when you don't have parents to yell at you. Everyone else is just surround sound. Besides, my sister always had my back.'

'Why do you always do this?' Hrishi asked almost angrily.

'Do what?' Radhi turned to him surprised.

'*Act* so tough. You did it when your parents died as well. You wouldn't let anyone near you.' Hrishi finished his drink in one long gulp. 'It's okay to be vulnerable sometimes, you know? You worry about there being a chip in your armour, but the real question is why have armour on, in the first place?' He patted his pocket for his car keys. 'Anyway, I had better leave now. Thank you for dinner,' he said, almost formally, then softening, he leaned forward to give her a hug. 'Take care, Radhi.'

Radhi nodded, too taken aback by the turn their conversation had taken.

'Tell me how it goes tomorrow?' he said at the door.

Radhi nodded again. He had given her the idea to visit the property registrar's office to check on Wagle's property dealings.

When he was gone, Radhi made herself another drink and went back to the window. She had enjoyed having Hrishi over more than she cared to admit to herself. His presence hadn't felt foreign in this space. It was almost as if he belonged there, with his head stuck inside her refrigerator, rifling for lemons. She took a deep breath of the warm, sea-scented air and wondered if there was any truth to what he had said. Her mind drifted back to her marriage and the two relationships that had followed. Bedi, her ex-husband, had often complained that she didn't let him in, that she suffered in silence, whereas the older and wiser Mackinsey had chipped away at the facade gently until he could shine a torch in and see for himself the cause of her troubles, and to Nishant she'd shown herself voluntarily, realizing that he could do no harm. But it had been just a glimpse, a game of peekaboo, more an appeasement than surrender. Was Hrishi right about her?

* * *

'Aah, dirty dishes!' Lila announced, when she walked into the kitchen the next morning. 'I don't think I'd ever say it, but the sight of these makes me so happy.'

Radhi, who had just finished hiding all traces of the alcohol she'd drunk the night before, rolled her eyes at her housekeeper. Her head throbbed, making her reluctant to speak.

'I'm serious, Didi. I'm glad you had some company for dinner last night. In fact, even better if it was *more* than dinner.' She wriggled her eyebrows suggestively, then suddenly she covered her mouth with her palm, and stared at Radhi alarmed as it occurred to her that the person who came for dinner might've stayed the night and heard their conversation.

'*Was* it more than dinner?' she asked in a low voice.

Radhi laughed, despite the headache. 'Relax. It was an old college friend — strictly, just dinner.'

'Why so "strictly"?' Lila teased, back to her original volume again, as she turned to attack the plates in the sink.

'Because he's married!' Radhi said. 'Jesus, you and your questions!' She was making a cup of black coffee with lemon for her hangover and hoping that Lila wouldn't ask why she didn't want her customary masala chai.

'Aah,' Lila said, after a few seconds, as she began to line up the clean plates in the drying rack. 'Aah,' she said again, with a smile.

Radhi was in no mood to play games but knew full well that her housekeeper wouldn't let it go. 'Okay. What?'

'You didn't say that you find him uninteresting or unattractive — the only reason it was strictly dinner is that he is *un*-available.'

Radhi began to shake her head, but the movement hurt, so she stopped. 'That's not true.'

'Which part? You think he is boring? Or ugly? Or is he available?'

'None of it!' Radhi said exasperated, her head throbbing. 'If you must know, I think he's good looking and interesting and warm and kind and sexy. But he's married! So *why* are we discussing this?'

Lila turned to face her. 'Just. Sometimes, it's good to know why we deny ourselves the things we want,' she said, all trace of mirth gone from her eyes.

CHAPTER 15

Thursday

'Thank you, darling, for seeing the old tyrant, yesterday,' Madhavi said, when Radhi answered her call.

'Oh, come now, Didi, the pleasure was all mine,' Radhi joked. She was hurrying through the corridors at North Star hoping to catch the rehearsals of the play in progress. 'Did they figure out what's wrong with her?'

'You mean other than her attitude, personality and whole approach to life?'

Radhi laughed, surprised to find Madhavi so worked up. She usually tried to be more zen about her mother-in-law's presence in her life. 'Okay, what did she do now?'

'She wants to treat all the hospital staff on her floor to lunch. And she wants my help to organize it — permissions, caterers, invitations — the whole jig — as if I'm not already dying with two kids and work.'

'But why?' Radhi frowned at the unusual request.

'She says, because they are taking such good care of her.'

'Give them a good tip, then! A special bonus. Why this whole song and dance?'

'Where's the fun in that, Radhi? There will be no attention. No public thank yous. No waah-waahs from her friends . . . It will be what Roma Bansal would consider a poor return on investment. Anyways, so listen, I need a favour. Will you please take Amayra to a birthday party on the twentieth?'

* * *

When Radhi reached the school hall, rehearsals were in full swing. After Ms. Venus's death, Mr. Bottlewalla had taken over the direction and the general responsibility of the play. He stood below the stage, arms crossed, script tightly rolled in one hand, listening intently to the dialogue on stage. The backdrop, hand-painted in browns and whites, was that of a plush office. The actor playing the politician sat on a swivel chair on one side of the desk, while a couple of students portraying the role of angry activists, stood across from him. As Radhi made her way to sit on one of the empty seats in the audience, Bottlewalla clapped his hands loudly to get the attention of the actors on the stage.

'Roshni, can you please start over? And this time, lean across the table and thump it hard to make your point,' He directed the lead actress, a nervous looking, bespectacled, ninth grader.

'Kia was so much better,' Radhi heard one of the students, a twelfth grader she wasn't familiar with, in the row ahead of her, whisper to the girl beside her.

'I know, right? She was such a natural,' said her friend.

'Pity, she dropped out,' said the first.

'Oh, did she *drop* out? I thought they replaced her because she's been unwell and not coming to school.'

'No, no, she's back now. But doesn't want to participate.'

'Why?'

'Not sure . . . but it's probably . . .' The girl tilted her head closer to her friend and dropped her voice even lower.

Unable to hear their conversation now, Radhi leaned back in her seat, thinking about Kia. She wondered if her refusal to participate was because of how close she was to Venus. Was she unhappy that Venus's script had been changed? Or was she still disturbed about the teacher's death? Radhi remembered how she had found Kia crying in the bathroom. She was a sensitive girl, no doubt—

Radhi sat up straight and frowned as something else occurred to her. The tearstains on that assignment, days ago, had also been Kia's, but Venus had still been alive that morning. Hadn't she? If yes, what had Kia been upset about then? Was it possible that Radhi had misconstrued Kia's tears all along? And if yes, did they tie back to any of the current happenings at school — Venus's murder, Soam's disappearance — did the girl know something about any of it?

The backdrop on the stage changed to a leafy compound sprawled under an art deco style balcony of a bungalow. As the activists began to sit cross-legged on the stage, with pickets and signboards, ready to protest outside the minister's home, Radhi quietly slipped out of the room. She made her way to the English Department, where she had filed all the assignments she had received from the students so far. She was still searching the harmonium-style folder for the file she was looking for, when Ms. Savant entered the room.

'Oh sorry, I didn't realize anyone was here,' the English teacher mumbled.

Radhi looked up to greet her, but she avoided Radhi's eyes as she made her way to her desk and Radhi realized that the woman was probably embarrassed about her breakdown the day before. Reluctant to cause her any further discomfort, Radhi remained focused on her own task and located the file she was after. Kia's tearstained sheet was dated for the same day that Venus died, but Radhi's class had been in the morning, and the head of the English Department had been hale and hearty at the time. So, what had Kia been crying about then?

'*Satyanash!*' Ms. Savant cursed loudly in her native Marathi.

Radhi looked up to see that she had spilled her bottle of water on her desk and was scrambling to stop the water from spreading. Radhi grabbed some tissues from her purse and hurried to Ms. Savant's side of the room, but already a few of her files were soaked wet. The two women worked in silence for a few minutes, mopping the water with tissues.

'Let's separate these sheets and spread them out, so they'll dry faster,' Radhi said, moving towards Ms. Venus's empty desk.

'I can do that,' Ms. Savant said, hurrying from behind her desk towards Radhi, her hand extended for the file.

But Radhi had already started laying out the sheets and stopped in surprise when she saw the rude drawings of male and female private parts on some of them. They were answer sheets on Chekhov's and Tolstoy's short stories, but peppered with male genitalia and large, female breasts. Automatically, Radhi's eyes travelled to the far right of the page to see who had submitted it, but those spaces were blank. She looked up to see Ms. Savant hovering around the desk, her eyes filling up rapidly with angry, ashamed tears.

'You should report this,' Radhi said, gently.

'And say what?' Ms. Savant brushed the tears from her eyes, impatiently. 'That I'm unable to control my classroom? That the students make fun of me?' She took the remaining papers from Radhi's hands and began to spread them haphazardly on the desk. 'There's nothing I can say which doesn't make me sound like an incompetent teacher!'

Suddenly, the English teacher sat down on Venus's chair and began to cry in earnest.

'It is all that Venus's fault! She poisoned the students' minds against me, I'm sure of it!'

'But why would she do that?' Radhi asked, feeling compelled to defend the dead teacher.

'She didn't respect me! I came through my father's contacts, no? So how could I possibly be any good? Do you know she once asked to look at my teaching notes and laughed at them?'

'Why?' Radhi was surprised to learn of Venus's behaviour but found she couldn't put it past her.

'She said that my notes sounded like they'd been lifted off the internet. That good teachers spent so much time with the texts they were teaching that their "reflections had an anecdotal quality" to them,' Savant said, using her fingers to make air quotes. 'I wanted to tell her that some of us have *people* to spend time with! That not all of us live with cats!'

Radhi found that she agreed with Venus's advice, however harshly it had been imparted, but she stayed silent. The English teacher was wiping her eyes with the pallu of her saree and beginning to calm down.

'I know she's said something to the students, why else would they behave this way?' She hit the desk with her hand as something new occurred to her. 'Tell me, have *you* faced any trouble with them?'

'Not really,' Radhi admitted with a wince.

'See, only me. I knew it!' Ms. Savant blew her nose with a tissue. 'Anyways, I believe given enough time things have a way of working out. See who's in her seat now, hmm?' she said, getting up from Venus's chair.

* * *

'Hi, is Ms. Fernandes free?' Radhi asked her secretary.

It was lunchtime, and Radhi hoped to get the early admissions letter for her niece from the principal, but no sooner had the secretary nodded than Ms. Fernandes' door flew open, and the principal hurried out of the room looking frazzled.

'Sarita, please can you locate all the senior school teachers and ask them to come to the staffroom?'

'Ms. Fernandes?' Radhi began, but the principal shook her head.

'I'm sorry, Radhika, not right now. I have an important announcement to make.' She turned in the direction of the staffroom without breaking her stride, indicating that Radhi should follow her.

'Mr. Bakshi, Mr. Bottlewalla, please join me,' Fernandes said to the two teachers who were standing outside the staffroom, deep in conversation.

'Everyone.' Ms. Fernandes clapped her hands loudly to get the attention of the teachers at various stages of finishing their lunch. 'Everyone, please may I have a moment of your time.'

A hush descended over the room as one by one the teachers noticed the principal and fell quiet.

'Soam Mehta's father has just informed me that he has put in a Missing Person advertisement in the *Gazette* for Soam, which will appear in the next couple of days. Apart from their own contact details, they'll have to mention that he was a student here at North Star and that he went missing from the vicinity of the school.' Fernandes raised her hand up to silence the soft murmur that had started among the teachers. 'Our security systems have no record of his ID being swiped at entry, which means he never entered the school that morning, but the Mehtas' driver has given a statement that he dropped Soam outside the school gate. That was the last anyone saw of him, so there's no way to keep the name of the school out of this ad. Which means—'

Fernandes paused now and looked around the room to make sure she had everyone's attention. But before she could resume, Kamble had walked into the room and come to stand beside her.

'Which means that there's bound to be some chatter about our school,' he said, taking over the conversation. 'Given our profile, journalists might come sniffing to see if they can make a story out of it — and it is your job to see that they can't.'

The art teacher raised her hand. 'I don't get it. What kind of story?'

'They might ask questions about the vap—' Fernandes began, but Kamble cut her off.

'No story. That's the point. If they reach out to any of you — say you know nothing of the matter. So, no comment. I don't want any of our teachers talking on behalf of the school.'

'But won't it look like we have something to hide?' Mr. Bakshi asked.

'The school will issue an official statement about this. We don't want any stray comments from any of you to be taken out of context. You know how these journalist types are. They can twist anything to make it more sensational.'

'And lastly, if anyone reaches out to you, please inform us,' Fernandes said.

'Yes, you can come directly to me,' Kamble added.

Radhi saw Fernandes bristle at that, but the principal kept her expression neutral as she wished the teachers a good day, before turning to follow Kamble out of the room. No sooner had the principal and MD of the school left, the staffroom erupted into a chorus of questions and speculations.

What was that about?

They seemed so tense.

It's because of the vaping, isn't it? They don't want North Star to get that *sort of a reputation.*

Do you really think it's just that?

What do you mean? What else could it be?

Well, last year was that suicide, and now they have a missing student . . .

At this last comment, Lily turned to the teacher who had spoken and hissed, 'What's the connection between the two? Soam's not dead. He just seems to be acting up. This is exactly why the management doesn't want us to speak to journalists.' She began to put away her empty lunch box and collect her things.

'What do you think, Mr. Bakshi?' she asked, turning to the chemistry teacher on her right.

He shrugged. 'Knowing Soam, this does seem more likely a bid for attention.'

'Oh, I don't know,' began one of the sports coaches. 'Soam is used to being the star player, but he's a responsible kid—'

'Responsible and hot-headed!' interjected one of the other coaches.

'Yes, I can't deny that. The apple hasn't fallen far from the tree in that respect,' said the first coach.

'No, no, the father is in a different league altogether! Have you seen him when he comes to watch the matches?'

'Yeah! Curses more than he cheers. We've had to tell him to watch his language around the kids.'

'Forget cursing, did you see him cuff that Romil's dad in the January match? Just because he appealed the umpire's decision to let Soam play?'

'I heard he—'

'Ms Zaveri?'

Everyone heard Kamble's voice before they realized he had entered the room again. Abruptly, the teachers fell quiet, no doubt wondering how much the MD had heard.

'May I please speak with you for a moment?' Kamble said.

'Sure.' Radhi rose to join him outside.

'Ms. Zaveri,' Kamble began without preamble. 'I just remembered that the National Editor of the *Gazette* is your friend — please will you put in a word for us? I really don't want this blown out of proportion.'

'Oh, I don't know if that will help at all,' Radhi said, surprised at the request and knowing just how scrupulous Hrishi was.

'But you will try?' Kamble pressed. 'These journalists are like hounds, if they think they've smelled a good story, they'll shred our reputation to pieces to find it.'

Radhi nodded silently, unwilling to commit to anything. The MD thanked her and walked away without any further conversation, seeming preoccupied.

The lunch bell rang just then, and one by one the teachers began to file out of the staffroom. Radhi regretted having missed the last of the conversation among the teachers. The stories about Mr. Mehta's temper had put a new thought in Radhi's head. If the man was willing to punch someone over his son's wicket, what would he do for his sport's captaincy?

Mr. Bakshi and Mr. Bottlewalla passed her by with curious smiles, and she smiled back. She had been wanting to talk to Mr. Bakshi about his meeting with Venus but hadn't had the chance. She grabbed her things from the now empty staffroom and made her way to the principal's office again. She knew that Fernandes was in crisis mode currently, and that Radhi's early admissions letter was probably low on her list of priorities, but Radhi didn't see that changing anytime soon. Already, by letting Kamble have the revised script, she had lost her leverage. Now, she needed to get her hands on that letter, before she made a single allegation of foul play. Because if Venus's death was really a murder like Radhi suspected then things at North Star were going to get much worse before they got better.

There was no one at the secretary's desk outside Ms. Fernandes' office. Radhi waited for a few minutes, thinking that perhaps the woman had gone to the washroom, but when the secretary didn't reappear, Radhi knocked on Ms. Fernandes' door.

'Not now, Sarita.' Ms. Fernandes' voice floated out, sounding weary.

'Ms. Fernandes, it's me, Radhika,' Radhi said, opening the door a crack.

The principal had been leaning back on her chair, eyes closed, a wet napkin covering her eyes and forehead. She straightened up as soon as she heard Radhi's voice, and the napkin slipped from her face.

'Sorry,' said Radhika, 'there was no one at the desk outside. Would you prefer I come back?'

Fernandes seemed about to tell her to go but then she sighed and pulled her chair towards her desk. 'No, I might as well get on with the day. Come in.'

'Are you not well?' Radhi asked as she took a seat in front of the principal.

'Migraine,' Fernandes said. 'Which no number of pills seem to be helping.'

'They're often stress induced, aren't they?'

'Yes, clearly.' Fernandes rubbed her forehead, then she opened a drawer and brought out a jar of balm. 'Do you mind if I apply some? I must warn you the smell is quite strong.'

'Please,' Radhi said. 'Go ahead.'

A strong smell of menthol filled the room as the principal scooped some of the balm with two fingers and applied it on her temples. 'Must smell a bit like your cigarettes, no?' she asked. Then, seeing Radhi's surprised expression, she added, 'What? You think I didn't know?'

Fernandes chuckled as she snapped the lid of the jar shut. 'I haven't run this school these last fifteen years without keeping a track of what happens outside our gates.' She put the jar back in the drawer and wiped her hands with a tissue. 'As your former teacher, I'm tempted to give you a little lecture right now, but I'm trying to pick my teachable moments.'

'And this isn't one of them?' Radhi asked with a smile.

'It would've been if you were fifteen . . . but now . . .' Fernandes shook her head, smiling back. 'Though even with fifteen-year-olds these days it's hard to tell.' She added a moment later, her face darkening.

Radhi waited for the principal to continue, but when she remained quiet, Radhi said, 'That's what Soam's punishment was about, wasn't it?'

Fernandes looked at Radhi then looked away and Radhi wondered whether she'd said the wrong thing. But then the principal sighed. 'Yes. That was supposed to be a teachable moment for him. That boy has so much potential as an athlete — he shouldn't have been anywhere near that vape. But just yelling at him wouldn't have solved anything. With teenagers you can't simply expect them to do as you say. Maybe because they aren't as much in awe of you anymore. So, you have to try other things. Like taking away something they hold dear . . . *that* always gets their attention.'

Fernandes pinched the bridge of her nose before rubbing the area gingerly. 'Of course, not everybody thinks the way I do.'

The principal's phone rang then, and Radhi saw Kamble's name on the screen. 'Yes, Satish?' Her tone was wary.

She waited for him to finish speaking. 'Why? I already told you I have it under control. You know, you really need to back off and let me do my job.' She hung up on the MD and placed her phone on her desk with some force.

'Sorry.' She shook her head as if to clear it. 'What is it you wanted to see me about?'

'I know this is a bad time,' Radhi began awkwardly, 'But I was wondering if my niece's early admissions letter is signed and ready?'

'Have you considered the job offer Satish made?' Fernandes asked, taking Radhi by surprise.

'Uhm . . . not yet. There's been a lot going on. But I will.'

Fernandes nodded. 'Our dear MD told me to dangle the letter as bait to convince you into taking the job. He said to hold off on giving it to you for as long as possible. But you know what? I'm not going to play his silly games.' She opened a drawer to her right side and brought out a sealed envelope in the North Star green and gold. She slid it towards Radhi. 'He shouldn't have offered the admission in exchange for a play script — that's not how schools are run — but now that he did, I'm not going to hold it back.'

Radhi took the envelope and smiled. 'Thanks, Ms. Fernandes. I appreciate it.'

* * *

After Radhi left, Fernandes put her elbows on her desk and covered her face with her hands. The action was in part to stop the pain and in part to examine the source of it. She had run the school successfully and independently for so many years that this new arrangement, which had Satish Kamble breathing down her neck in the guise of learning the ropes, was frustrating every fibre of her being. She knew why his father had called him back, of course. But knowing didn't make it easier. He had no business coming into the staffroom today. It was insulting, him trying to talk and take over when she was right there to get the job done. She'd given fifteen years of her life to the school and made it what it was. And now, the father and son couldn't wait to see the back of her. Just as they had been glad to see Venus gone. Fernandes felt something wet streaking her cheeks and realized with a start that they were tears.

CHAPTER 16

With the admissions letter snugly in her bag, Radhi made her way briskly to the school canteen. In her pursuit of Fernandes and the letter, she had missed lunch. Now, she was starving and craving something hot and greasy, and not the salad that she'd asked Lila to pack in her tiffin that day. The North Star canteen was one of the only places in the school that was without any kind of frills. A large and airy hall with broad windows, it was lined with rows of long wooden tables and benches, its form dedicated entirely to its function. At this time of the day, it was mostly empty, with the students back in their classes after lunch. Radhi bought herself a plate of medu vadas, which came with bowls of sambhaar and coconut chutney, and sat at one of the empty tables. She was about to take a bite of her food when she noticed Kia at one of the other tables, sitting alone.

Radhi walked up to her. 'Do you mind if I sit here?'

Kia nodded once she'd got over her initial surprise. The teachers rarely ate in the school canteen.

'How come no class?' Radhi asked as she put her tray on the table.

'I'm sitting this one out.' Kia shrugged, twirling the Maggi noodles on her plate.

And then, because Radhi was looking at her expectantly, she added, 'We've got swimming right now, and I'm on my period.'

'I heard you dropped out of the play,' Radhi said, after they had sat together in silence for a few minutes.

Kia shrugged again. 'Yeah.'

'Everyone was saying you were very good.'

Kia shrugged a third time but didn't say anything. Her mood was sullen.

Radhi reminded herself to be patient. That teenagers didn't always make the best communicators. She finished her medu vadas in silence. Then she tried again. 'Can I ask you something?'

Kia nodded.

'Why were you upset, that day? In the bathroom? I had thought it was because of Ms. Venus's death — but now, I'm not so sure.'

That got the girl's attention. She looked up from her plate before looking back down again.

'It's personal,' she said, after a while.

Radhi leaned back into her seat and took a sip of her water. There was no fighting a teenager's assertion of privacy, but still she tried. 'I hope it wasn't boy trouble — boys really aren't worth crying over, you know?'

'It wasn't.'

'Good. By the way, I liked your assignment on food a lot. The writing was almost poetic.'

'Thanks.'

'Ms. Venus would've been proud.'

At that, Kia looked at her, burst into tears, jumped up and ran away, leaving Radhi staring after her, thoroughly zapped.

* * *

Radhi had reached a stage in the whole affair where she could really do with some answers. Every question she asked seemed to sprout two more of its own, leaving her, if it was possible, further behind than where she had started. Still thinking about Kia, Radhi made her way back to the staffroom. She had finished her classes for the day, but she was hoping to find an opportunity to speak with Mr. Bakshi. However, the only teachers present in the room were Ms. Lily, Ms. Savant and Ms. Farah, all of whom looked up when Radhi entered.

'Miss Zaveri! Thank God it's only you,' the art teacher said. 'We were worried Ms. Fernandes had come back again.'

'We are planning a farewell for Ms. Fernandes,' Ms. Lily explained.

'Ah, understood,' said Radhi with a smile.

'Would you like to help with it?' Ms. Savant asked, perhaps to return the kindness Radhi had shown her the day before.

'No, no, let's not bother Ms. Zaveri,' Ms. Lily said. 'She's just here for a couple of months and she barely knows the principal.'

'Oh, I've known her for a very long time, in fact,' said Radhi. 'She used to be our maths teacher in my old school. I'd love to help.'

Ms. Lily raised her eyebrows. 'I had no idea. How lovely!'

'That settles it then,' Ms. Farah concluded. 'You can be part of our planning committee. We are meeting this evening at Ms. Lily's house.'

'Yes, you are welcome to join in,' Ms. Lily said.

* * *

'This school is really something, man,' Hrishi began without preamble when Radhi picked up his call on her way to the property registrar's office.

'What happened?'

'Fernandes called Neha and told *her* to ask *me* to avoid any stories on North Star. Can you imagine the nerve?'

Radhi chuckled. 'Kamble asked *me* to do the same thing. I'm to convince you to avoid writing about North Star in the coming days. He doesn't know that that's going to have the exact opposite effect.'

'Now Neha is after my life to comply, of course. We had a huge fight when I told her I was going to do no such thing. She doesn't know what we suspect about Venus's death. What a mess!'

He was quiet for a while, then he said, 'Listen, I'm sorry about the way I left yesterday. It was a bit abrupt.'

'That's fine.'

'But I meant what I said. Vulnerability is a strength, not a weakness. You've got to let people in. Okay?'

'Yessir,' Radhi said, lightly.

'Joke all you want, but you know I'm right . . . Anyways, were you able to go to the office for land records?'

'I am on my way there.'

'Okay, tell me what you find out.'

* * *

Radhi waited inside the Maharashtra government's land record management office. It was a poorly lit, narrow room, with a single row of desks and chairs, all facing the entrance. The wall behind the desks was lined with wooden, floor-to-ceiling filing cabinets with glass doors. Venus's article had said that Wagle took advantage of his ministerial post and was in the habit of routinely directing development agencies to parcel out government land to further his own interests. The article had urged the government to look into it. It cited as an example a mall in Mahalaxmi which was allegedly built on land originally assigned for a cemetery. While it was difficult to get records of the minister's personal land holdings, what Radhi hoped to find out was all the land allotments made during his tenure as a minister for city and industrial development.

The clerk in charge was shelling peas when Radhi walked in. There was a computer on her desk, a bunch of files and beside that a quickly growing mound of empty peapods. Even as she listened to Radhi's request, her fingers did not stop their brisk movements. At first, Radhi was a little irritated at how unprofessional everything seemed. Yet, the efficiency with which she typed out Radhi's request into the computer, moved the polythene bag of peas from her lap to the floor and went into a back room to pull out the required records, left Radhi feeling a little embarrassed. She hadn't thought about how these women had two full-time jobs, one outside the home, and the other inside it, where chances were that the whole family depended on them for cooking, cleaning, groceries and child rearing.

It took Radhi a while to understand the system under which the information had been recorded. But once she had spent an hour or so poring over it all in some detail, the numbers began to make sense. There was a total of seven columns on every page: the date on which the lease for the land had been signed, the size of the land parcel, its address with the exact pin code, the purpose it had been allotted for, the duration of the lease, the name and address of the company or individual who had received the allotment and the development agency which had made the allotment. Along with, of course, was the price per square feet. As she went through the pages, names of familiar areas and buildings jumped out at her. One, however, made her stop and straighten up. Right at the top of the eighth page, alongside a 20,000 square-foot plot of land on Temple Hill, allotted almost twenty-five years ago, was the name Sri Ravi Kamble.

Radhi paused and read through the entry again. Suddenly, it was clear to her why the Kambles wanted to curry favour with Wagle. Why they had invited him as chief guest to the school despite his obvious unpopularity at the moment. Why they had been horrified with Venus's script and demanded that she change it. Why Kamble had taken pains to tell Hrishi that the opinions expressed in Venus's article were entirely her own and that the school had nothing to do with it. Radhi took a look around. The clerk on duty had finished shelling the peas and was now clearing out her desk while talking to the officer beside her. Nobody seemed to be paying Radhi any attention. She brought out her phone and took a picture of the sheet. Here was finally a strong, believable motive for why the Kambles would want to shut Venus up.

CHAPTER 17

As her car made its way towards Lily's house, Radhi's mind was still on what she had learned about the Kambles, and it was only when Ramzan bhai pulled the car over that Radhi realized with a start just how close Lily's building was to where Venus had lived. Lily lived in the same banyan-tree-lined Bandra lane as Venus, just a few buildings ahead. She remembered then that Lily and Venus were part of the same church and wondered if Lily knew more about Venus's personal life than the others at school. She got out of the car, letting Ramzan bhai drive off to find parking, then belatedly realized that she'd arrived almost ten minutes early. She considered waiting at a café for a few minutes before heading up, knowing just how particular the maths teacher was. But on one side of the building was a laundry with a grey sun logo, on the other side was a repair shop with appliance spelled as 'applianse', and across the street a garbage disposal truck was making its way into the lane, its stench announcing its arrival even before it had stopped. She decided to head up.

Lily had her hair in rollers when she opened the door.

'Sorry,' Radhi said as she handed her a box of brownies. 'I got here a bit early.'

'No worries, will you give me a few minutes?' Lily touched her hair self-consciously with a smile. 'I was just getting ready.'

She was dressed in a purple floral dress and seemed much warmer than her usual, measured self. While she went back into her bedroom, Radhi looked around the modest but neat living room, taking in the old-fashioned, mosaic-tiled flooring, the matching brown Rexine sofas on opposite sides and the horizontal, glass cabinet below the television set, where little knick-knacks in glass, porcelain and plastic were arranged in precise rows. On the top of the cabinet, beside the TV, were picture frames with photographs of a little girl and Lily with a man.

'That's Tony, my husband,' Lily said when she emerged from her room and saw Radhi looking at the pictures. 'He passed away a couple of years ago.'

'Oh . . . I'm sorry to hear that . . . And that's your daughter?'

'Yes. Tara. She's almost nine. It's just me and her now.' Lily fluffed some cushions and adjusted the flower vase on the centre table. 'She's at my parents' home right now. They live right here, in the next lane.'

'It must be a relief to have them around, isn't it?'

'Oh, you have no idea.' Lily brought out a tray with a jug of water and glasses, which she offered to Radhi before heading back to the kitchen. 'I'll just get started with the tea, so that it's ready before the others get here.'

'Sure,' said Radhi, taking a seat on the sofa which looked right into the kitchen so she could talk to the maths teacher while the latter worked.

Radhi watched as Lily put the water to boil, added the sugar and the chai masala, then went on her toes to reach for the tea leaves container from a higher shelf. She added the tea leaves, then placed the container, on a lower shelf, right next to the sugar. There was something odd about this movement, something strange, but before Radhi could put a finger on it, the doorbell rang and Ms. Farah and Ms. Savant, along with Mr. Bottlewalla and a couple of other teachers, were at the door.

'You know, I was a bit surprised when they decided to go ahead with the party, considering all that's been going on,' Ms. Farah said, once pleasantries had been exchanged and everyone was seated comfortably around the living room.

'Me too,' Ms. Lily admitted. 'I half expected the senior Kamble to organize one of his biryani lunches in the school canteen and be done with it.'

'For Ms. Fernandes?' Mr. Bottlewalla scoffed. 'They wouldn't dare! Before she joined, do you know what our school ranking was?' He continued without waiting for an answer. 'Twenty-eighth in the country. And now?' Mr. Bottlewalla shook his head. 'The Kambles know what they owe her.'

'Are either of them doing speeches?' Ms. Savant asked.

Mr. Bottlewalla frowned. 'They've asked me to say a few words.' He scratched his cheek. 'I'm already missing Ms. Venus. She had such an ease for speaking in public.'

'Liked the sound of her own voice, you mean,' Ms. Savant muttered, then she bit her lip. 'Sorry, I know some of you were fond of her.'

For the next hour or so, they discussed themes for Fernandes's party. Everyone agreed that given the principal's love for her garden, something with plants was a must. But what? As they brainstormed, they came up with a flower-themed bingo where the prizes would be seeds and saplings. And a 'Find Your Pair' game where the guests who drew the fruit cards had to go about the room finding the people who held the relevant parent tree cards. The party would take place outdoors on the school premises and someone suggested a white canopy to give it an English garden party feel. When it came to food, the ideas were so many and so contrasting that Lily excused herself to go to the kitchen and Radhi had to ask if there was a budget they were working with.

'Not really,' said Ms. Farah. 'The younger Kamble has given us a free rein.'

'See, they do want to give her a grand send-off,' said one of the other teachers.

Ms. Farah smirked. 'More like, he'll be glad to see the back of her.'

'Why do you say that? They don't get along?' asked Ms. Savant.

'I think it's mutual. He was brought in to look over her shoulder after that . . . uh . . . incident last year, which she can't stand. And *she* pushes back on any new idea from him, which he is sick of.'

'By the incident, you mean . . . the suicide?' Savant asked.

A loud crash sounded from the kitchen, and everyone turned to see Ms. Lily picking up pieces of a broken plate from the floor. 'It's all good, all good . . . I'll be out in a second,' the maths teacher called out before anyone could offer to help.

'Yes, that.' Ms. Farah turned back to Savant. 'The senior Kamble thought Fernandes didn't handle it the way she should've.'

'Why?' Savant asked.

'There were theories that the school—'

'Aren't we going a bit off topic, here?' Lily said, carrying out a tray with some store-bought vegetable puffs and coconut macarons, along with the brownies which Radhi had got her. 'Ms. Fernandes is not without her faults. She can be arrogant and stubborn. But the school is what it is, because of her.'

'True,' Ms. Farah conceded. 'She's been a good mentor to you, no?'

Ms. Lily nodded. 'Especially after Tony passed. I was in such a shambles. She really looked out for me.'

For the next few minutes, the teachers munched and made notes of their ideas, and soon the discussion turned to the guestlist. All the primary and secondary school teachers were invited, along with the forty parents who were part of the parent-teacher association.

'I believe the Kambles want to invite some of their own contacts as well. They've given me a list,' said Ms. Lily.

She got up and walked to her room, emerging a moment later with a sheet of paper.

'Obviously,' said one of the teachers, taking the sheet from her, 'they aren't going to miss any opportunity to network.'

'So that makes it about eighty-odd people.' One of the teachers waved the Kamble guest list in front of them, bringing the topic back to the party.

'May I see that?' Radhi extended her arm.

She took the sheet and scanned it for the one name she was sure would be on it. She was not disappointed.

* * *

Hrishi was already waiting for Radhi when she reached the new brewery in Fort. She had called him to tell him what she'd learned at the land records office, but he had suggested meeting instead.

'Isn't this a little loud to talk?' Radhi asked, speaking over the music when she'd taken a seat across from him.

'I've been dying to check it out and Neha hates beer,' Hrishi said, sheepishly.

When they had both got a pint each in front of them, Radhi brought out her phone, swiped it to the photograph she'd taken of Wagle's land allotment to Kamble, and slid it towards Hrishi who whistled after he had studied it for a few minutes.

'So, to get this straight. Wagle directed the MMRDA to allot Kamble some land to build a charitable educational institute on it. A not-for-profit. But Kamble did the exact opposite?'

Radhi nodded and took a sip of her drink.

'And since no legal action has been taken against Kamble for starting a private school, we can assume Wagle has received or continues to receive some kind of compensation or kickback from them.'

Radhi nodded, again.

'Wow,' said Hrishi, leaning back into his chair, his beer forgotten. 'This is huge Radhi — and throws such a new light on the Kambles.'

'That's not all,' Radhi said. She pointed to her phone again. 'Look at the term of the lease.'

'Twenty-five years.' Hrishi looked up from the phone. 'Which means . . . it's up for renewal—'

'Next year,' Radhi completed his thought.

* * *

Friday

On the morning of the Interschool Drama Competition, Radhi hurried backstage, an hour before the event was about to start. She was supposed to have got there sooner, but the beer she'd consumed the night before had made her head throb in the morning and she'd had to slow down her movements to prevent it from hurting more. Hrishi and she had sat late into the night, debating how they could use the information she'd found to get to the bottom of Venus's death. They'd both agreed that to involve the police at this stage would be premature, seeing as they did not have any actual proof, just a tentative theory. Radhi had left their discussion reluctantly, knowing that she had an early morning. Mr. Bottlewalla had requested her help to do a run through of the whole script with the students. He was going to be busy organizing the actors from the other participating schools, so that their backdrop and costume changes happened in the right order. By the time Radhi reached the lobby outside the greenroom, the place was steeped in a sort of mad pre-show chaos typical, she imagined, of any kind of production. Searching for familiar faces, she moved and pushed her way through the crush of people with a series of apologetic excuse mes, until she found the North Star actors in the music room, which had been clearly marked off-limits with a sign and yellow tape.

'There you guys are!' she said, relieved to see that they were ready with full costume and makeup. 'I've been looking for you.'

'Sorry, Miss,' said one of the students. 'But it's crazy outside with all those randos from the other schools.'

Radhi raised her eyebrows at the language but didn't comment. She got out a copy of her script from her bag. 'Shall we?'

For the next fifteen minutes or so, they stood in a circle and rehearsed their lines with expressions and voice modulation but no movements, because of the lack of space.

Just before the final act, there was a soft knock on the door and Fernandes walked into the room.

'Break a leg, children!' Fernandes looked around the room, smiling at the students. 'Though, you know what I always say about North Starians, right? "We don't need anyone to wish us luck, because . . . ?"'

'We make our own luck!' the students completed her sentence together, in a chorus, in what was clearly a familiar rejoinder.

Fernandes beamed back at them. 'That's right! Now, go win this thing for me.' She patted Radhi's shoulder before she left the room. 'Thank you for doing this.'

Radhi spent another quarter of an hour with the students until she felt that practising the lines any more would make them sound fatigued on stage.

'Now give those throats some rest,' she said. 'And good luck! Even if you're making your own, a little freebie won't hurt anyone.' She chuckled as she left the room.

Making her way outside again, she stood for a moment, observing the bustle of backstage. Props were being carried to and fro, actors were rehearsing their lines, makeup artists were applying finishing touches and, in a corner by a window, taking it all in with a wistful expression on her face, was the lone figure of Kia. Radhi made her way to stand beside the girl who gave her a small smile.

'Why did you drop out? You clearly love it so much,' Radhi asked Kia after a few minutes.

'Because I was angry,' Kia replied, without turning to her.

'At?' Radhi asked, surprised. 'Mr. Bottlewalla?'

Kia shook her head impatiently. 'I was angry at the school. At Ms. Fernandes. Ms. Lily. Everybody.'

'Why?'

Kia didn't answer immediately, and Radhi thought that maybe the teenager was done talking to her, but then she spoke again, her voice lower and her eyes rapidly filling with tears. 'Because they've asked me to leave North Star.'

'But why?' Radhi frowned, surprised.

'Because I'm stupid, obviously,' Kia said, before turning on her heel and running out of the room.

Radhi slowly made her way in the opposite direction to the assembly hall where the drama competition was about to start. The place was packed to the seams and buzzing with excitement. Students of North Star sat beside contingents from other schools in tightly laid out rows of chairs, while the teachers either sat or stood flanking them on both sides. Ms. Fernandes, the Kambles, father and son, sat in the front row, a vacant seat between them for the chief guest. Radhi found an empty chair next to Ms. Farah and took a seat. She was disturbed about how upset Kia had seemed and hoped the girl was okay. She had tried to go after her, but a group of students carrying a projector and lights had come in between them and, by the time they made their way through the back-stage crowd, the girl was gone.

Uneasy, Radhi leaned in towards the art teacher, 'Tell me, Ms. Farah, does the school sometimes ask students to leave?'

Surprised, perhaps because of how unrelated the question was to the occasion, it took a moment for the art teacher to answer her. 'You mean does the school suspend students? Ye—'

'No, not suspend,' Radhi interrupted her. 'I mean leave for good . . . maybe because their grades aren't good enough?'

The art teacher blinked rapidly as she tried to process how to answer Radhi's question. 'Uh . . . well . . . not officially, no, but in some cases the school does give a nudge in that direction. You know what I mean?' she said, choosing her words with care.

Radhi certainly didn't know what she meant. But before she could ask, the lights had dimmed, and the speakers sprang alive with the announcement that the chief guest had arrived, and the show was about to start.

Dressed in a starched white kurta, a khadi jacket and Nehru cap, Wagle was the quintessential Indian politician as he walked to the front of the room with folded hands and an entourage of lackeys. If Radhi had any doubts about how qualified he was to judge a drama competition, they were erased immediately at the sight of his crocodile smile. Clearly, the man was an expert. He greeted the audience, thanked the Kambles for inviting him and lit the inaugural lamp on the stage with the ease of a consummate actor.

CHAPTER 18

'Inspector,' Radhi said when Shinde picked up the call, 'you know how you said your senior was under pressure to close this case?'

'Yes . . .' he answered, cautiously.

'Could it be coming from Wagle?'

'Ramakant Wagle? The politician?'

'Yes.'

Shinde paused to think. 'Hmm, it's possible . . . Why?'

Quickly, Radhi told him about his connection with the Kambles, leaving out the illegal parts. Those she wanted to hang on to for later. When he'd agreed to dig around, she asked him if he'd had any luck with finding Venus's doctor.

'Yes,' he said. 'As a matter of fact, those reports we found led me straight to her general physician, a Dr. Bharati Rao.'

Shinde paused here. Radhi sensed that he was waiting for someone to pass.

'And?'

'And she said Venus was in good shape. No serious issues. Just the regular calcium and vitamin deficiencies which come with age. She seemed very shocked to hear about how she had passed.'

'So, this confirms what we have been saying all along!' said Radhi. 'Why didn't you tell me sooner?'

'Because there's more.' Shinde sounded smug. 'You know how I was wondering about the newspaper in Venus's apartment and who could have turned it?'

'Yes . . .'

'Well, it got me thinking that since there were no signs of forced entry, what if someone had a spare key to Venus's place. Single people sometimes may give a key to a friend or relative for emergencies. No? So, we checked with the neighbours. But they didn't have it. They told us to check with the women she attended church with.'

Shinde paused again — and this time it was for effect.

'Well?' Radhi said, impatiently.

Shinde chuckled. 'Well, it seems like someone does have her key.'

'Who?'

'That's what I was going to find out next. I'll call you if we learn anything.'

'Thank you, Inspector.'

'See, madam, we do know how to do our jobs.'

Now, it was Radhi's turn to chuckle. 'I never had any doubts.'

Radhi hung up, amazed not only at the information Shinde had given her but also at the fact that she had actually managed to share a moment of levity with him, however brief it may have been. She had snuck out of the school for a quick smoke after the drama competition. Now, she made her way back, thoughtfully.

The atmosphere in the staff room was celebratory. North Star had been awarded first place in the competition and the teachers, even though most of them had had nothing to do with the event, were swept up by the boisterous mood of the students. Radhi had wondered how the school, as the host, would establish fair play and avoid allegations of partiality, but it had been achieved easily enough. Each school that performed had been given a numerical code, so that no names had been announced on stage and the judge had no way of knowing which school was which.

As everyone congratulated Mr. Bottlewalla, he flushed pink, enjoying the attention, but protested graciously to include Radhi in the victory. 'It was all thanks to the solid script, guys. First, what Ms. Venus wrote and then how Ms. Zaveri built upon it.'

'Honestly, I didn't have to do much,' Radhi said, 'The flesh and bones of the script were so robust that all I made were cosmetic changes. The kids did a fab job though!'

'Please, Ms. Zaveri, you were a life saver, so stop being so modest please.' Ms. Farah smiled at Radhi. 'But yes, Ms. Venus was really something else, everything she touched became gold.'

Ms. Savant who was in conversation with the music teacher, turned at that and rolled her eyes, but for once she held her tongue. The conversation continued in this vein for the entirety of the staff tea break. Eventually the teachers started dispersing one by one until only Mr. Bakshi, Ms. Lily, Mr. Bottlewalla and Ms. Farah remained. Radhi, who had been trying to get Mr. Bakshi alone for days now, decided that it was probably never going to get more private than this.

'I was thinking it would be such a triumph for Ms. Venus if she were here today,' Radhi began in a circumspect manner.

'So true,' said Mr. Bottlewalla, refilling his coffee mug for what was probably the fourth time that hour. 'We won the gold trophy, no less.'

'I don't know about that,' said Mr. Bakshi. 'Her eye was not on the literal prize. She was far more interested in embarrassing the politician.'

'It seemed to be a favourite pastime of hers,' Ms. Lily said, drily.

'What? Embarrassing people?' Mr. Bottlewalla laughed. 'I wouldn't go that far . . . but yes, she didn't hesitate in calling people out.'

'You know, I still keep thinking about how she passed away. It was just so sudden.' Radhi turned to face the chemistry teacher. 'Mr. Bakshi, when you went to meet her that evening, how did she seem to you?'

'When?' Mr. Bakshi stopped doodling on the paper napkin in front of him.

'The day she died — did she seem very worked up to you?'

'No idea . . . I never met her that day,' the chemistry teacher answered, casually enough, but he'd gone very still.

Radhi studied him, surprised. Somehow, she hadn't expected him to lie so baldly to her face. The part of her that considered him a friend had almost hoped he'd have a valid reason for why he hadn't told the police about meeting Venus. She considered calling him out there and then but thought better of it. A confrontation would probably yield better results if they were alone.

'Ms. Venus was always worked up about *something* or the other,' Mr. Bottlewalla was saying, oblivious to how tense Mr. Bakshi seemed. 'Some people are just built like that. Stress magnets, I call them.' He chuckled at his own cleverness. 'And some people are like me.' He patted his rotund belly and grinned. 'Happy go lucky.'

'In my experience, it has a lot to do with your sun sign,' said Ms. Farah. 'Scorpios, like Ms. Venus, can be intense. While Cancerians, like me, are often very sensitive.'

'And creative,' added Ms. Lily with a smile. 'My daughter's also June born.'

'Speaking of birthdays,' Radhi said on an impulse, 'I'm having a little dinner tomorrow night to bring in mine. I know it's a bit last minute, but I'd love for all of you to come.'

* * *

Radhi was in her car, on her way home, still thinking about how stiffly Mr. Bakshi had accepted her invitation. It was clear that he hadn't wanted to come and had almost begun to make an excuse, but Mr. Bottlewalla and Ms. Farah had immediately protested and told him not to be a spoilsport.

Radhi had no inkling about why Mr. Bakshi had lied, but now his discomfort alone was intriguing to her. Picking up her phone, she dialled her sister's number.

'Didi, can I add a few people to tomorrow's guestlist?' Radhi said to Madhavi when she answered her call.

'Of course,' her sister said immediately, sounding pleasantly surprised. 'Who do you want to call?'

When Radhi had told her about the North Star teachers, she sounded less enthused. 'Are you sure? I didn't know you were that close . . .'

'Not close, exactly,' Radhi began, 'but—

'Oh, wait a minute,' Madhavi interrupted her, 'This is about Venus's death, isn't it? You're trying to get to the bottom of it—'

'Yes, well—'

'Jesus, Radhi, can't you have a nice birthday celebration without thinking about murder and murderers?'

'In fact, mystery parties are quite the rage, Didi,' Radhi joked, trying to cajole her sister. 'People hire party planners and actors and plant clues and whatnot to get the theme right, and here I have all of it ready-made . . .'

'Okay, stop. Stop. Fine,' Madhavi said, exasperated. 'It's your party, you want them, you got them. I'll let the caterers know. But what are you hoping to find out?'

'I don't know yet,' Radhi admitted. 'There are all these undercurrents just below the surface. I can feel the tension, but I can't understand it.'

She told her sister about how Ms. Lily had been hunting among Venus's things, and about how she'd denied finding any article but had seemed to know exactly what article Radhi had been asking about. And she told her about Mr. Bakshi who'd lied about meeting with Venus on the day of her death.

'Tell me, Didi, do you know anyone who works at Victoria High?'

'The girl's school on Grant Road?' Madhavi mused. 'Yes, as a matter of fact, I do. There's a woman at my yoga class who's taught there forever. Why?'

'Mr. Bakshi used to work there at the same time as Ms. Venus. I want to know if they were close or if there's any kind of history there.'

'I'll check,' said Madhavi. 'And I'll inform the caterers.'

Radhi thanked her sister and then asked Ramzan bhai to turn the car towards the mall. It had just occurred to her that she had nothing new to wear for her own party.

* * *

Radhi lay on the bed on her stomach, typing furiously. She had just hammered out two chapters of her new book and was now making notes for a third. On the floor beside her, shopping bags lay like fallen dominoes, strewn in a glorious pile-up of colour. There was the unmistakable Hermes orange, the cream with the embossed gold of Burberry and the rich cobalt of her new favourite Indian designer brand, Nicobar. She'd come home with bright, linen shirts the colours of limes and strawberries, short dresses in tussar and pastel crepes with pearl details and trimmings of lace. There were crisp cotton kurtas with bell sleeves, Chinese collars and A-lines, to be paired with pleated dhotis and straight raw silk pants. And to go with them all there were strappy stilettoes and ballerina shoes with bold bows and buckles.

Radhi sighed contently and raised herself to a seated position, surveying her haul with a smile. It had been so long since she'd set foot in a store that she'd all but forgotten how nourishing a new dress could be for the soul. It was ironic, she knew, to equate the swipe of a credit card with a spiritual experience and yet she felt that the simple motions of trying on something new was an affirmation of life itself. The glimpsing of an unfamiliar version of yourself in the mirror, a moment ripe with possibility. Even if that hope was as flimsy as the chiffon on you, even if it lasted just as long as the swish of a zipper coming down, there was still promise in that moment of a whole new fate.

Radhi threw herself down on the bed again, this time on her back with her arms crossed behind her head, her thoughts traversing the length of her day — from new book to new clothes to the new guestlist for her party — coming to stop at the play that morning.

She knew now that the Kambles were indebted to Wagle for the school land, which was why they couldn't have let Venus retain the original script of the play, but was that where their policing stopped? What if they had found out that she planned to write about him in the paper? What if they'd tried to stop her and she hadn't listened? How far were they willing to go to protect Wagle then? Or maybe all they did was warn the minister that a damaging article about him was going to come out. Maybe, somehow, what happened next was the minister's doing?

Radhi rolled back on to her stomach and fired up her laptop again. She wondered if Venus's next article had been about Wagle and what it could have said. She began to read about the minister, curious about his background. A product of the Deccan, Wagle was born and brought up in Pune. The third son of a railways clerk, he had dropped out of college in the second year to join the local branch of a major political party. Here, he had proven that he had a knack for the complicated leveraging and manoeuvring of favours, flattery and string-pulling that was so essential to Indian politics and had quickly risen through the ranks, from local leader to branch head to municipal corporator to minister. He had sixteen court cases pending against him and had married twice. His first wife had died of pneumonia within a few years of marriage. With his second and current wife, he had two sons and a daughter. Both sons had entered politics and joined their father's party, while the daughter was married to a local businessman. As Radhi went from his professional history to the personal, a photograph of Wagle at the opening of an animal hospital caught her eye. She looked at it again and gasped, then read the caption below, just to be sure. Standing beside Wagle, as he cut the red ribbon, were his wife and daughter. Kiran Wagle and Seema Wagle-Savant. Ms. Savant.

The same Ms. Savant, whom Venus had given a hard time because she had got the job through her father's connections. Ms. Savant, who was convinced that Ms. Venus had turned the students against her and who was angry at Ms. Venus for her script and the planned humiliation of her father. The same Ms. Savant who had discovered Venus's dead body on the day she was murdered.

CHAPTER 19

Suddenly, Radhi's mind was buzzing with a thousand questions. So far, her impression of Savant had been that of a bumbling teacher, essentially harmless, regardless of how disgruntled she seemed with Venus and the students. But now, she couldn't be sure. How had it been for Savant to know that her father was all set to be the subject of ridicule at the school? If Venus didn't know of her connection to the politician, she may have voiced her opinions frank and unfiltered. Hell, knowing Venus, Radhi doubted even that would've stopped her. It was entirely possible that Venus knew and had powered through her plans with the play, regardless. In either case, it couldn't have been easy being Wagle's daughter. Surely, it had rankled her. But what had she done about it? Tell her father? Tell the Kambles? And when the Kambles scrapped the play? Had Venus ranted against all the 'bloody politicians and bureaucrats' with Savant present? Radhi could imagine it of the Head of the English Department, easily. How had Savant felt then?

Radhi sucked her breath in as something else occurred to her. The article that Venus had written and the phone call she had made to Thomas, the editor at the *Gazette*, had Savant witnessed those too? If Venus didn't know about

Savant's connection to Wagle, there was every chance that Savant, who shared the English Department room with her, had seen her work on that article. Or worse, had read it. It would've been entirely feasible with Venus in and out of the room for her classes. How angry had it made her? And what had she done then? Tell the Kambles or her father, again? Or had she decided to do something about it herself?

Radhi bit her lip when she remembered the new article Venus had written. Did Savant know about that too? Is that why she had come back that night? And was that the reason Radhi hadn't been able to find it? Because it had already been found and destroyed?

Radhi glanced at her phone. She was itching to share this new information with Hrishi and to hear his thoughts on it. But it was well past midnight. She didn't dare call him at home. She was also curious to know if Shinde had found out anything interesting about Wagle. But regardless of how cooperative he'd been lately, he wasn't likely to take her call at this time, either. Sighing, Radhi shut her laptop. She had promised the students who had participated in the play that she'd drop by for their celebratory brunch, the next morning. She shut her eyes, but sleep evaded her completely. Though for once, she didn't mind.

* * *

Saturday

When Radhi made her way inside the Nutcracker, a popular café at Kala Ghoda, the next day, the brunch was well underway.

'Come, Ms. Zaveri, come!' Mr. Bottlewalla boomed from the head of the table. 'Everyone, shift up, and make space. Ms. Zaveri, the avo-on-toast here is superb and so are the burrito bowls!'

When Radhi had greeted everyone and taken a seat, she was surprised to find Kia to her left.

'Kia! I am happy to see you here.'

The girl blushed. 'Yeah, my friends insisted I come because I was part of the original thing.'

'They were right.' Radhi smiled but left it at that. She had questions about what the girl had told her the day before she ran away, but she didn't want to risk upsetting her again.

The conversation on the table moved from the play to the performances of the other schools, to their ongoing rivalries in sports to the would-be sports captain, Soam Mehta. Everyone expressed surprise that he hadn't still been found, before the discussion turned to Ms. Savant and how she had left the classroom crying the other day.

'Why do you all trouble her so much?' Mr. Bottlewalla asked, in between bites of his burrito wrap.

'She asks for it, sir!' said one of the students. 'She wants so badly to be our friend that she forgets she's our teacher.'

'Yeah, the other day she told us Shakespeare knock-knock jokes . . . isn't that lame?' said another.

'Would you rather have a teacher who didn't care?' Mr. Bottlewalla asked, his tone only half admonishing as if a part of him was just a little bit glad that he wasn't the unpopular teacher.

Radhi had been listening, but her attention was divided between the conversation on the table and Kia's movements to her left. She really wanted to complete their conversation, and at one point, she felt like she'd get the chance when Kia excused herself to visit the ladies' room. Radhi was about to follow her but one of her friends went with her, and she lost the opportunity.

As the meal was drawing to a close, a waiter arrived with a cake and the students burst into the Happy Birthday song, and Radhi realized with a mixture of surprise and embarrassment that they were singing for her.

'My birthday's tomorrow, you guys . . .' Radhi began, but her protests were drowned by the loud birthday song that had now begun playing on the speakers of the café.

As soon as she had blown out the candle and cut her cake, a couple of the kids smeared some cake on her face, while the others clapped.

'Eew!' said Radhi, as she wiped her cheeks and forehead with tissue.

'Some of it has even gone in your hair, Miss,' said Kia, trying to help her get it out. 'You'll need a mirror to reach it all.'

Radhi excused herself to go to the bathroom and Kia followed her to help.

It was only when Radhi was all cleaned up that Kia spoke. 'I'm sorry I ran away like that, yesterday.'

'That's fine,' said Radhi, watching her in the mirror. 'But are you okay? Can you tell me a little bit more about why they asked you to leave? Maybe I can help?'

Kia shook her head sadly. 'It's no use, Miss. My parents have also tried.'

When Radhi continued to look at her expectantly, Kia continued. 'It's my maths marks. They bring down my whole average. And that impacts the average of the whole class. As well as the overall results of the school.' Kia leaned against the bathroom wall. 'Ms. Lily tried working with me. Gave me extra classes in school, but . . .' Kia shrugged. 'I just suck at numbers. Theorems, algebra, ratios, it all goes over my head! So, now the school has asked me to leave. Ms. Lily told my parents that the school would write me a good recommendation letter to help with admissions in some other school.' Kia was crying now. 'But I don't want to go to a different school. All my friends are here! And it is so humiliating to be asked to go like this. Ms. Venus was going to help me, but she's dead! So, there's no way out of it now.'

Kia looked despondent. Radhi handed her a tissue.

'How was Ms. Venus going to help?'

'She was going to ask Ms. Lily to reconsider. My marks in English literature and even in other languages are pretty good. With English I am usually top of the class, so Ms. Venus knew I am not stupid. She told me she would convince

Ms. Lily and if Ms. Lily didn't agree, Ms. Venus said she had a plan B.'

'Plan B?' Radhi repeated, suddenly alert. She had heard Venus utter these same words before, in a different context. 'What did she say she was going to do?'

Kia shrugged. 'She didn't say. She just told me to not worry, because she had a way of dissuading Ms. Lily from sending me away.'

'So that's why you were crying that day in the bathroom?'

Kia nodded. 'I was upset because Ms. Venus didn't get a chance to try her Plan B,' she said, splashing some water on her face.

As Radhi and Kia made their way back to the others, Radhi thought about what Venus's plan B could have been and if she had already threatened Ms. Lily with it. Was it possible that her death was a consequence of that? She started as another thought occurred to her. Quickly, she brought out her phone and texted Shinde.

Did you find out who had Ms. Venus's key? The woman from the church — was her name Ms. Lily, by any chance?

It was a few minutes before Shinde responded.

Not Lily. One Mary D'Souza. We are meeting her today.'

Radhi hung up the phone disappointed. Something in her gut said that Venus's plan B was important. But what was it?

* * *

Radhi arrived home on the evening of her party to find her apartment darkened except for the glow of lamps and the strings of fairly lights which draped the length and breadth of her bookcase and bar and continued gently around her monstera and fig plants giving their leaves a beautiful sheen. Little bulbous glass vases of baby pink chrysanthemums and white gypsophila were placed in corners and on the ledges of both the windows, while soft, sitar music wafted from the speakers. The whole place smelled of night jasmine in bloom.

Radhi stood for a moment at the door taking it all in. She knew the flowers were Lila's doing and the music was her sister's. Her housekeeper knew exactly how Radhi liked her flower arrangements, and Madhavi knew why she adored Pt. Ravi Shankar. He had been their dad's favourite.

'Well, don't just stand there,' said Lila. 'Unless you're planning to receive your guests like this.'

Radhi looked down at the baggy sweatpants and T-shirt she had on and grinned. 'You've made the house so pretty that I might just get away with it.' She hugged her housekeeper.

'Is that Radhi?' Her sister came out of the kitchen, with a small platter in her hands. 'I was just trying some of the food the caterers have begun to assemble. Here . . .' She gave Radhi a bite of a dim sum stuffed with spicy mushrooms and tofu.

'Mmm . . . this is sooo good,' Radhi said, covering her half full mouth with one hand.

'Wait till you try the Vietnamese summer rolls,' Madhavi extended the platter towards Radhi. 'They've got strips of mango and avocado in them, and you have to have it with this yum peanut sauce.'

Lila and Madhavi had banished Radhi from her apartment that afternoon as they got the place ready for the party. Radhi had spent the last few hours at a spa getting a deep tissue massage, followed by steam, sauna and, at the end of it all, she'd got her hair done at the spa salon. She'd returned home feeling rejuvenated.

'All of this looks just lovely!' Radhi said to her sister and Lila. 'Thank you, guys!'

'Lila did most of it,' Madhavi said, and the housekeeper protested with a good-natured, 'Rubbish, Didi,' before going back to the kitchen to yell at the caterers who were messing up her kitchen.

'Come, if you really want to thank me, you can do it after you've seen your birthday gift.' Madhavi took Radhi by her hand into the bedroom and sat her down on her bed. She went back out into the living room, returning with a small, square, blue, velvet box which she placed in Radhi's hands.

When Radhi saw the golden 'Z' with the elaborate flourish on it, she immediately knew what was in the box. The logo of their father's company, which her sister now ran, could only mean jewellery.

'Didi!' Radhi gasped when she saw the emerald and baguette studded parrots. 'This is too much!'

'So, what if it is?' Madhavi grinned. 'I'm allowed to spoil my little sister every now and then, aren't I? Do you like them?'

Radhi held up one of the parrots to her ear and turned to look in the mirror. 'They're gorgeous,' she said. 'I don't think even Mom and Dad would spoil me the way you do. But . . .' She put the earring back in the box and paused dramatically. 'This time, even I've got something for you.'

'What? No, no . . .' Madhavi frowned. 'It's *your* birthday, *you* are the one who gets gifts, or have you forgotten how birthdays work?'

Radhi chuckled and was about to get up to bring out the North Star early admissions letter from her bag, when Lila came to ask for Madhavi's help in the kitchen.

'Let's talk later.' Madhavi gave Radhi a peck on her cheek, 'Get ready.'

Alone in her room, Radhi slipped into one of her new dresses, a cream-coloured shift of the softest crepe, which was long enough for a house party, but short enough to show off her long legs. She'd had her hair taken up in a messy, high bun which accentuated her neck and made her cheekbones look even sharper than they were. Now she slipped on the new earrings her sister had just gifted her and paused to study her reflection in the mirror. She knew she looked good, but there was a puffiness to her face, especially under the eyes, thanks to all the excess drinking, which needed to be addressed. She picked up her eyeshadow pallet and gave herself dramatic, smoky eyes, following it up with a subtle pink lipstick. Finally, content with her appearance, she drew the curtains and opened the windows for one last smoke before the party started. With her sister and aunt and other family members in attendance, this was probably going to be her only chance all night.

* * *

The party was in full swing, the guests dotted Radhi's living room in clusters. Radhi's friends from college, the few she'd managed to stay in touch with over the years, were in one corner, a large gaggle of cousins, the ones she was fond of and the ones she could just about tolerate, made up another little group where her sister and brother-in-law stood talking with them, and the teachers from North Star formed a third. Her favourite aunt Vrinda, who had been like a second mother to Radhi and Madhavi after their parents' death, had dropped by and left early, pointing out to Radhi that the average age of the room was thirty-five, a good two decades younger than her. As luck would have it, another aunt, who Madhavi had insisted they invite seeing as they were inviting Vrinda, had been taken ill with a stomach bug and had to cancel last minute — a true birthday gift from her in Radhi's opinion. There were only two absences which Radhi felt acutely, her best friend Sanjana, who'd moved to London after her father's unnatural death, and Hrishi, who had promised he'd come but hadn't so far.

A pair of servers did the rounds of the room with appetizers and cocktails. Madhavi, who had also hired a bar tender for the evening to mix drinks for people, had been surprised to see how well-stocked Radhi's bar was. She'd raised an eyebrow at Radhi's collection of red wines, but other than that, had held her tongue. Radhi's nieces had sent her a card with a magnifying glass, so that she'd 'always know the truth of how loved she was', while George had sent her a gift voucher for a writers' retreat happening in the Himalayas. And her cake cutting, which was the most embarrassing part of any birthday celebration for Radhi, had taken place without much ado — all things considered, she had to admit she was having a fantastic time.

Now she was with the North Star teachers. Ms. Farah had just finished gushing over Radhi's vast collection of books, Ms. Lily had told Radhi that she loved the décor and Mr. Bottlewalla had repeatedly complimented Radhi on the finger food, taking multiple helpings to prove his point. Even Mr. Bakshi, who had started out the evening looking uncomfortable, had relaxed enough to comment on the apartment's stunning sea view. Now, Radhi felt that the only way this party could get better was if she could get some answers about Venus's death. She decided to be a bit more direct this time.

'Mr. Bakshi, I didn't know that you and Ms. Venus both used to teach at Victoria High.'

The chemistry teacher had just taken a bite of his dim sum, which he now swallowed abruptly and began to cough.

'Oh yes!' said Mr. Bottlewalla before Mr. Bakshi could respond. 'Ms. Venus, Mr. Bakshi and even I! Though that was more than a decade ago, and I joined a couple of years after Mr. Bakshi had left. But we've all worked in the same schools at some point or other.'

'True, there's always a steady rotation,' said Ms. Farah, 'considering there aren't that many schools on Temple Hill. What with the astronomical cost of real estate in these parts.'

'Speaking of,' said Mr. Bottlewalla, addressing himself to the art teacher, 'did your landlord agree to the new lease?'

Radhi watched, frustrated, as the conversation veered towards the many woes of homeowners in Mumbai. Mr. Bakshi who had now regained his composure, excused himself to go to the washroom. He'd been discomfited by her question, that much she was sure of, but she was no closer to finding out why. Finally, when she was ready to admit that nothing new would come out of the evening, the conversation moved to the topic of Soam Mehta, who apparently, when he was in grade two or three, had hidden in the art supplies closet and had had the whole housekeeping staff in the school looking for him.

191

'The art supplies closet, really?' Ms. Lily asked.

'Yes! I was the one who finally found him,' Ms. Farah said.

'But why?' Radhi asked, surprised.

'He thought he'd get in big trouble for not completing some Marathi homework. So, he ran to the art studio before Marathi class and stayed there for almost two hours, until we found him.'

'That long!'

'I think at that age, children don't have the right grasp on the passage of time,' Lily said, taking a sip of her mojito, 'He probably didn't realize that the Marathi period was long over.'

'He'd drawn a cricket pitch with an umpire and wickets, while sitting there in the near dark, with just a peep of light coming in because he'd kept the door ajar,' said the art teacher.

'I think he came to the art studio because of all the art therapy you used to do together. Probably felt safe,' Mr. Bottlewalla said, before taking a Thai salad canape from a passing server.

'Why therapy?' Radhi asked.

'He was an anxious kid,' Ms. Farah said. 'The art calmed him down. I worked with him for a year or so, then the sports took over. And it seemed to do the same job.'

A server came up to them with mini bowls of a lemony water-chestnut salad, almost at the same time that Mr. Bakshi rejoined them. And the group was silent for a few minutes while they sampled the new dish.

'By the way, I was curious to know under what circumstances does the school ask students to leave?' Radhi asked, looking at no one in particular.

The art teacher glanced at Ms. Lily almost at the same time as Mr. Bakshi asked, 'What do you mean?'

Radhi shrugged and said with a studied casualness, 'I've heard that students in the higher classes are sometimes asked to leave school if their grades aren't up to the mark?'

'Kia told you, right?' Ms. Lily said, almost at the same time as Mr. Bakshi said, 'That's not exactly true.'

Both the teachers glanced at each other and Ms. Lily flushed.

'It's not just grades. There are many other things that the school keeps in mind before taking such a decision.' Mr. Bakshi clarified. 'And these decisions are very rare.'

Radhi wondered if Ms. Lily would add anything, but the maths teacher remained quiet and, unless Radhi was imagining it, tensed.

CHAPTER 20

Radhi sat on the sofa, her heels off, feet on the centre table in front of her, relishing the complete quiet of the now empty house. She'd switched off the lamps, but the fairy lights still flickered, casting a gentle glow over the room. Turning older felt different every year. There were times when she'd dreaded it and others, when she'd approached it with a hesitant hope, but for this birthday she had been afraid. This year had been about realizing that her choices had consequences. When she'd been in the thick of it, making those choices and taking those decisions, she had been merely coping. But now that she was more settled, she was beginning to understand what her actions would come to mean.

She considered her decision to move to India. Sure, she'd received some taunts and titters from relatives, and the new proximity to family meant that her actions were more observed and needed to be more restrained. But she loved that she got to spend time with her nieces. She now knew who Amayra's favourite Disney princess was and the name of her sister's favourite hair stylist. She could gossip with her sister about everyday things because now that she was back home, she was privy to those inconsequential details of her life. It had also been a pleasure to reconnect with old friends.

She'd been afraid that she'd changed too much for them to have any real connection now, but in the interim that she'd been away her friends had changed and grown too, and it had been nice, for the most part, to discover who they had become and find that she still liked them.

Radhi took a sip of her wine and reminded herself that her drinking had its consequences too. She made a birthday resolution to break out of this habit she'd fallen into and sealed it with another sip. Smiling to herself at the irony of it.

The doorbell startled her from her ruminations. Her eyes travelled to the clock. It was well past one. She walked to the door, put her eye to the peephole and gasped. Hrishi stood outside, one hand in the pocket of his khakis and the other, holding a huge bouquet of oriental lilies.

'Thank God you weren't sleeping!' Hrishi said as he took in Radhi's dress and hair. 'And thank God the party is over too,' he said, looking beyond her into the empty house. 'I couldn't bear to socialize right now.'

Still not over her surprise, Radhi opened the door wider to let him in.

'Happy birthday,' he said, handing over the flowers before stepping forward to give her a hug.

'Thank you,' Radhi said, breathing in his scent of coffee, cigarettes and Old Spice and feeling something unnameable stir in the pit of her stomach.

'Right up until I rang your doorbell, I thought it was a good idea to come,' he said, as he followed her into the living room. 'But now I feel it was a bit lunatic.'

'Lunatic or no, I'm so glad you are here.' Radhi turned to grin at him. 'But surprised, also. Drink?'

He nodded and she went to the bar to get him a gin and tonic, before refilling her own glass with more wine. They sat side by side on the sofa, she, with her legs tucked in, watching him curiously.

'The place looks nice.' He nodded at the flowers and lights. 'Good party?'

'It was lovely. I'm glad I did it. I wondered where you were.'

He took a sip of his drink before answering. 'We were meant to come together . . . Neha and me. But then we got into this big row, and she refused to come. And she didn't want me to go either, but I . . .' He sighed as if this was something he'd struggled against. 'But I wanted to.' He held her gaze for the briefest of moments before looking away.

'What happened?' Radhi asked. Suddenly, she felt it was important that she know why they'd fought.

Hrishi didn't answer immediately. He seemed conflicted, as if he was struggling to make up his mind about something. Radhi studied his familiar careworn face and felt an alarming twinge of longing to touch it.

'What happened, Hrishi?' she asked again, softly.

'Neha realized I knew you from college.'

'Meaning?'

'While I was telling her who we could expect to meet at your party, she realized you were the Radhika from my college days.'

Radhi frowned. 'How does it matter where we know each other from?'

Hrishi ran a hand through his hair. 'Sorry, I know I'm being cryptic — but it's just embarrassing.'

He was quiet for a moment before speaking again. 'You know that copy of *Gone with the Wind* which you lost in college?'

Radhi nodded, she'd loved the book and had hunted high and low for it.

'Well, I had it. I don't know how it got into my bag, but when I saw the last page, I didn't feel like giving it back.'

Radhi thought back to what she'd written on the last page and blushed.

'You had doodled our names with a heart between them, over and over again and filled the whole page. And I loved seeing it.'

Radhi remembered clearly the economics class she'd spent intertwining the H & R of their names together, in bright pink, and smiled shyly at the memory. 'This was around the time that we—'

'Kissed,' he said, completing her sentence and looking at her for a moment before continuing. 'Yeah, well, so Neha found the book among my things when we first got married and grilled me about why I had kept it.'

'Why did you?'

'Well, initially, I had meant to tease you about it. But then—'

'But then my parents died, and I turned into a bitch of the first order,' Radhi said, lightly.

'Yeah, something like that.' He laughed. 'Honestly? I always thought that you'd . . . that we'd . . . get back together eventually. That once you'd worked through your grief, we'd resume where we left off . . .'

'You didn't anticipate the bitch-mode to last as long as it did,' Radhi said, remembering how angry she'd been and how she'd shunned all her friends and shut herself off with angry books and music and dark thoughts.

'Hey, you were heartbroken,' Hrishi said gently. 'Anyway, I used to love looking at that page, so I kept the book . . . Eventually, of course I forgot about it, but then, a few years ago, Neha found it and wanted to know all about you.'

'So that day at the office, when she met me, she didn't realize . . .'

'Yeah, she put two and two together this evening, and said it was too awkward to be friends with my old flame, and was angry at me for insisting we come to your party . . . Jesus . . .' Hrishi said, putting his drink down and shaking his head. 'It sounds so bloody awful when said aloud, doesn't it? I mean what kind of jerk puts their wife in such a position?'

'Hey . . . hey,' Radhi put her hand on his knee. 'Go easy on yourself okay . . . You work very hard at this, you're a good guy . . .'

'Am I, though?' Hrishi turned to look at her. 'I never did throw the book away. I just told her I did, when in fact I took it to work and kept it there.'

'Why?' Radhi asked, her voice catching in her throat.

'I couldn't,' he whispered, his expression so full of anguish that it knocked the breath right out of her.

Almost as one, they moved towards each other. The kiss that followed, was laden with so many unspoken words that it went on and on, gathering in intensity until every coherent thought had been driven out of Radhi's mind, leaving her only with an acute awareness of his hand on her bare knee and how her skin burned where he touched it. At one point, he pulled her on to his lap and groaned her name into her ear. She'd never heard her name spoken like this. It scorched her ear and the skin on her arms broke into goosebumps, even while her face, her lips and her whole body felt like it was on fire, her consciousness focused only on the callouses of his palm which had now travelled to her thigh and was brandishing the skin there. And the salt of his tears which she could taste on her tongue. Or were they her own?

* * *

The next morning Radhi woke up to find Hrishi, fully dressed, sitting at the edge of her bed, his head in his hands.

'Hey,' she pulled her quilt around herself and went to sit by him, slipping her hand into his hair. 'What is it?'

He turned to her, the expression on his face so tortured, that she immediately withdrew. 'Wha—'

'I'm sorry,' he said, 'I've become the kind of man I've always abhorred. I've cheated on my marriage with no thought to my child. No thought to our families. Or to the future. I've been unfair to Neha. Unfair to you . . .'

He took her hand in his and tucked a stray strand of hair behind her ears, but at his next words, Radhi felt her heart sink and the room darken despite the sunlight streaming into it. 'I'm a child of divorce. I know what a broken home feels like. I swore I'd do better by my child. And now . . .' He shook his head. 'It's laughable how royally I've fucked things up.'

Radhi withdrew her hand from his even though the slightest touch of his skin felt like sustenance to her and without that contact, she suddenly felt bereft.

'Hrishi,' she said, then repeated when he refused to look at her, 'Hrishi, listen to me. Yes, we fucked up, but your child need not have a broken home because of it. It was one night. Just one night. Beautiful, but nothing in comparison to the life you've worked so hard to build with Neha. You've put in so much to make this marriage work . . . and this? Us? Last night? It doesn't have to mean anything, we . . .'

Radhi had been so intent in making her point that she didn't realize when his eyes hardened with shock and pain. 'Doesn't mean anything?' his voice barely above a whisper. 'Are we really going to do this again?'

Radhi stared at him, mute. She had said it was nothing, because she thought that was what he wanted to hear, what he needed to hear. Now, looking at the furious expression on his face, she wished desperately she could take it back.

'Hrishi, I didn't mean it. Of course it matters!'

But Hrishi wasn't listening. He was on his feet, running his fingers through his hair, tucking his shirt into his trousers. Radhi made to move towards him.

'Do you really not see this for what it is?' He shrugged her hand away from his shoulder. 'Or is something within you so broken that you can't?'

She stepped back as if she'd been slapped.

He paused to look at her, his eyes brimming with hurt and anger and something else. 'I'm sorry,' he said, before shutting the door behind him.

Radhi sat back down on the bed, stricken.

'I'm sorry, too,' she whispered out loud to the empty room.

He was gone, and now she'd never have the chance to tell him how life-altering the previous night had been. How she had never experienced anything like it before. How feverish, how transported and yet how alive she'd been at his touch. How after so many years she still thought about their kiss, and it still made her heart thud harder. And how she had imagined this night with him countless times. And how it had surpassed everything she had dreamed of.

CHAPTER 21

'Don't tell me you were still sleeping,' Madhavi said when Radhi answered her phone.

It was past noon, and Radhi had spent the whole morning in bed, ignoring calls from people trying to wish her happy birthday, groggy, depleted, alternating between crying and replaying feverishly the night that had passed. The first time they made love, it had been urgent, intense. The second time round, they'd slowed down. Hrishi had paused to look at her body, and she'd closed her eyes, shyly, until he'd forced her to open them again.

'Radhi, are you there?'

'Yes, sorry Di.' Radhi cleared her throat. 'Tell me.'

'Okay, really quickly, two things: First, you're supposed to take Amayra for that pool party, today, you remember, no?'

'Yes. Yes, I do,' Radhi lied, covering her eyes with her hands, still trying to get her bearings.

'I don't know why you don't keep a calendar like other functioning adults,' Madhavi said, catching Radhi out. 'Maybe that should've been your birthday gift, instead of diamonds.'

Radhi groaned but didn't bother to defend herself.

'And secondly, I have news about your Mr. Bakshi. My friend who works at Victoria High said Mr. Bakshi left school under mysterious circumstances.'

'Oh?' Radhi sat up in bed and propped a pillow behind herself.

'The rumour is, he was having an affair with a student.'

'What?'

'Now remember, he was very young himself. Twenty-two, twenty-three and the student was seventeen. But it was against all the rules. Hell, teachers aren't allowed to date each other, so a fling with a student must've been so scandalous.'

'What happened then?'

'He was asked to resign. The school didn't take any other action against him because the girl's parents didn't want to make a big hue and cry. Besides, they got married a few years later, anyway.'

'Hmm . . . that's interesting,' Radhi said, thoughtfully.

'No — what's interesting is who turned him in,' Madhavi said, finally playing her trump card.

'Who?' Radhi asked even though she had a fair inkling of where Madhavi was headed.

'Ms. Venus. She's the one who reported it. And that's not all . . .'

* * *

As Radhi showered, she thought back to the last piece of information Madhavi had shared with her. Apparently, after having been asked to resign, the young and hot-headed Bakshi had stormed into the staffroom, called Venus an unfeeling, meddling bitch, and predicted that she would pay for this someday. All of which sounded very damning in the light of Venus's suspicious death, if not for the fact that it had happened twenty years ago. Somehow, it seemed unlikely that someone would hold on to a grudge for that many years. Especially because both of them had been working at North Star for some time now. And there were bound to have been plenty of opportunities during that time. Unless, she thought, unless . . . something had triggered it.

Radhi wished she had someone to talk this through with. She thought of Hrishi and felt a fresh pang of grief. Immediately all thought of Bakshi and Venus flew out of her mind, as it occurred to her that all morning, with all the regret she had felt at having ruined things with Hrishi or at having wasted all those years they could've been together, not once had she regretted that she'd been with a married man. She'd met Neha, they'd spoken, and still Radhi felt no guilt on her account. Even now, when she thought about it, there was no part of her that wouldn't do it again. As Radhi put the finishing touches on her makeup and looked at herself in the mirror, it scared her to know this about herself.

* * *

Had Radhi been thinking clearly, the venue details Madhavi texted her would have provided the first clue. But consumed as she was with trying to solve a murder, if not the question of her own deeply problematic love life, she had assumed that the poolside birthday she was taking Amayra to would involve a bunch of kids splashing about in a pool, followed by food and cake. Which was naive, she now realized, even for someone who hadn't attended a kids' birthday party in recent years, because this, after all, was Temple Hill. And anyone remotely familiar with the neighbourhood could reasonably expect a six-year-old's birthday planned like a full-blown society wedding.

For the sake of this party, the parents of the birthday girl had taken over the pool, both decks and the adjoining lawns of a luxury five-star hotel. And as if the sheer sprawl of the thing wasn't enough, they'd converted it into 'Sia's World of Pink', announcing it with a six-foot-long, vinyl banner at the entrance, lest anyone miss it. Reams and reams of streamers and bright owl lanterns, all in pink, hung from the branches of frangipani trees. Pink balloon sculptures of mermaids, flamingos and starfish dotted the lawns, while in the pool, pink, life-sized winged unicorns, dolphins and turtles waited for the kids to take notice. Waiters patrolled the perimeter of the pool with platters of French fries, cheese corn balls and tall glasses of neon-pink drinks, at the beck and call of the children, who all but ignored them, their somersaults and dives into the water, fuelled almost entirely by the sugar from gurgling chocolate fountains, pink marshmallows and ice cream counters with pink softy dispensing machines. A live DJ was taking requests, churning out one TikTok song after another. And to make it all bearable Radhi supposed, for the adults at the party, they'd provided an open bar. Her mouth went dry at the sight of the alcohol, and it was with an effort she forced herself to look to the other side of the pool, where a gaggle of mums in oversized sunglasses chatted animatedly.

'Come, maasi, let's go,' Amayra said, emerging from the changing room in her swimsuit. She held up her swimming cap, and Radhi tied her hair into a bun before helping her put on the cap.

'I need those,' Amayra said, pointing to where a pool attendant was blowing up arm floaties for the kids who needed them.

They walked towards the man and once Amayra had inflated turtles on both arms, she went running to join her friends, while Radhi stood and watched, reluctant to join the group of adults on the other side.

'Radhi?' a woman's voice called from behind and this time, Radhi recognized it at once.

'Vedika,' she said when she turned, greeting her former classmate with a cool nod.

'I'm so glad I ran into you.' Vedika extended one billowy arm of her batik silk kaftan in an attempt at a half hug. When Radhi didn't respond, she let her arm drop.

'Listen, I felt bad about how we left things the last time. I just want you to know you're very brave.'

Radhi peered at whatever was visible of her face behind the large sunglasses and beach hat, to catch any hint of insincere emotion, but was surprised to not find any.

'Thank you,' she said, still with some reservation.

'You've come with your niece?'

'Yes. My sister had to be elsewhere.'

'I think it's wonderful how your sister can depend on you. Some sort of support system is so necessary while raising kids! I don't know what I'd do without my parents,' Vedika said, steering Radhi towards where the other mums were standing. 'Every time we have a late night, or when we need to travel or if I'm not well, I just send my boys off to my mum's.'

There it was again, Radhi thought, that gnawing guilt in the pit of her stomach for how much she'd robbed her sister of. She swiped a martini glass from a passing waiter and made a face when it turned out to have no alcohol.

'Maasi, hi!' Amayra waved at her from the pool, as they passed.

Radhi stopped to wave back before touching Vedika's arm. 'Hey, can we get a real drink?'

'Of course.' The other woman turned towards the bar. 'I heard you've been teaching at North Star. How's that going? You must get a lot of behind-the-scenes goss, no?'

'Some . . . Nothing very exciting.'

'What's the story on that Soam Mehta?'

Radhi frowned. 'Hasn't come home yet. His poor mother's falling to pieces,' she said, before ordering their drinks at the bar. 'It's sad, really.'

'Some of the parents in our batch were saying the school was very harsh with him,' Vedika said. 'Not that any one of them would criticize openly.'

'Too scared of consequences, again?'

Vedika nodded. 'It's the Kambles. I hear the junior Kamble is worse than his father. Takes these things too personally. Singles people out and calls them in for a "conversation" if he hears anything,' she said making air quotes with her fingers. 'Ms. Fernandes is the other extreme, though. She refuses to acknowledge a problem unless *she* considers it one.' Vedika shrugged. 'I can't decide whose approach I prefer.'

'This Soam running away is a problem all right.' Radhi shook her head, 'What a crazy thing to do.'

'Honestly? I don't blame him.' Vedika took their pink cosmos from the counter and gave one glass to Radhi before continuing. 'The father's such a terror.'

'Oh, you know them?' Radhi asked before taking a long and very welcome sip of her drink.

'Not me, my husband. They go to the same gym,' Vedika said as the two of them stepped away from the bar and walked towards the lawn. 'He is always talking about his son. Bragging about his achievements . . . his rigorous schedule. Constantly comparing with others. That kind of pressure can't be good for anyone.'

'And he's what? All of fifteen?' Radhi asked, appalled.

'That's now. All his coaching and training must have started a decade ago.' Vedika reminded her.

'Five . . . that's how old Amayra is now,' Radhi said in wonderment.

'By the way, the Mehtas are not *that* much of an anomaly.' Vedika stirred her cocktail with her index finger and licked it, before taking a sip of her drink. 'He is aggressive, sure. But there are mums at this party who have their five-year-olds learning Chopin with the express purpose of putting it on their college admission essays.'

She waved at a few mothers walking towards them. 'See, that one, in the navy green jumpsuit?' she asked Radhi, who nodded. 'She enrolled her five-year-old for a Mandarin class. And was annoyed when the teacher said it was too early.'

Before Radhi could express her incredulity, they were joined by a pair of mums and the conversation had drifted to the upcoming school exams, the new shoe vendor the school had engaged and gossip about the parents whose child's party they were currently attending. *Too cliché* was the general consensus on the pink theme. Radhi marvelled at the human proclivity to find something to diss. Regardless of how much money had been spent, how lavish the venue, how elaborate the buffet with its counters of mini burgers and mini pizzas and mini idlis for the kids and everything in their original sizes for the grown-ups, there'd always be something to find fault with. Simply, she sometimes suspected, because it made for easier conversation.

Radhi scanned the pool for Amayra. The child was sitting on the ledge, her feet dangling in the water, licking at a trickle of ice cream running down her hand from her cone. Her thoughts went back to what Vedika had said about Soam's father, making Radhi wonder, not for the first time, whether the man's ambition had anything to do with Venus's death. She wondered what sort of environment at home forced a child to run away. How afraid the child must have been, how entirely sure of being misunderstood. There was a thought at the edge of Radhi's consciousness about Soam and where he could've gone, but before she could take a hold of it, her attention was caught by the conversation around her.

'This time, they've really gone all out for Grandparents' Day.'

'Yeah . . . it's a grand musical, I hear.'

'Matilda, no? But isn't it annoying that we don't get to see it?'

'At the last PTA, I suggested they record the whole thing on video and then share a link with parents.'

'Or better still make it live! In this day and age, surely that's not too tall an ask.'

Radhi wasn't sure when she stopped listening, just that her gut felt like it had been sucker punched. Reeling, she backed away from the group. *Grandparents' Day. Oh God. Oh God.*

In all the years she'd struggled with the debilitating guilt of robbing her sister of parents, she'd never once considered what she'd snatched from her nieces. The girls didn't have one whole set of grandparents because of her. And she knew Roma Bansal, Madhavi's self-absorbed mother-in-law, with all her imagined health problems and mania for male heirs, couldn't possibly fill the void.

Radhi didn't realize, when she'd stumbled to the bar, that she was standing in front of the bartender, and he was looking at her expectantly. All her resolve from the previous evening crumbled in the face of her own villainy. She asked for a gin on the rocks and then because she didn't want the other mothers to see her veer away from the acceptable-at-four-thirty-in-the-afternoon cocktails, she had her drink in one quick gulp. It burned her throat but did nothing to settle the mad churn of emotions in her stomach.

'Maasi!' Amayra called. 'See me!'

Radhi watched as the child jumped into the pool, her sleeve floaties pushing her upwards almost immediately. Radhi raised an arm to wave at her.

'Maasi, look again!' The child climbed out of the pool and positioned herself for another jump.

Radhi thought of her own nani, her mother's mother, and was instantly consumed by the jasmine scent of her talc. Her nani's house was where she'd first fallen in love with stories. At mealtimes, at naptime and at bedtime, Radhi would demand stories, and her nani would regale her with tales of gods and wise men and powerful queens. Stories from history, mythology and the Jain scriptures. Of magic and valour and morals. And Radhi would lap it all up, along with her food.

As she watched Amayra now, it horrified Radhi that her nieces had never had that, would never have it. Would never know the shocking indulgence of a grandparent.

'One more,' she told the bartender, quietly.

'Maasi, look!' Amayra called again, this time holding a friend's hand, before they jumped in together.

Radhi smiled at her and waved weakly. She thought of what a terrific nani her own mother would've made. She imagined Amayra on her mother's lap, the same broad forehead and large eyes on both of them. Art would probably be their thing. Her mum had a fine hand and together, she imagined, they'd sketch and shade lion manes and banyan trees and moonlit lakes, just like Radhi and her sister had done when they were young.

'One more, please.' Radhi pushed her empty glass towards the bartender and earned a curious glance from a waiter picking up a tray of piña coladas.

She didn't care. She imagined the girls at their nani's house for Diwali, making rangoli with her mum. Learning how to fill in the intricate chalk design with fine, colourful powders, scattering petals, placing diyas. How much richer would the girls' lives have been had their grandparents been alive? Her heart ached as her thoughts went to her father. He'd have bought the girls their first musical instruments, she was sure of it. And introduced them to all the great gharaanas of Indian classical music — regardless of how much the girls protested or how boring they found it, he would've insisted on practice, on daily riyaaz.

'Is that your daughter?' Radhi could hear the bartender talking to her, but she couldn't register his words. Her ears were filled with the strains of sitar and her father's voice raised in Raag Malhaar.

'Excuse me, ma'am?' The bartender spoke louder this time. But more than his volume, it was the sense of urgency in his voice that finally broke through the haze of Radhi's thoughts.

'Is that your daughter?' he asked, pointing to a small crowd of children and parents that was fast gathering around the pool.

Radhi got up with a lurch, losing her balance as the heel of her right shoe got stuck in the grass. She fell, her reflexes too sluggish, too alcohol-ridden, to check her sprawl. The bartender, perhaps because he was aware of the number of drinks she'd consumed, was by her side in a minute, helping her as she scrambled to get up. But she brushed aside his arm the moment she was upright again, feeling a terrible, blind panic rise within her at the sight of the gathered people. She hobbled her way to the pool, her heel broken, too drunk to realize that removing both sandals would get her there much quicker.

CHAPTER 22

'Excuse me. Excuse me,' she hissed urgently as she pushed her way into the crowd, her knees almost buckling with relief at the sight of Amayra sitting upright on the ledge of the pool. She was coughing and crying and shivering despite the towel someone had wrapped around her but other than that appeared unharmed. One of the mothers was rubbing her back while another held out a glass of water for her to drink.

'Ssshhh, it's all right darling, maasi is here.' Radhi knelt beside her, taking her into her arms in a tight hug.

The child clung to her and pressed her face into Radhi's neck, howling even louder. Radhi held her for a few minutes before drawing away to examine her. She wiped her tear-smeared face with her hands.

'Are you okay?' she asked.

The child didn't answer but one of the mothers did. 'I think she's fine, just shocked.'

'But she got lucky . . .' said someone else.

'Yeah, thank God the other kids yelled when they did.'

It turned out that after trying out a series of jumps with the floaties on, Amayra had decided to try one without them. Her friends, who'd egged her on, thought she was horsing around when they saw her thrash her arms in the water, but eventually they realized she was really floundering, and they called out to the lifeguard. Radhi didn't know whether it was the terror of realizing what could've happened, or the deluge of relief flooding through her that it didn't, or the copious amounts of alcohol in her bloodstream that affected her, but a tremor went through her body, and she clutched Amayra and began to cry. Gentle tears at first, that fast turned into great big, heaving sobs.

At one point, someone urged them to get up. Radhi tottered trying to lift Amayra up. The alcohol had drained the strength from her arms. She removed the other shoe from her foot in an attempt to steady herself and hoped that the mothers would chalk up her lack of balance to her uneven footwear. One of the mothers picked Amayra up, and together they made their way into the changing room.

* * *

'Where are they?' Madhavi's voice reached them before they saw her.

Somebody seemed to have called her and told her what had happened. She rushed in, scanned her child before pressing her to herself. Her eyes met Radhi's and took in their haunted expression.

'It's okay,' she whispered. 'It's okay.' She seemed to be talking to them and to herself.

Straightening up, she leaned in to give Radhi a hug, but she pulled away almost immediately, with a puzzled look.

Radhi knew her breath reeked of alcohol, and she felt her face burn with the shame of it. As she met her sister's eyes, she saw Madhavi's concern transform into realization, and then to something else. Radhi's stomach dropped in fear. They rode back home in silence. The air in the car as still as a grave. Only Amayra spoke from time to time. Sharing stories from the party, her shock and fear dissipated in the face of two helpings of cake. Madhavi nodded and smiled, giving the impression of listening but Radhi could tell from the tightness around her mouth that her mind was on what she was holding back. Whatever it was that she wanted to say to her sister, was not for Amayra's ears.

Back home, Radhi ran to her room as soon as Lila opened the door. Surprised and concerned, the housekeeper followed her.

'What happened, Didi? Are you okay?' She knocked on the door several times before Radhi answered.

'Yes, please just let me be!'

'But what happened?' Lila tried again, but Radhi refused to say.

She was crying, her face buried in her pillow, feeling a kind of self-loathing she hadn't felt in a long time. She'd been unbelievably careless and self-centred. Had she no self-control, no sense of responsibility, no consideration of consequences? Her mind went to what would have happened if Amayra hadn't been pulled out from the water in time and reeled back in horror almost instantly.

It was such a dark and terrifying place that Radhi feared she'd go mad with grief and guilt, if she paused to consider it even for a moment. All she knew was that she had screwed up in one of those massively colossal ways that there was no going back from. She wondered if her sister would ever speak to her again. And if she did, would she ever trust her? She stayed in bed all evening and all night. Curtains drawn. Room dark. Unable to face anything about herself which light could illuminate. She knew that Lila had come knocking several times to check on her, and to offer her dinner and then milk. But the knocks had seemed to come as if from a great distance. Radhi wasn't sure if she'd answered. The only voice she was completely cognizant of was her own inner voice, and it was harsh and livid.

Her thoughts veered and skittered nauseatingly, one minute lingering at that moment at the birthday party before the crowd parted to reveal Amayra, the next to her night with Hrishi, her hands in his hair, his lips on her shoulder, to her parched throat which craved more alcohol despite everything, or perhaps because of the absolution it provided from it all.

But she didn't find an iota of solace, no matter how often her mind swerved. Or how much her body twisted and turned. At some point, drained and sore from the self-flagellation, her thoughts went to Venus's murder and the missing boy. And they stayed there, murder motives and culprits, far less dangerous than the harm she wished upon herself.

* * *

Monday

The doorbell rang angrily and repeatedly, waking Radhi up, disoriented and confused. Her eyelids were crusty, stuck together and it was with some difficulty that she opened them. From the way the light slanted into the room, she knew it was late, almost noon, but that was all she had time to consider, before the events of the previous day came flooding back to her, and she squeezed her eyes shut again as if in physical pain. The doorbell stopped ringing. Radhi heard the main door open and muffled anxious voices outside. Nervous, because she had a faint idea of who it could be, she got out of bed. In the living room, Lila stood by the door in a crumpled saree, looking strangely guilty, with Madhavi by her side. Radhi felt her heart sink.

'Sit.' Her sister pointed her to the sofa before she could say anything. Then, turning, 'Lila, you can go home now. And thank you for calling me.' Madhvi squeezed the housekeeper's shoulder.

As Radhi watched Lila collect her purse and things, she realized with a growing sense of shame that Lila was wearing the same clothes as the previous evening which meant she hadn't gone home to her son last night.

'Sorry, Lila,' Radhi said to her quietly, 'I didn't mean to worry you.'

'It's fine, Didi.' Lila met her eyes. 'I'm sorry too. I didn't want to tell on you,' she said, before she shut the door behind her.

'Since when has this been going on?' Madhavi asked, once the sisters were alone and sitting across from each other.

'Since when has what—' Radhi began.

'The drinking.' Madhavi cut her off, her voice like the serrated edge of a blade.

'I don—'

'Please Radhi, cut the crap, okay?'

Radhi winced as the ugly words from her sister swirled about them in the bright light of the day.

'I . . . I'm not sure.' Radhi couldn't bring herself to admit the truth. Not because she was worried about how angry it would make her sister, but because of how much it would hurt her.

'Lila tells me it's been going for months now. She said you take the trash out before she gets here on the days you've been drinking, so that you can dispose of the bottle.'

Radhi opened her mouth to ask how the housekeeper knew, but her sister silenced her with her next words.

'She said she checked the trash bags and that it's been happening far too often now.' Madhavi's face, as she confronted her sister, was devoid of all expression, and Radhi knew it was a sign of how livid she was. They'd always been on the opposite sides of the spectrum in how they expressed their anger. While Radhi got all hot and emotional, her sister turned colder the madder she got.

'Why?' Madhavi asked, letting the word hang there in all its stark awfulness.

'It helped me sleep,' Radhi said, finally. 'I've had trouble sleeping and without a therapist's note, there was no way to get the pills.'

Madhavi frowned. 'I thought you refused therapy, because you were doing well. You began writing again, you were dating Nishant . . . You said you were in a good place!'

'I was! I am. The writing makes me so happy. It keeps me sane. But—'

'But what, Radhi? You have a supportive family here. You love what you do. You even had a shot at a new beginning with Nishant, but you didn't take it!'

'I know, I know. I'm grateful for my life here. I swear I am!'

'So grateful that you have to drink yourself to sleep?!' The coolness in Madhavi's voice had been replaced by frustration. She got up and began pacing the room. 'So, what's bothering you then? Is there something I don't know? Something new?'

'No! Nothing new.'

Madhavi was silent for a few moments studying her sister's face. 'Surely, you aren't still thinking about the accident?'

Radhi looked back at her, miserably. Her silence more telling than anything she could say.

'Oh, for heaven's sake, Radhi!' Madhavi erupted, throwing her hands up in the air. 'It's been more than fifteen years! Are you never going to get over it? You are not the only one who lost their parents that day, you know? I miss them too! Like phantom limbs. All the bloody time. Every single minute of every single day. But that doesn't mean I become a raging alcoholic! You know why? You know why? Because I have people who love me and depend on me. And that includes you.' Madhavi paused to look at Radhi, her eyes filling with hot, angry tears, which she wiped impatiently. Her voice turned softer, but harder. 'Do you know I wasn't able to grieve for them properly because of you? You had gone to such a shambles that I had to stay strong for your sake. I would cry in the bathroom because I didn't want you to see me like that.'

Radhi stared at her sister, stricken. Wrecked as she had been by her own guilt and pain and consumed with rage at herself and the world at large, she hadn't paid attention to what her sister had been going through.

'Didi,' she whispered, 'I had no idea . . .'

'How could you? I never let it become your burden.' Madhavi's anger seemed to have got a new lease of life. 'But can you say the same about yourself? You wallowed and wallowed in self-pity, and it became my job to pull you out of it. Why? We *both* lost our parents that day, didn't we? Didn't we, Radhi?'

'But I'm the only one responsible for it,' Radhi said, after a long, fraught moment of complete silence. She wiped her wet face with her sleeve, she hadn't realized when she'd begun to cry.

Madhavi clutched her head, angry and frustrated and sat back down on her seat. 'You took years of therapy to disabuse yourself of this notion. It's called survivor's guilt. You already *know* this, but you refuse to accept it. It's like you thrive on this guilt. Don't you think you're giving yourself far too much importance in the grand scheme of things?'

Radhi shook her head. Her voice, when she spoke, quivered, as if what she wanted to say was far too heavy for the words to carry on their own. 'You're wrong. I did have a part to play. What I never told you or any of the therapists is that they never wanted to go to Pune that weekend. They tried to talk me out of it. But I was hell-bent on participating. So, Mama said that Papa would come along, while she stayed at home with you. But I insisted they both come. I was so sure I was going to win, I wanted them both there . . .'

Radhi paused and looked at Madhavi who was looking at her strangely. But she continued, hurrying to say the words before she lost her nerve, 'So you see, if I hadn't forced them *both*, you'd still have at least one parent alive today. And Amayra would have at least one grandparent to take to school on Grandparents' Day!'

Madhavi's eyes widened. She began to speak then paused before starting again. 'Is that . . . is that what triggered it?'

But Radhi couldn't answer. Now that she had said what she had bottled within for so many years, it was as if something in her had let loose and the tears wouldn't stop flowing.

Madhavi got up and came to sit beside her on the sofa. 'In that case, there's something I need to tell you too.' She waited until Radhi had stopped crying long enough to hear her, before continuing. 'You know how you forced Mama to come along?'

Radhi nodded.

'Well, I forced her to go.' Madhavi's voice broke as she said this. 'I wanted the house empty to throw a party for my friends. So, I pleaded and promised her that I'd be good, that I'd behave myself, that they needed to start trusting me more, and that's how I convinced her to go with you.'

Radhi clutched her sister's hands and stared at her for a long time as if she couldn't process the words that had been spoken. She had lived with the crushing weight of this guilt for so long that now that it had been suddenly lifted, she felt lightheaded, unable to steady herself or her emotions.

'So . . . so it's really not my fault?' she said finally, in the slightest of whispers, terrified that if she spoke any louder, she would jinx it, and it would become untrue.

Madhavi sighed sadly and shook her head. 'It was no one's fault. Not even the truck driver who rammed into them.' She put an arm around Radhi. 'It was meant to happen. They were meant to go. We were meant to grow up with each other. And my girls were meant to have a wonderful, wonderful and *sober* maasi instead of grandparents.'

Both sisters smiled at that, and then they held each other and cried for a long time.

CHAPTER 23

Radhi drummed her fingers on her desk, as she read through the words of the new chapters she'd just written. It had been a few hours since Madhavi had left, and at first Radhi had just lain on the couch, spent and drained, but as the hours passed, that feeling of having been wrung out and emptied had changed into a sort of lightness and Radhi had found that she could breathe with an ease she hadn't experienced in a long time. She had showered then and had sat down to work and, as she had suspected, the words had seemed to flow with an effortlessness which she didn't dare to question or inspect too closely. Now, happy with what she'd written, she cracked her knuckles and stood up and stretched her back. Her mind immediately wandered to Venus and North Star. It was a bank holiday that day, so she didn't have to go to school, but she found that the dead teacher was always on the periphery of her thoughts — the fact that she had no one to mourn her made Radhi feel more responsible to find out what had really happened to her. She brought out her diary and Soam's name jumped out at her — immediately pulling her to the night before and the thought she'd had just before she fell asleep.

Rushing to her room, she brought out the folder of assignments which she'd taken to carrying in her bag, so that she could review and grade them whenever she had some spare time. Quickly, she flipped to the exercise she had set the students of Soam's class the day before he went missing. She pulled Soam's sheet from the pile and read it one go. Then she read it again. By the time she finished it, she was certain she knew where the missing boy had gone.

* * *

Mrs. Mehta clutched her husband's arm with one hand and pressed her handkerchief to her mouth with the other, as they sat across from Radhi waiting for her to read them their son's last assignment.

'I have a theory of where Soam could be,' Radhi had said to them when she rang the doorbell to their apartment and found to her relief that the Mehtas were home. Now, she cleared her throat and began reading aloud:

> *My safe place is a two-storey bungalow made of marble. It's got balconies in every room and a large terrace that overlooks a sugarcane field. It is far away from the bustle of the city, in a small town with fewer cars and better weather than Mumbai. The lane outside is quiet and wide enough to play cricket. Though there are never enough people for a full match, there are enough kids like me who visit in their winter holidays, and we end up having a good time.*
>
> *There is a dairy close by, so the milk is thick and creamy and the lassi and paneer are to die for. We play cards in the afternoons, when the grown-ups are taking a nap. Judgement, Black Queen, Bluff and whatnot. Sometimes, we line up all the spare mattresses in a row in the living room and have somersault competitions and wrestling matches. At other times, we play hide-and-seek. The house has many dark corners and dusty storerooms, which are rarely used, except when we lay in wait for our annoying little cousin and jump out to scare him.*

Radhi looked up from the page to find Mrs. Mehta crying. 'So, this place rings a bell? You're familiar with it?' she asked.

Mrs. Mehta nodded. 'My parents used to own a bunga-low in Devlali. It's near Nasik. We used to go there with my brother's family every winter. And the kids used to do all of this, that he describes. I can't believe he writes so well.'

'So, do you think he could've gone there?' Radhi asked eagerly.

Mrs. Mehta shook her head. 'No, I don't think so.'

Her husband added, 'We sold this bungalow some years ago. The upkeep was too much trouble. Haven't been to Devlali since.'

Radhi bit her lip. She'd been so sure that Soam was hiding in his safe place. Now she felt bad that she'd come rushing here and raised their hopes.

'Sorry, I really thought he'd be here — especially since the place was on his mind that day.'

'No, please don't apologize — I am glad *someone's* think-ing about him. The police for sure aren't,' Mrs. Mehta said.

'Oh, don't start this again, Komal,' Mr. Mehta, turned to his wife, irritated. 'The police are doing their job. You are just upset with them because they've insinuated that your darling prince was up to no good. Just wait till I get my hands on that boy. He'll have hell to pay for.'

'This!' Mrs. Mehta scowled at her husband. 'This is the reason he's run away. Don't you still get it, you bloody fool?'

'Don't you blame your shortcomings on me!' Mr. Mehta swatted the arm of the couch with his hand and got up. 'You had one job. To raise these boys right. I've not expected any-thing else from you. You've had every luxury and resource at your disposal. And still you've failed, yo—'

'How dare you?' Mrs. Mehta yelled at him.

'What about friends?' Radhi interrupted them, desper-ate to get out of this uncomfortably private conversation and alarmed at how quickly it had escalated.

The Mehtas turned to stare at her as if they'd both for-gotten she was there.

'Friends?' Mrs. Mehta blinked.

'Yes,' Radhi hurried on. 'He mentions in his assignment that he used to play cricket with some boys in the neighbourhood. Did he have a good friend there? Someone who still has a bungalow there and who would let Soam crash there for a few days?'

Mrs. Mehta looked at her husband and the man sat back down again. 'Yes, as a matter of fact, most of the old families still own their bungalows,' he said.

'He had many friends there,' Mrs. Mehta said. 'There was one boy in particular, Swaraj. They were close, and I know they've kept in touch over the years.' She got up and rushed out of the room, returning a few moments later with a mobile phone.

'This is Soam's,' she explained to Radhi as she hurriedly scrolled through his contact list. 'Here it is — Swaraj Choksi!' She handed the phone to her husband who used his own phone to dial the number.

The two women watched as he spoke to the boy on the other side. They watched as his shoulders slumped and the permanently angry knot on his forehead dissolved into relief and his eyes suddenly began to shine with something that looked suspiciously like tears. Still on the phone, he met his wife's eyes and nodded.

CHAPTER 24

That evening, Radhi paced around the house trying to not think about alcohol. She'd returned home from the Mehtas a couple of hours ago and already she'd watched two episodes of *Monk*, following it up with a beautiful film called *The Swimmers*, about two Syrian sisters with an Olympic dream. Now, she had shut the television and was looking for something else to distract her. Something other than her phone, which she'd switched off to prevent herself from constantly checking her WhatsApp for a message from Hrishi. She may have told him it was 'just one night', but she would never be able to relegate it to that space in her head where she stored her casual flirtations. She'd written to him to tell him that she hadn't meant what she said, asking him to meet her just once more so that she could explain. And then she'd written again, saying the same thing in different words. She told herself she wasn't begging. But she knew what it was. She'd waited for a few hours for a response, which didn't come. Finally, in frustration, she'd switched off her phone — part of it, to salvage some remnants of her own dignity. She knew she'd eventually have to check it. Mrs. Mehta had promised her that she would text as soon as they had their son with them. She had hugged and thanked Radhi profusely for her help, while her husband stood behind awkwardly, not used to expressions of gratitude. The couple had left for Devlali almost immediately. They'd half begged, half threatened Soam's friend not to say anything to their son.

Mrs. Mehta had chalked up Radhi's interest in the boy to concern for his welfare, but she probably didn't realize that this was only the half of it. The fact was that Radhi strongly suspected Soam knew something about Venus's death. He'd gone up to her room that evening — that much she was certain of — but what had happened then? Had Venus caught him at some mischief? Had she confronted him? Had he done something stupid? Or had he not gone in at all? Had he witnessed something he shouldn't have? That was what Radhi wanted to find out.

Sighing, she walked to her bookcase. She didn't want to read anything too dense. The lack of sleep, and all the crying, in the last twenty-four hours, not to mention the television she'd already watched, had left her eyes tired and scratchy. And yet, she needed to immerse herself in something or she'd drive herself crazy. She picked up Venus's book of poems and walked to her couch. Again, she encountered the number five. Again, she turned to that page. And again, she read the poem on the transience of a flower. But this time, the hair on her arms stood up as a new thought occurred to her. What if Venus had been pointing to a specific person with that scrawl? What if the five wasn't the point, rather, where it led was. What if the flower on page five was a reference to a person's name?

Lily. Lily D'Souza.

Could the maths teacher be involved in some way with Ms. Venus's death?

Radhi reached for her phone. She didn't know who it was she planned on calling or what she planned to say. It was more a mindless action, something to do with her hands while her mind tried to work out the implications of this new thought. As soon as she switched on her phone though, a flurry of pings filled the room. She scrolled through the messages from her sister who was checking on how she was doing without the alcohol, and from George, who was urging her to check her email. There wasn't a single message from Hrishi. But there was one from Shinde.

Met the lady who had the key. She says the key has been with her the whole time. Saw a photo in a frame at her place, which will interest you. Call me when you see this, pls.

Radhi cursed him for keeping her in suspense and dialled his number. But while waiting for him to pick up, she had a hunch.

'It's Ms. Lily, isn't it?' she asked, when he answered the phone.

'Uhm . . . yes, Mary, the woman who had the key, is Ms. Lily's mother.' He sounded irritated that she had guessed, but his curiosity got the better of him. 'How did you know?'

'I knew Lily and Ms. Venus were part of the same church and that Ms. Lily's parents live close by to her, so the chances were they probably go to the same church as well.'

She told him about Ms. Venus's scrawl. She didn't expect him to really appreciate it, but she didn't have Hrishi, and she really needed a sounding board, someone to tell her that she wasn't completely crazy. She also told him about how she had found Lily looking among Venus's things after her death.

'What if Venus's plan B was another article — something inflammatory against the school and Ms. Lily in particular, for asking students to leave because of their weak academic performance?' Radhi asked, voicing aloud the question that had been on the edge of her consciousness all this time. 'In fact, what if Venus threatened her with it? That would also explain why Lily didn't ask 'what article' when I mentioned that Ms. Venus had written one. She had probably been looking for it that day!'

Shinde waited until she was all talked out. Then he asked the question, she knew it would all boil down to eventually. 'All of this is possible, madam, but where is the proof?'

Radhi was quiet for a few moments then she said, 'What about fingerprints? If she went to Venus's apartment, there are bound to be prints, no?'

'But how do I collect them? The boss is certainly not going to give me permission.'

'Isn't there any other way? Something that will escape his radar?'

Shinde started to protest but Radhi changed tack. 'An officer with your kind of experience — surely, you must know how to do it offline. Or know of people who can help?'

'Of course, I do.' Shinde snapped. 'But it would be such a risk.'

'But what if you did find something? Can you imagine the rewards?'

Radhi stayed on the phone for a few more minutes, until she had convinced the inspector to get the fingerprints. But she knew that even if he did get a match, it would be incomplete without the article to support it.

What was in that article? she asked herself, for what was probably for the nth time that night.

* * *

Tuesday

Radhi spent the next day in school, her head low, but eyes and ears open for anything that would give her some inkling about why Venus had been murdered. So far, she had suspected Kamble, Savant and Lily in turn. Each of them seemed to have a plausible motive and yet, there was nothing to tie any of them down to anything. Even Mrs. Mehta, who had messaged her to say that they had brought their son home, had not responded to Radhi's request that she be allowed to talk to her son. Radhi had grown increasingly frustrated as the day progressed, until Shinde had called in the second half of the day with the information she'd been waiting for. She'd hung up with him, dialled Lily's number

225

almost immediately and asked her if she could drop by her home that evening.

Lily opened the door in a long maxi dress. Her daughter was doing her homework at the dining table. She said hello to Radhi before taking her books inside.

'So?' said Lily with a curious smile, when they were seated across from each other.

Radhi hadn't told her why she needed to speak with her, just that she needed to do it in private. Now, she took a deep breath and plunged in.

'Ms. Lily, there's no easy way to ask this — so I am going to come right out and say it. Okay?'

Lily's smile faltered. 'Yes . . . please do. I would appreciate directness.'

'Ms. Lily, did you go to Ms. Venus's apartment after her death?'

The shock on Lily's face was impossible to mistake for anything else. Whatever it was that she had expected from this conversation, it wasn't this. Her eyes widened and the colour drained from her cheeks.

'I . . . I . . . no, of course not. Why would I? What made you say that?'

Radhi stayed quiet, giving her a chance to speak the truth. But Ms. Lily just sat there, her fingers digging into the arms of her chair.

'You've never gone to her house?'

Ms. Lily blinked. 'No . . . I didn't say that . . . I went once, a few years ago for a church meeting.'

'How, then, can you explain why the police have found your fingerprints all around the place?'

Lily stared at her mute. She'd begun to sweat freely despite the fan overhead on full speed. She opened her mouth to speak a few times, but no sound came out.

'I needed some paperwork . . . for the church,' she managed, finally. 'I know I shouldn't have gone into her house like that . . . but I . . . I didn't see any harm.'

'You were there for the article, Ms. Lily.' Radhi countered. 'Can we please just be honest with each other?'

Lily jerked back as if she'd been slapped. 'I don't know what article you're talking about.' She stood up. 'And I don't appreciate you coming here and making baseless allegations. Now, if you'll excuse me, I have to help my daughter with her homework.'

Radhi stood up slowly. Her eyes not leaving Lily's face.

'I think you're lying, Ms. Lily. I think Ms. Venus wrote an article, which contains something you don't want people to know.'

'You don't know what you're talking about.'

'But I'm going to find out.'

'Why? Why are you doing this?' Lily asked in a hoarse whisper.

'For Ms. Venus,' Radhi said.

'But what does it matter? She's dead.'

'Dead or murdered?'

The last thing Radhi saw as Lily shut the door in her face, was how petrified the maths teacher seemed.

* * *

Lily sat back down on the sofa, shell-shocked after Radhi had gone. If this were a clean, hard, algebra problem, her mind could examine all the variables before coming up with the right solution. But life wasn't maths. The sum total of different things didn't always add up to the whole. For the life of her, Lily couldn't fathom how things had gone so awfully wrong, and the terrible part she had played in them. With a shaking hand, Lily reached for her phone.

* * *

Radhi had just reorganized her bookshelf. Now she was desperately looking for something else to keep her busy and her mind off her parched throat. All her usual pastimes, books, jigsaw puzzles and crosswords, required her to stay still and concentrate, which she was finding hard to do. She could have cooked or baked, but she found she wanted to avoid the sight of food. She needed something that would keep her physically busy and tire her out, like cleaning, but the kitchen, as usual, was spic and span thanks to Lila's attentions, as was the study. She made her way to her own bedroom and shut the door — putting more distance between herself and the mango wood drinks cabinet.

She opened her wardrobe and stood in front of it, hands on waist. She hadn't much paid attention to it ever since she'd moved to India and first set it up. Now she began to rifle through the drawers where she kept all her jewellery. Starting with the one that held her gold pieces, which she wore only for weddings and other family functions, and then the one with her silver jewellery, which she was always more drawn to and tended to wear in the day to day. Her silver earrings collection was her one true indulgence. Unlike the gold, which she'd mostly inherited from her mother and received in marriage from her ex-husband, the silver collection was what she had built for herself over the years, picking up danglers and studs and hoops in the shape of peacocks and parrots and lotuses from her travels across the world.

Radhi worked methodically for almost two hours. Moving to Indian formal wear after she was done with the jewellery, sorting through sarees and blouses and kurtas and anything else she could lay her hands on, Sighing, she dragged one of the armchairs in her room close to her wardrobe and climbed up, ready to attack the shelves which stored her party bags and clutches, next. But no sooner had she raised her arm, she put it back down and swore under her breath. An image of Lily with her arm raised came to her mind, instantly taking her back to the evening at Lily's house when the maths teacher had gone to the kitchen to make tea for them. She'd had to go on her toes and extend her hand for the sugar canister which was two shelves above the tea leaves and the cardamom pods.

And Radhi remembered finding it odd then but hadn't quite figured why, until now. Now she wondered why something as basic and staple as sugar had been placed on an inconvenient high shelf instead of with the tea and cardamom, when all three ingredients would go into the boiling water for the tea together. It made no sense when it came to how kitchens were usually organized. Especially, for someone as precise and methodical as Lily.

The only explanation Radhi could think of was that the maths teacher hadn't placed it there. Someone else had. Someone who was familiar enough to make tea in that kitchen — and who was at least six feet tall.

Radhi didn't sleep that night. It had been right in front of her throughout. She was amazed that she hadn't seen it.

CHAPTER 25

Wednesday

Mr. Bakshi sat opposite Radhi, a wary expression on his face. They were at a café near the school where Radhi had requested that they meet during the school lunch hour. With his arms folded across his chest, he seemed guarded. As if he already knew that he wasn't going to like what she had to say.

'I'll be straight with you, Mr. Bakshi,' Radhi began without preamble, feeling acutely that the time for niceties had passed. 'A student saw you meet with Ms. Venus on the day she died. But when I asked you about it, you lied. May I ask why?'

Mr. Bakshi frowned. The two of them had always been friendly, but now when he spoke there was an unpleasant edge to his voice. 'Honestly, Ms. Zaveri. I don't see how that's any business of yours.'

'Would you rather answer the police?' Radhi asked, evenly.

'It was a personal matter — what does it have to do with Venus's death?'

'That's what I'm trying to find out. So? Are you going to tell me, or do you prefer Shinde?' Radhi held up her phone. 'He's just a call away.'

Radhi had expected Mr. Bakshi to cooperate at the mention of the police, but the chemistry teacher turned out to be made of sterner stuff. He leaned back on his seat and regarded her coolly. 'I don't intend on telling the police anything either. Not unless there's something they want to charge me with.'

Radhi watched the stubborn set of Bakshi's mouth. She changed tack.

'You're having an affair with Ms. Lily, aren't you?'

Bakshi had been drumming his fingers on the table. Now, his hand froze.

'Says who? Don't tell me you're going by some stupid bathroom graffiti.'

'I haven't seen any graffiti, but I've seen other stuff.'

'Oh yeah?' Bakshi challenged.

'Like how you get Italian food in your tiffin the morning after Ms. Lily's been to an Italian restaurant for dinner, or the way your shirts are laundered at the Sun laundry which is right below Ms. Lily's house but nowhere close to where you stay.'

Mr. Bakshi straightened up. 'What the hell are you talking about?'

'Ms. Venus saw you two together, near Ms. Lily's house ... didn't she? And she threatened to tell the school authorities?'

This last part had been guesswork. But from the confusion, anger and fear that danced on his face, Radhi was sure she was on to something. She pressed on.

'Teachers aren't allowed to date. If Venus told everyone, it would be a scandal because you're married. Not to mention the affair you were accused of in the past. I doubt your career would have survived another such accusation, isn't it?'

Radhi waited, half expecting the chemistry teacher to protest but he remained quiet, watching her intently.

'That's what you went to talk to Ms. Venus about, isn't it? And when she didn't listen — because she's Venus — what did you do?'

'I didn't have to do anything!' said Mr. Bakshi. 'She died, didn't she?'

With this statement, Mr. Bakshi had finally lost his cool and given away more than he intended to. He stared at Radhi, realizing with what seemed to be a growing sense of horror, that he'd just admitted to the affair.'

'Did she just die, though?' asked Radhi quietly.

The chemistry teacher went very still. 'What are you saying, exactly?'

'It was cyanide poisoning. It just looked like heart failure.'

Mr. Bakshi stared at her for a long moment and then he stood up.

'Do you actually have proof for any of this, Ms. Zaveri? Because otherwise, this is beginning to sound like one of your creative writing exercises.'

When Radhi didn't answer, he gave her a curt nod. 'I thought not. Goodbye, Ms. Zaveri.'

As Radhi watched him walk out of the café, two things were clear to her. The first was that Mr. Bakshi was right. Without concrete proof, none of this would add up to anything. And second, that when it came to procuring cyanide, there couldn't be anyone with easier access to a lab than a chemistry teacher.

* * *

Mr. Bakshi walked out of the café, his heart hammering inside his chest. He'd never been this afraid in his life. When Lily had called him about that woman, he hadn't realized just how deep into it she was. She only needed to breathe a word about this to Fernandes and everything would be finished. His job and his marriage, both exploding and disintegrating, as if in an experiment gone horribly wrong. Inside his pocket, he let his key dig deep into his palm, the pain doing little to distract him from his troubles. First Venus and now this woman, would he never be able to rid his life of busybodies? He had reached the school but didn't enter. Instead, he took a turn and walked away. Needing to think.

* * *

Radhi had put her phone on silent during her conversation with Mr. Bakshi. She checked it now and was alarmed to find three missed calls from Shinde.

'Finally, you've found the time to call me back!' Shinde said as soon as he answered the phone. His voice sounded high-pitched and unnatural.

'What's happened?'

'What I most feared! They know. *He* knows! And now I am in deep shit! What are we goi—'

'Inspector . . . Inspector, please,' Radhi interrupted him. 'Calm down for a moment. I don't understand.'

Shinde paused and began again. 'My station manager knows that I've been investigating this case behind his back. Somehow, he found out about the fingerprints and now he says he'll have to take action against me for insubordination.'

'How did he find—'

'I don't know, okay?! It's not important. What's important is that I am screwed. My promotion has gone out of the window. And now I need to worry about my job! Which means you have to worry about it!'

'Let me think about this for a minute, will you?'

'The time for thinking has gone, madam! Now it's time to act. I've been listening to all your theories. Now, we need some proof. Or poof! I'm done for. And remember your close friend from the paper? The editor? Now is the time for him to materialize. He needs to come here asking questions and putting pressure on the higher-ups or I will lose my job!'

Shinde went on in the same vein for a few minutes more, and it was with some effort that Radhi calmed him down enough to get off the phone. She was sweating by the time she finished the short walk from the café to the school and knew that it was due only partly to the April heat. She couldn't get Hrishi involved, not when he hadn't responded to any of her messages. But she would find a way to prove that there had been foul play even if it killed her.

* * *

'Ms. Zaveri?'

Radhi looked up to see Satish Kamble pause at the door of the English Department, before entering. She shut the diary she had been writing in and put it away. All her notes on Savant and Wagle and Kamble himself were in there and the last thing she needed was for it to fall into the wrong hands.

'Can we talk for a minute, please?' Satish Kamble folded his hands across his chest and leaned against one of the walls.

Radhi had chosen to spend her free time in the English Department because being in the staffroom with Ms. Lily or Mr. Bakshi after their recent confrontation would've been uncomfortable, to say the least. But judging from the expression on Kamble's face, this conversation didn't seem like it was going to be pleasant, either. She took a deep breath and braced herself.

'It's been brought to my attention that you've approached the police saying that Ms. Venus died of foul play?'

Radhi cursed Shinde for having dragged her name in, but she couldn't blame the man. He would have had to justify his actions in some way.

'I have,' she said.

'Would you like to tell me about it?' Kamble asked, icily.

In a few words, Radhi told him about how Venus's symptoms were consistent with cyanide poisoning and how one of her coffee cups had gone missing.

Kamble was quiet for a whole minute before he spoke. 'So, you think someone murdered her?'

'Yes.'

'Who?'

'I don't know yet.'

Kamble shook his head. 'Ms. Zaveri, this is sounding too far-fetched, even for a writer of fiction. This is a school, filled with educators and kids, not murderers.'

'Educators have been known to break the law, you know. Ask your father, if you don't believe me.'

Kamble's eyes narrowed. 'What's my father got to do with this?'

'He built a private school on land meant for a public educational institute. He made millions in school fees when this was supposed to be not-for-profit for underprivileged children. That's a felony right there,' Radhi said.

Kamble left the wall and came closer, to stand with his hands on her desk. Looming over her. 'My father has given this city a wonderful educational institute which benefits hundreds of students every year. North Star is the topmost school in the country. And sometimes, if we need to work around our outdated laws and policies, then so be it. There are worse crimes than that.'

'So, the benefit to your bank balance is just incidental, is it?'

'People pay because it's a good school. We work hard to make it one.' Kamble spat each word out separately. 'You didn't seem to have a problem with it when you wrangled an admission letter for your niece, if I remember correctly.'

'That's before I knew about the murder.'

'Just because we broke the law once, doesn't mean we are murderers, Ms. Zaveri.' Kamble left Radhi's desk to pace around the room. 'By raising these questions and making these risky accusations you are dangerously close to ruining the reputation my father has worked so hard to build!'

'Is that what Ms. Venus had also threatened to do? Is that what got her killed?'

Kamble turned to her furiously. 'How dare you?'

'I know about how your lease is up for renewal. And why you need Wagle,' Radhi said quietly. 'Venus was threatening to make things very difficult with Wagle, isn't it?'

For the first time since he had entered the room, Kamble's face registered something other than anger.

'How could you kno—' he sputtered to a stop. Then he took a deep breath and gathered himself. 'Please don't come back to this school tomorrow onwards.'

As Radhi watched Kamble leave, it was fast coming home to her that she had dug a very deep hole for herself. In the last twenty-four hours, she had made many enemies, and twice as many accusations. And despite all the ugly confrontations, she was no closer to the truth than when she had started out. Lily, Bakshi, Mr. Mehta, Kamble, Savant, all of them seemed to have a motive to kill Venus, but all of them couldn't have done it. So, who had?

Radhi wished she could have a smoke. It would clear her mind and help her make sense of this gargantuan mess. She checked her phone. There was still nothing from Hrishi or Mrs. Mehta. But there were dozens of messages from Shinde, all in the previous vein. She was to help him get out of this mess she had buried him under. Radhi brought out a cigarette and rolled it between her fingers, drawing some comfort from its familiar shape and smell. She wished there was somewhere on the school campus she could grab a quick smoke. After her conversation with Kamble, she was suddenly afraid that if she left the school grounds, the security might not let her back in. Hadn't Soam and Brij gone to vape in an old bio lab when Venus caught them? She got out of her chair and walked out of the room, stopping only to get directions from one of the students, who pointed her towards the staircase. The bio lab was on the top floor.

Radhi made her way up, her cigarette and lighter clutched tightly in her palm. But as she reached the topmost floor, all thought of smoking suddenly evaporated from her mind, replaced by a terrible, urgent, new question — which became all the more concrete, when Radhi entered the dusty old lab at the very end of the corridor and took in its state of disuse.

What had Venus, Head of the English Department, come to do in a biology lab? The two classrooms beside it also seemed latched and abandoned. What business then did Venus have to be on this floor, and in this room? Radhi could think of only one.

CHAPTER 26

Radhi entered the biology lab and looked around, taking in the old, human skeleton in the glass case, the rusty microscopes, the peeling, grey charts of human organs illustrated in graphic detail and the jars and bottles of dead insects floating in formaldehyde that lined the shelves of the wooden cabinets on both walls. And then, she began to hunt. A hunt, which took shockingly little time. Because no sooner had she started did she find a bundle of papers with Venus's distinct scrawl inside one of the drawers of the teacher's desk. Quickly, she went through them to arrive at a sheet of paper with a headline, subhead and date. It was the article she had been looking for, the one Venus had planned on submitting to the *Gazette*. Only, it wasn't written by her.

* * *

When Radhi had read it, she sat there for a long while, working out what to do. Then with a deep breath and a prayer, she went to meet Soam Mehta. If there was anyone who had seen something, it was him.

* * *

Mrs. Mehta didn't seem happy to see Radhi, but she let her in without a fuss.

'I'm sorry I haven't responded to your messages. It's just been a lot for our family,' she explained, as she offered her some water. 'We just needed some alone time together.'

She went out of the room to get Soam, who came out a few moments later, followed by his father. Radhi would have preferred to speak to the boy alone, but his parents flanked him on either side of the couch and looked like they had no intention of going anywhere.

Soam seemed embarrassed about the fuss he had caused and spoke haltingly about why he'd run away. He admitted that he'd gone up to the English Department to deface Venus's prized poster and had hidden outside for a long time, waiting for the room to clear out. But without any luck. Someone or the other always seemed to be in. Finally, he'd seen his father go in and had heard a terrible row ensue. Voices were raised and threats were made. And at one point, Soam had seen Mr. Mehta fling a paperweight from Ms. Venus's desk on to the floor.

'That's when I left,' Soam said, looking at his father. 'I got scared seeing how angry you were.'

Mr. Mehta winced but held his tongue, and Mrs. Mehta took up the story, 'Then the next day, when we received the news of Ms. Venus passing away from heart failure, Soam began to worry that maybe his father had had something to do with it.'

Mr. Mehta shifted uncomfortably in his seat and looked at his hands.

'Soam was scared about what would happen if some-one found out about his father's visit and felt like he was somehow responsible for the mess,' Mrs. Mehta continued, rubbing her son's arm gently as she spoke. 'And instead of coming and talking to me about it, he decided to run away.'

Soam shook his head. 'I'm sorry, Mama, I wasn't think-ing straight. I thought if I could just go away for a few days, I could figure what to do.'

'There was nothing to be done! She didn't get a heart attack just because I went there and made some noi—' Mr. Mehta began to speak, but his wife silenced him with a sharp look.

'I think you've done enough already.' She turned to Radhi. 'So, you see, this was all just a big misunderstanding. My son didn't do anything wrong, even though he'd gone up to make mischief. And my husband—' She looked at him and then back. 'He has agreed to take a backseat when it comes to the remainder of Soam's schooling.'

Radhi had heard the whole story without interrupting them. The boy seemed to be telling the truth and for once, Mr. Mehta seemed embarrassed by his role in the entire affair. She finally asked Soam the one question which she hoped would help her solve the whole thing.

'When you were hiding outside, did Ms. Venus leave the room for anything?'

The boy appeared to think for a moment, then he nodded.

'And was anyone in there, during that time?'

The boy nodded again.

* * *

Back in her car, after leaving the Mehtas' home, Radhi sent out four messages. One to Fernandes, another to Kamble, a third to Shinde, and finally, one to Hrishi. He deserved to know. Then she went back home to wait. Now, she had the proof Kamble had mocked her about, but there was much she needed to think through. And she needed to speak to Kia and the Lit Kids. There were some questions she had for them.

Two hours later, in the late evening, when all students and teachers had left for the day, she instructed Ramzan bhai to take her back to North Star. She carried Ms. Venus's book of poems with her.

CHAPTER 27

Ms. Fernandes was eating a blueberry cheesecake when Radhi walked into her office.

'My one true indulgence.' She smiled at Radhi as her visitor took a seat across from her. 'I thought I deserved a little celebratory treat, today. You and I, both, from what I gather.'

When Radhi looked at her blankly, she clarified, 'I hear, you were very instrumental in bringing Soam Mehta home.'

'Oh that.' Radhi smiled back.

'Yes, I must say, thank you. I can't even begin to describe what a relief it was to hear from the Mehtas today.' Fernandes removed a slice of cake from a box beside her, placed it on a plate and slid it towards Radhi. 'Here, have some. With all the hullabaloo over that boy's disappearance, my BP had shot up so much!' Fernandes shook her head as if she couldn't believe it was over. 'I think I'll finally be able to sleep tonight.'

She took another spoonful of her cake. 'Go on, take a bite. It's delicious.'

She waited until Radhi had eaten some.

'An old Parsi lady in my building makes it. I used to bring a few slices home every Saturday. But not anymore. Now, I need to worry about my sugar.'

'It's delicious,' Radhi said, eating distractedly, her mind already on the conversation that lay ahead.

'So, tell me, what is it you wanted to see me about?' Fernandes asked, but then she raised her hand. 'Oh, but before I forget, I wanted to know if you've considered our job offer? Satish may not have gone about it the right way, but the more I think about it, the more I feel you will make a fantastic teacher.'

It took Radhi a moment to remember what Fernandes was talking about, and then she almost giggled at the absurdity of the request, given the number of enemies she'd made at the school, in the last two days.

'Not yet. Sorry, I've been a bit preoccupied.' She took two more bites of the cake and pushed her plate aside. From inside her bag, she removed a copy of the article she had found in the old bio lab and slid it towards the principal.

'Please read it,' she said, when Fernandes glanced at her quizzically.

As the principal read, the expression on her face remained unnaturally neutral. When she raised her eyes though, something dangerous flickered in there. 'It's utter rubbish, of course. The ramblings of a disturbed child. Where did you find it?'

Radhi ignored her question. 'Is it, though? This is the girl whose sister committed suicide last year, isn't it? I think it is very pointed and precise. Her sister was depressed after she was asked to leave the school. Her suicide was a direct result of that. She blames the school, its intense academic pressures and in particular, the obsession with high maths scores. That's it.' Radhi leaned back and folded her arms across her chest. 'It can't get any clearer than that.'

Fernandes rolled her eyes at that. 'Haven't you understood anything from this whole Soam Mehta incident? When things go wrong, people always need someone to blame. That's how they cope. That's how they survive.'

'In this case, though, the blame seems to have been placed at the right feet, no?' Radhi countered. 'This kid had difficulty with math, she worried obsessively about her grades and, when she couldn't cope, Ms. Lily asked her to leave the school. The child couldn't accept it and went into depression.

'At first, I thought it was all Ms. Lily's fault, but that couldn't be right. She doesn't have that kind of power. Neither to take such a critical decision, nor to stay on after such disastrous results. No, it had to be someone higher up. Someone who is obsessed with how the school performs because their sense of self is so inextricably tied to it. You are the one who has been pressurizing Ms. Lily to ensure that every batch gets the best maths grades.'

Fernandes put her fork down and cleaned her mouth carefully with tissue paper before speaking again. 'I told Venus also, when she came to me rambling about this, that it was best to stay out of it. We've done this every year. Asked the runt of the litter to leave if they couldn't keep up. I have worked so hard to raise this school to the position it is at. I won't have some stupid tragedy bring it down like that.'

'But she didn't listen, did she?'

'Fool that she was, she threatened to have this published in a national newspaper!' Fernandes snarled. 'Can you imagine? Her pig-headedness would've have ruined everything. The reputation of this school. Its future. Not to mention, my legacy. This is all people would've remembered me for. Because I'll tell you one more thing about the masses. They have piddly, goldfish memories. Those parents you see swarming around me at school events? They would've fixated on this one unfortunate thing and entirely forgotten everything else I've done for this school.'

'So . . . you poisoned her?' Radhi said, loosening the top button of her shirt, and rifling in her bag for her bottle of water. Her mouth suddenly felt very dry.

Fernandes smirked at that. 'I was half afraid, but half expecting you to arrive at this. When Kamble came to me to tell me what a raving lunatic you were. How you were insisting that Venus hadn't died of natural causes, I wanted to tell him that you were always one of my smartest students. I knew then that you'd piece it together eventually.'

Fernandes got up and began pacing the room. 'So, what gave it away?'

Radhi rubbed her temples and took another sip of water. Her head felt heavy, and she sensed the beginning of a headache. Instead of answering the principal, she brought out Venus's book of poems and opened it to the front page.

'Ms. Venus knew, you know? While she was dying, she realized what you had done.'

Fernandes peered at the shaky '5' and frowned, not understanding.

Radhi turned to the fifth page of the book and pointed to the title. 'She was trying to point us to a 'Flower'. She was probably scared that if she wrote your name and you found the book on her desk, you'd take it. So, she had to leave a clue. Something, not immediately obvious. At first, I didn't understand. Then I thought it was Ms. Lily, until I finally remembered you. Rose Fernandes.'

Fernandes scoffed. 'English teachers and their word games. Is that all you have? What about how I did it?' Now that the truth was out in the open, Fernandes seemed almost proud of what she'd almost got away with.

'You crushed apricot seeds into her coffee powder.'

Fernandes gaped at her for a moment. 'That's good, very good,' she said slowly. 'And how did you arrive at that?' She seemed to think she was Radhi's maths teacher again and wanted to know if her student had arrived at the solution by the proper method.

Radhi took a few more sips from her bottle, somehow no amount of water seemed to be helping. The dryness in her mouth had now moved to her throat.

'I knew it was cyanide poisoning. All her symptoms were consistent with that. But who had access to cyanide? It's not like one can go into a chemist and buy some. You can either make it in a lab or extract it from plants. Apple seeds and apricot seeds both contain cyanide.'

243

Fernandes was nodding. As if encouraging Radhi to follow that train of thought.

Radhi rubbed the spot between her eyes which had begun to throb. 'I remembered seeing apricot plants in the school garden on the day of the Garden Fest. And I know how knowledgeable you are about plants and gardening. All you had to do is crush some seeds and add it to something with a stronger taste. Ms. Venus's penchant for her coffee was well known. You just needed to add it to her ground beans and then go back and take the cup and replace the beans.'

Fernandes gave a little clap. 'Well done.'

'I wish I could say the same about you,' Radhi said. 'How could you have just killed her?'

Fernandes scowled at that. 'What did you expect me to do? Let her go ahead and ruin something that's taken a lifetime to build?' She shook her head. 'There are consequences to everything. Even godforsaken idealism. However well-intentioned it is. Hundreds of students go to school here. Scores of teachers depend on it for their livelihoods. Do you think this school would have survived a scandal like this? We would've become a laughingstock. *I* would've become a laughing stock.'

'It was always about you and your pride, wasn't it?' Radhi opened and closed her eyes, she could see Fernandes in front of her, but her features had lost their clarity.

'Until you give your whole life to something, don't come and judge me,' Fernandes said, then she bit her lip. 'Of course, you may never have the opportunity now.'

'What?' Radhi asked, the light in the room was hurting her eyes, and her vision had become even blurrier. 'What did you say?'

Fernandes got up, slid out from behind her desk and walked towards the door of her office. She locked it and then turned to face Radhi, her arms folded across her chest.

'I'm sorry, Radhika. Despite your cleverness, you would've been wise to remember that you were my student, and I was your teacher. Always a step ahead of you. With all the research you seemed to have done on poisons, did

Belladonna ever come up? Its berries are deadly. Your blue-berry pie wasn't blueberry at all. Mine, of course, was the regular variety. When Kamble called me to tell me about your little chat with him, I knew it was only a matter of time before you were on to me. And I'm nothing, if not prepared. By the time we finish our chat here, you will be beyond help.'

It took Radhi a moment to process what the principal was saying. But by then she'd lost her capacity to focus. Her face felt hot and flushed. And her heart was beating fast. Too fast. She tried to stand but all strength seemed to have left her body. 'So will you,' was all she managed.

'What's that?' Fernandes asked.

But before Radhi could repeat her words, she had lost consciousness.

* * *

The first thing Radhi smelled when she woke up was a com-bination of lavender mingled with antiseptic. She stirred and winced at the tug of the IV tube in her hand.

'Radhi! Oh, thank God! Thank God!' Madhavi's wor-ried face loomed over for a moment before she disappeared and reappeared a few moments later with a nurse.

As the nurse checked Radhi's vitals and fiddled with the knobs and tubes, Radhi tried to get her bearings. Her head felt heavy and foggy, and it was a moment before her conversation with Fernandes came back to her.

'Didi,' she called to Madhavi and tried to get up.

'Shh!' Madhavi said. 'Stay still for a minute.'

When the nurse had ascertained that everything was as it should be, and given her a few sips of water, she pressed the lever on the side of Radhi's bed so that it rolled up halfway into a semi-reclining position.

'Didi, what happened? At the school?' Radhi asked, her voice weak and hoarse and entirely unlike her own.

Madhavi didn't answer her. Her clothes were rumpled, her hair mussed, and she looked like she hadn't slept all night. She bent down to kiss Radhi on her forehead. 'I will kill you if you ever try to die on me again. Okay?'

Radhi tried to chuckle, but her throat hurt. 'It was Fernandes . . . who . . . who did it.'

'Yes, yes, we know. The police have taken her. And I'll tell you everything that happened. But first, you need to meet someone.'

Madhavi disappeared again and this time in her place Hrishi entered the room.

He stood at a distance, unshaven, shirt untucked, hair standing, a haunted expression on his face.

'I'm not contagious, you know.' Radhi smiled weakly.

He took a step towards her and then another. 'Thank you,' he whispered, his eyes not leaving her face.

'Uhm . . . I think the words you might be looking for are "Get well soon"?'

He smiled at that. 'Thank you for not dying. Not now . . . not after . . . not after everything that happened. I don't know what I'd have done.'

Radhi tried to respond but he shushed her with a gentle finger to her lips. 'There's plenty of time to talk about all of that. But first the police need to talk to you.'

Radhi leaned back on her pillow and closed her eyes, gathering her strength for the conversation that lay ahead.

'Has someone told you, I saved your life?' Shinde said, swaggering into the room a few minutes later, a constable in tow. 'The doctors said if we had come even ten minutes later, they couldn't guarantee the outcome.'

Radhi smiled weakly at him. 'Hello, Inspector.'

'It's going to be Additional Director General of Police, soon.' He twirled his moustache.

'Congratulations,' Radhi said. 'I'm glad you saw my message, in time.'

'Oh yes. I had to bully the guards to let me into the school. But when we came to Fernandes' office, it was locked. We knocked and banged and called out, but she didn't answer. And I almost began to think that no one was in there. But then, luckily, that Satish Kamble showed up.'

Radhi nodded. 'I had asked him to. As backup.'

Shinde pulled a chair and sat down with a humph. 'You don't trust me, still. After I almost lost my job because of you.'

Radhi didn't have the energy to argue.

'Anyways, he located a set of master keys, and we used one of them to enter her office. You were sprawled on the floor, dead to the world, and you won't believe what she was doing.'

'What?'

'Watering all the plants in her office. She looked a bit mental.'

Radhi was silent for a while as she thought about her last conversation with the principal. 'What did she plan to do with my body after I was dead?' Radhi asked after a few minutes.

'She had told the school gardener to dig a long pit in the garden for some new plants. We think she planned to drag you there that night and bury you. And then plant some saplings over the patch.'

The inspector motioned for the constable to step forward. 'We need to take a statement. Can you tell us what happened when you went to meet her?'

Radhi shuddered thinking about how cold and remorseless Fernandes had seemed at the end. Slowly, in some detail, she took Shinde through her conversation with the principal. 'I have the original article at home. I got the kid's number, the one who wrote the article, from some students at school. Ms. Venus had convinced her parents to publish it finally, so that it could help other students.'

Radhi leaned back again, feeling drained. Madhavi who had been hovering at the door, came in and looked pointedly at the inspector who took the hint.

'Just one last thing,' he said, getting up. 'We have enough on Fernandes to keep her locked up on attempted murder charges. But what about the proof for Venus's murder? Even if she confessed to you, we'll probably need more in court.'

'Inspector, please can we do this tomorrow?' Madhavi protested.

'It's fine, Didi,' Radhi said, then she turned towards the inspector. 'Soam Mehta. He saw her fiddling with the coffee machine when Venus was out of the room. He didn't realize what she was doing, at the time.'

Shinde nodded and was about to leave when Radhi said, 'Check Fernandes's home for Venus's missing mug. It won't be in her kitchen. Check the windowsills. If she hasn't thrown it away, she probably planted something in it.' Shinde nodded again, this time his smile held something that looked very much like respect.

* * *

The next morning Radhi woke up to find Hrishi in her hospital room. He was reading a book when she came to. She didn't call out to him immediately, choosing instead to study his profile. His face seemed tired, careworn, and there were bags under his eyes from lack of sleep. She wondered if he'd been here all the hours that she'd been asleep and what his wife thought of that. Her throat hurt and her mouth was parched for water, but other than that she felt much stronger than before. As she shifted and tried to raise herself, the movement attracted Hrishi's attention, and his face lit up.

'Do you need something?' He came to stand beside her as she pressed the lever beside her bed to sit up. 'Should I call the nurse?'

'Just water, please,' Radhi said.

Hrishi poured water from a bottle into a cup with a straw. 'They're most likely going to discharge you day after,' he said, as she drank deeply, even though the water hurt her throat.

When she was settled again, he dragged his chair closer to her bed and sat facing her.

248

'Listen, I'm so, so sorry that I didn't respond to your messages. I was being a jerk — you didn't deserve tha—'

'No, you were hurt, I understand . . .'

Hrishi shook his head gently to silence her. 'Don't make excuses for me, Radhi. I cheated on my wife, was furious and disgusted with myself and projected it on you. Truth is, I had no business walking out on you like that. Not when I showed up at your house in the middle of the night, knowing very well where it might lead. Not when being with you was the most healing, exhilarating experience of my life.'

He paused, took her hand in his and held her gaze intently. Radhi felt her face grow warm, but before she could say anything, a nurse came in to check on her and give her her medication.

When she had left, Radhi said, 'I didn't mean what I said that day, that it was just a night. It was . . .' She faltered and sighed. 'It was so, so much more than that.'

'I know,' Hrishi said. 'I think I knew it even then, when you were saying it. But it was just so much easier to believe your words and stomp out of there. So much easier to go back to my marriage.'

At the mention of his marriage, he looked down as if he was struggling with something. The silence stretched, but this time, Radhi didn't hurry to fill it up. She waited until he continued.

'It was easier to go back . . . but harder to stay. My heart just wasn't in it. And, if I'm being honest, hasn't been in it for a long time now. I was trying hard to make it work for Anoushka's sake, but I realize now that I wasn't being fair to Neha. I was holding back on us, and she sensed it. And when she challenged me about it, I resented it. But the truth was, she was right, all along. I was just not as invested as her.'

'Did you tell her? About us?' Radhi asked slowly as she finally realized what Hrishi was saying and felt a sudden, unexpected, crushing guilt.

Hrishi shook his head. 'When I told her that I wanted out, I didn't want you to be the reason. Neha and I have other problems which have nothing to do with you. And I wanted to make sure she saw those clearly. But I will . . . I have to.'

Radhi remained quiet. She had finally encountered the guilt that had eluded her after the night she'd spent with Hrishi. At the time, it had been shunted by how badly she had wanted him and how right it had felt. But now it presented itself to her in the harsh light of day, unmistakable for anything else. She'd lived with guilt before, had let it seep into every part of her life and mark every bright day of her existence. But this time, she sensed a change within her. A shift, tectonic in nature, slight but forceful, that offered to obstruct the guilt from marring her days. Urging her to give herself a fair shot at happiness, for once in her life.

Hrishi got up from his chair and began to pace the room. 'I am going to need some time to sort out my life. But when things are more settled, can we explore this . . . this thing between us and see if it's real?'

When Radhi didn't answer immediately, Hrishi said, 'I know I have no right to ask you to wait . . . but I can't bear to think that we were this close, and we didn't find out.'

* * *

Lily hesitated at the door of Radhi's hospital room, the next morning, seeming nervous and entirely unlike her usual, poised self.

Radhi, who was feeling significantly better, smiled at her, encouraging her to come in.

'Sorry, I wasn't sure if I . . . if I . . . if you'd be feeling up to it . . .' she said, as she took a seat beside Radhi's hospital bed and lapsed into silence.

'I'm glad you've come.' Radhi took a sip of her water, giving the maths teacher an opportunity to collect herself.

'I feel I owe you an apology . . .' Lily said, after a few minutes. 'For failing to do the math.' She tucked a stray strand of hair behind her ear and swallowed. 'I suppose I was just really distracted by Ms. Venus's interference in my relationship with Mr. Bakshi. And just so relieved when she passed that I completely failed to see all the signs that had added up to her death.

'I've really struggled with my role in Rashi's suicide. But I told myself I was just following Ms. Fernandes's orders. That surely there had to be other factors contributing to that child's depression . . .' Lily ran a hand over her face. 'I have a daughter myself. The thought of what those parents must have gone through still keeps me up at night.' She looked Radhi in the eye, 'I really didn't want to ask Kia to leave. But Ms. Fernandes said that we couldn't let one incident derail how we've always done things at North Star.'

Lily got up and began pacing the room. 'When Ms. Venus told me about the article, I was secretly relieved. I thought surely Ms. Fernandes would relent now and Kia would be able to stay. But then Ms. Venus passed. And the whole situation just resolved itself. Both the article and my relationship with Mr. Bakshi were safe. I couldn't believe how lucky I had been.' Lily shook her head and came back to take a seat next to Radhi. 'Had I just done the math, I would've realized that the probability of something like this happening was next to nil! That something was off.' She clutched the edges of Radhi's hospital bed. 'But you have to believe me when I say that not for a moment did I suspect that Ms. Venus was murdered, let alone that Ms. Fernandes had something to do with it!'

'I believe you,' said Radhi, 'I know how much you respected Fernandes. Your mind wouldn't go there.'

'Thank you,' Ms. Lily whispered, her eyes watering up. She got up to leave but at the door she turned. 'Mr. Bakshi couldn't make it . . . but he sends his regards.'

Radhi smiled and nodded. She knew that last part was a lie, but she couldn't blame Mr. Bakshi for not wanting to see her. Their last conversation had been far too unpleasant, and perhaps it rankled even more, because they had been friends.'

Radhi didn't have much time to dwell on it because soon after Ms. Lily's departure there was another knock on her door and Satish Kamble walked in with a huge bouquet of flowers.

* * *

'What is this?' Madhavi put down the cup of tea in her hand to pick up the North Star envelope that Radhi had just placed in front of her.

They were at Radhi's house, a few days after her discharge from the hospital, and Lila had just served them their afternoon tea with masala sandwiches stuffed with a spicy potato filling. Radhi flashed her sister a mysterious smile as she began to open it.

'What? When — I mean *how* did you get this?!' Madhavi asked in a rush after she'd read the contents of the early admissions letter and registered what it meant.

After Radhi had told her about her deal with Kamble, Madhavi asked, 'And he's still going to honour this? After everything that's happened?'

'Yep. It's all part of the agreement we've reached.'

Madhavi looked at her expectantly and she elaborated. 'You know that article about the girl who committed suicide which Venus had planned on publishing?'

Madhavi nodded.

'Well, I've agreed I won't give it to the *Gazette*, provided he makes some changes to the school.'

'Like?'

'Like they can't ask academically weak students to leave the school just to keep their average up. Which means, Kia gets to stay. Then they're going to start a counselling centre at the school, so kids like Brij and Soam can get the help they need instead of harsh punishments which don't address the core of the problem.'

'So does that mean that kid gets his sports captaincy back?'

'Yes, provided Soam takes the counselling and works hard.'

252

'And what about Mr. Bakshi and Ms. Lily?'

Radhi shrugged. 'I didn't tell Kamble about them. I thought about it — a lot, in fact. But I find that I feel differently about this stuff than Ms. Venus. Sure, the rules exist for a reason, but why should our existence always be so bound and bridled? I mean who are they really harming? And who knows what drew them to each other? Was it loneliness or something else? I don't see why we need to judge. I've had enough of that happen to me in my own life.'

Madhavi nodded thoughtfully. 'Speaking of your life . . . how's Hrishi? Seeing him at the hospital looking so disconsolate was quite the surprise. If I weren't so wretched myself, I would've investigated further.'

Radhi smiled at that. 'We are figuring things out. It's complicated. But something about it feels inevitable.' She scrunched her nose. 'Does that make sense?'

'Sure. You have to explore where it goes.'

Both sisters were quiet for a few moments. Then Madhavi asked what had clearly been worrying her. 'And the drinking?'

'Not a drop since that day,' Radhi said, looking her in the eye. 'I'm looking for a good therapist.'

'Good.' Madhavi sighed, looking relieved. 'Very good.' She picked up a piece of the sandwich and bit into it. 'Lila!' she called out into the kitchen. 'I will have one more of these, please. I suddenly feel very hungry!' Madhavi glanced at the admission letter again and the grin on her face faltered. 'But what about the stuff you found about Kamble and Wagle? Aren't they going to be in trouble for that?'

'They are.' Radhi shrugged. 'I've given Shinde whatever I've found. There will be a lot of legal manoeuvring involved, and they will have to pay a hefty fine. But Kamble is a lawyer, he'll manage, I think. He seemed more concerned about that suicide article.'

'So, Hrishi was okay not to run it?'

Radhi shrugged again. 'It wasn't his decision to make. It was mine. I have the article, and I think more good will come of it, if I hang on to it. Hold it over the school's head so they make more responsible decisions. Besides, Hrishi is running a new story on Wagle. They've found several other irregularities in his dealings. We might still be able to save that park, he thinks.'

'That park is a boon for us,' Lila said walking into the living room with more sandwiches and a bowl of gulab jamuns. 'It's where Shiv plays cricket with his friends. Without it, where would they play? On the road?

'Here Madhavi didi, eat something sweet to celebrate Didi's good news,' she said, placing the gulab jamuns in front of them.

'What good news is this now?' Madhavi turned to Radhi surprised.

'We hadn't got to that, yet.' Radhi smiled. 'I've just heard back from George. My book has received rave reviews and now the publisher wants to offer me a three-book deal.'

'Darling! That's fantastic!' Madhavi got up to give Radhi a hug. 'Aren't you glad now that you were at that school helping out your sister?'

THE END

ACKNOWLEDGEMENTS

Thank you, dear reader, for continuing to read the Temple Hill mysteries and for sticking with Radhi and (me), as we antagonize nosy aunties, munch on delicious, fried snacks and create a lot of personal drama, while we solve murders. Writing book three felt like a big milestone, one that I would never have reached without the support of so many wonderful people.

Many thank-you-hugs are owed to:

Laura Coulman, my editor at Joffe Books, for her incredibly gentle steering of the book. Her confidence in my judgement, helped me trust myself better, and for that, I'm so grateful.

To Jon Appleton and Laura again, for their insightful and detailed editorial inputs.

To Hanna and Sasha and the whole team at Joffe Books for all the magic they do to bring the Temple Hill mysteries to readers.

To Cherie Chapman for the fabulous cover art.

To Kanishka Gupta, my literary agent, for being such a steadfast champion of my books.

To Delna, Rachna, Neha, Hetvi, Diya and Sanaya for all the delicious stories they shared about school life and more.

To Pooja, for always wanting to help. Murder methods, endorsements, whatever I need.

To my favouritest early reader, Deepti, for always being so generous with her time, and unfailing in her kindness.

To Em, for the love and sunshine. For being so proud. And for getting it when mumma is lost on Temple Hill.

To my husband, Maulik, for a thousand different things, but always, always, always for the faith.

GLOSSARY OF INDIAN ENGLISH USAGE

3bhk: Indian real estate term meaning three bedrooms, a hall (living room) and kitchen

Bhagwan: Sanskrit word for deity or figure of religious worship

bhel/bhelpuri: crunchy, puffed rice snack

bussin: African American English word meaning excellent or delicious

chaiwallah: tea seller

chakri: crispy, spiral-shaped snack

champak: a type of magnolia tree

dal/daal: lentil dish

Deccan, the: The Deccan Plateau, also referring to the southern peninsula of India more broadly

dhokla: savoury, sponge dish

dhoti: a garment worn by men, wrapped around the waist and legs, with the look of trousers

diya: oil lamp

gharaanas: a line of musicians, spanning generations, linked to a particular musical style

gulab jamuns: a fried dessert made with milk and syrup

idli: rice cake

ikat: Southeast Asian, dyed fabric

kajal: black powder used as eyeliner or for marking the forehead

kachori: fried, stuffed pastry

kalamkari: traditional, hand-painted cotton

kathak: classical dance

khadi: hand-spun cloth, famously worn by Mahatma Gandhi

khaman dhoklas: a similar dish to dhoklas, made with curry leaves

laddu: a round, sweet snack eaten during Diwali festival
managalsutra: necklace worn by married Hindu women
maasi: aunt
masala: a mixture of spices
masala chai: sweet, spiced tea
medu vada: savoury fritter
methi puri: crisp bread made with fenugreek leaves
Nehru cap: a white, side cap, pointed at the front and back, famously worn by Mahatma Gandhi
Padma Sri: award recognising citizens' contributions in society
panipuri: street food snack filled with mashed potato, onions and spices
papads: papadam/poppadom
peon: orderly/odd jobs worker
pulao: rice pilaf
Raag Malhaar: a traditional musical structure associated with heavy rain
rangoli: traditional pattern-making on a floor or tabletop.
Rani pink: fuchsia or hot pink colour
ras: mango puree
riyaaz: rehearsal
sambhaar: South Indian lentil stew
Sanganeri print: floral textile patterns from Sanganer, in Jaipur
santoor: a percussion string instrument
satynash: a curse word, meaning destruction or ruin
sheeshum: North Indian rosewood
tabla: hand drums
tussar: a type of silk

THE JOFFE BOOKS STORY

We began in 2014 when Jasper agreed to publish his mum's much-rejected romance novel and it became a bestseller.

Since then we've grown into the largest independent publisher in the UK. We're extremely proud to publish some of the very best writers in the world, including Joy Ellis, Faith Martin, Caro Ramsay, Helen Forrester, Simon Brett and Robert Goddard. Everyone at Joffe Books loves reading and we never forget that it all begins with the magic of an author telling a story.

We are proud to publish talented first-time authors, as well as established writers whose books we love introducing to a new generation of readers.

We won Trade Publisher of the Year at the Independent Publishing Awards in 2023 and Best Publisher Award in 2024 at the People's Book Prize. We have been shortlisted for Independent Publisher of the Year at the British Book Awards for the last five years, and were shortlisted for the Diversity and Inclusivity Award at the 2022 Independent Publishing Awards. In 2023 we were shortlisted for Publisher of the Year at the RNA Industry Awards, and in 2024 we were shortlisted at the CWA Daggers for the Best Crime and Mystery Publisher.

We built this company with your help, and we love to hear from you, so please email us about absolutely anything bookish at feedback@joffebooks.com.

If you want to receive free books every Friday and hear about all our new releases, join our mailing list here: www.joffebooks.com/freebooks.

And when you tell your friends about us, just remember: it's pronounced Joffe as in coffee or toffee!